# THE

# SHATTERED

# STAR:

## STARLIGHT AND SHADOW

This is a work of fiction. Names, characters, places, and incidents are the product of the author's imagination or are used fictitiously. Any resemblance to actual persons, living or dead, events, or locales is purely coincidental.

Copyright © 2025 by Skyler R Ostrom

Published in the United States

ISBN: 9781968493011 (Paperback) | 9781968493004 (ebook)| 9781968493028 (Hardcover)

First edition

# THE
# SHATTERED
# STAR:
## STARLIGHT AND SHADOW

By

SKYLER R OSTROM

For those who *care*,
But can't find the words to show it.

# THE
# SHATTERED
# STAR:
## STARLIGHT AND SHADOW

# Chapter 1:
## Infantry

Sebis burned white under the midday sun as Kael marched toward the end of his old life. The city had grown in the last few years, and the Vallen home had gone from being surrounded by farmland to hovering on the outskirts of the growing mass of plastic and metal. Earthen bricks clapped under Auctor's feet as he trailed behind with their mother. They pressed through masses of people, laboring and worshiping, always under the ever-present gaze of Starlit shepherds.

A weight pressed down upon Kael. He had grown up here, with friends, family, and a home, and was leaving it all behind.

A hand grabbed him and pulled. He fell backward into his brother's arms. Hover trucks whined as they flew past, gusting air that brushed their faces as the brothers stood.

There was annoyance in Auctor's expression. "You walked right out in front of the truck! You know I won't be there to save you after tomorrow." Releasing Kael, he turned and walked down the adjoining street.

Their mother grabbed Kael, looking him up and down. "You must pay more attention. Do you have any idea what that would do to me?"

He hugged her without a word.

Following Auctor, they turned the corner. A road stretched toward the horizon and ended at the recruitment plaza.

Kael ran to catch up to Auctor. "Thank you. I wasn't paying attention."

Keeping his pace, Auctor stared ahead.

Few people milled about on the street ahead, and identical buildings lined either side. And were sharp edges of white and green plastic. Many of which were two story multi-family residences, built on the ground of old torn down wooden farm houses. A pile of the reddish-brown bricks sat where a work crew had dug underground to work on the pipes.

Kael's nose wrinkled and his stomach turned at the rot clinging to the air; the scent of fresh bread was woven with sewage. The smell faded as they passed the work crew repairing the underground line. It didn't matter if it was bread or nutrient blocks, it all smelled terrible in the sewer.

Kael glanced at Auctor, saw his odd stare, then looked away. "Mom, do you think he'll know I joined?"

"If he's still out there, he'll know." Her voice sounded distant, as if she were far off in thought.

"We barely knew him. Why do you want to follow him?"

Kael scowled at Auctor. "Don't talk about him like that." He frowned at the ground for a few steps. "It's not him I'm following, it's the idea. The dream of bringing light to the Starless."

"Auctor, leave your brother be. It's hard enough, him leaving, without you two fighting."

"I don't see how his enlisting in the corps helps us."

"Haven't you ever wished to do something greater?" Kael asked, looking up from the ground at his brother.

After hesitating for a moment, Auctor replied, "Why should I care about them? Let idealism and fantasies of glory and honor take others. What I have here is real. Shepherds aren't a concern as long as I worship and follow the law. I live the life I want."

Kael clenched his fists, imagining the countless Starless existing without direction or meaning, waiting to be saved. The idea of staying home, of family, of love, filled him with warmth and comfort. However, this comfort was overshadowed by the thought of living out his days

tending the same soil, buried beneath the weight of his unfulfilled purpose—his desire to follow his father's footsteps.

Kael slid to a halt. "What about the life I want?"

"You get to make the choice, Kael, I don't. I'm stuck here when
you're free to leave. I know what you will say—'Next year I can join
you.' It isn't good enough."

"You know how long I've waited for this day. I can't wait another
year."

Hands on her hips, their mother scowled. "That's enough out of
you two. I refuse to spend Kael's last few hours with us listening to you
argue."

Swallowing, Kael looked down again.

"I won't change your mind?" Auctor demanded.

Meeting Auctor's eye, Kael winced. "I can't stay."

Resignation flashed in Auctor's eyes before they returned to cool
gray fortresses betraying no feeling.

"You don't have to accompany me to recruitment."

Auctor shrugged. "Why shouldn't I? My older brother doesn't
take his first steps into the corps every day. Besides, I might learn
something."

Their mother rubbed her eyes tiredly. "Give him time. He'll come
around."

"I hope so."

Buildings shook as a transport shuttle launched from the nearby
pad. Sun glinted on the sleek silver cockpit; a hard line ran along its
side, ending at the angular cowlings wrapping the engines. The shuttle
spewed verdant plasma as it rose into the sky and faded from sight.

His heart pounded. Tomorrow, he would be flying off into the
horizon, transported out into the heavens near and between the stars
and taken to places where the God Ruler's armies would quell the
heretical hordes. He could picture it: charging forth, dressed head to
toe in a full array of battle gear, fighting side by side with others brave
enough to bring God's light to the darkened masses.

On the monitors outside the recruitment bureau, where scenes
played on repeat, he'd seen men and women shining in beams of glori-

ous starlight, accepting the willing masses of Starless into the Star's embrace. He pictured himself in those scenes, a glint of armor under the radiant sun, standing tall, chin tilted, gazing hard into the distance. The smells of dust and steel flooded his imagination, and anticipation tingled in his fingertips.

Pushing on through the crowds, they reached the recruitment plaza. Kael marveled at the wide open space. Every time he'd been here, it'd amazed him. The smell of lilacs hung in the air like honey, thick and sweet. Earthen bricks gave way to smooth marble stretching across the plaza. Marble statues stood at twice a man's height in the likeness of God. The glint of a golden star hovering above each statue caught his eye. They represented the Star's light, keeping God forever warm in its embrace.

Moving past the statues, he grabbed his mother's hand. A round, steel, gray building protruded from the ground like an obscene blister. Yellow-tinted glass windows wrapped around its exterior. The entryway bore a sign on which bold letters were written in the ancient covenant script: "Starlit Recruitment."

Inside the building, the air shifted, losing its sweet smell. Auctor and their mother found seats while Kael stood in line. Uniformed men and women sat in a row of identical gray desks, calling prospective recruits from the line. The floor looked like black stone but felt like plastic under his feet. After a woman waved him forward, he sat in a chair opposite her.

Her face was blank, and she nodded in greeting. "Name and age." Her voice was flat.

"Kael Vallen, eighteen tomorrow."

She entered information into a computer. "Family and age."

"Father, Ezra Vallen, forty-two. Mother, Ixia Vallen, thirty-nine. Brother, Auctor Vallen, seventeen."

"Your father is in the corps?"

"Yes."

She glanced at Kael then returned her gaze to the dull glow of the computer. "What branch of the corps are you interested in?"

"I want to help Starless accept the Star's embrace."

4

"Infantry."

He looked around as she input data. Soon, the computer made an affirmative chime and spat out a card small enough to fit in a pocket. After examining the card, the woman handed it to Kael.

It was cold to the touch, like metal. One side had information etched into it, and the other was a glowing display screen. It held Kael's name, age, identification number, and DEX modifier.

"This card links to our system. Any changes to your record or DEX will reflect on the display. DEX is the corps's acronym for Deployment and Expertise Identifier. It defines rank, primary role, and expertise, if any. As a recruit, your DEX is D0 I X0. Rank recruit, infantry, no expertise." She stood and saluted. "What is your admonition, recruit?"

Standing, Kael returned the salute. "As long as the Star burns, his will guides the faithful beyond the unknown."

The woman smiled. "Welcome to the corps, recruit. May you prevail in the Star's light and stand against the darkness of shadow. Report to the plaza tomorrow at midday, bring nothing except the uniform you're issued." She handed him a new uniform bundled with a pair of boots. "Dismissed."

Across the room, Auctor was slipping a paper into his pocket. After waving at him and their mother, Kael left the building. His heart raced like it would burst any second. Adrenaline flooded his body, and his feet were moving before he could think. He sprinted down the street. And for the first time, he was untethered from Sebis, his home, past, and doubts, leaving everything behind with every step. When he stopped, his breath came in heaving gasps. Kael smiled and looked at the sky.

Auctor and their mother caught up with him halfway down the street.

"Why did you run?" Auctor asked, eyebrows raised.

"What were those papers you put in your pocket?" Kael asked back.

Auctor glanced at their mother. "Nothing important."

Kael laughed between gasps. "I ran because I'm excited."

Auctor smirked. "Good for you, Kael. Don't trip over your enthusiasm."

Kael laughed again, the sound light and free, earlier doubts about leaving Sebis forgotten.

# Chapter 2:
## Shell

*"If one walks the path of shadow, do they not become shells without light to fill them, and if the shell is all that remains... why are they not hollow?"*
—question of one who found a new home at the prison Eesbex

Darkness filled Auctor's vision as he walked the forest path, but Syrelis's double moons provided enough light for him to navigate the labyrinth. He knew these woods, and every sound and shadowed shape lurking in the dark.

A familiar cliff face stretched upward, like it was reaching for the stars above. Auctor approached the cave entrance at the cliff base. His breath was even and calm and his heart steady, but his senses were heightened, alert to the nearing danger.

The caves were filled with Zirb, a dangerous, predatory animal, that stood waist high to a human. Much akin to spiders, they had hard charcoal exoskeletons covered in sparse white wiry hair. Eight legs if you didn't count the double jointed arm like pincer that sprouted from their foreheads between two rows of eleven eyes. And two fangs each a forearms length they used to inject their paralytic venom. Zirb were nocturnal, aggressive, and territorial. During the day, they slept, and people, including Auctor, collected their large eggs in relative safety. Now, they were awake and hungry.

His plan was proceeding without a hitch. Looking behind him, he saw the silhouettes of Zirb skittering between trees and over boulders. On reaching the cliff face, he began to climb. The rocks were jagged and cold against his fingers as he pulled his body upward. Vibrations from his assent would reach the creatures, who would emerge to investigate.

Finding a perfect vantage point, he sat just as the Zirb emerged from the cave entrance below him. He watched, motionless, while chaos broke and the creatures fought for their lives, succumbing to the Zirb he lured here from the other side of the forest. Auctor waited while the creatures devoured their kill. After some time, the remaining Zirb crawled toward their nest, slow and sated.

Auctor climbed down; the carnage lay before him as a testament to his genius. A thin smirk lingered upon his lips. Once the cave was clear, Auctor entered it. It was dark and damp, and the *drip-drip* of water echoed along the rough walls. He made his way forward to the heart of the nest, where thick moss had been collected in neat piles. A heavy, musty odor assaulted his nose as he approached the scattered eggs and placed them into his pack.

After exiting the cave, he navigated through the mass of bodies strewn about. Faint earthy and mineral smells perked Auctor's senses as he passed. Blue blood soaked the ground where Zirb had been ripped limb from limb and feasted upon. He stopped at the tree line and turned to look at his work one last time.

He marched back home and arrived before sunrise. Entering a storage shed, he set his pack on the dirt floor, and placed each egg on the shelves lining one wall. Fourteen in all. Smiling, his thoughts drifted back to the ease of manipulating those creatures to kill one another.

Hearing his family rousing from the house, his smile faded. He scowled at the wall, and his breath came hard and fast. His mind darted, looking for answers out of his grasp. He had tried to make Kael stay and failed.

Auctor balled his fists, and heat flashed in his cheeks. Striking out, he smashed an egg, sending the liquid inside spraying across the room and himself. He stared at the crushed shell as the egg dripped from his hand.

Then he smiled again. The papers he had taken yesterday might be helpful. If he couldn't make Kael stay, maybe he could find a way to enlist.

Pots and pans clanged in the kitchen. Auctor picked up a Zirb egg, shaking off the remaining viscous slime from his hands. His family would think he was thoughtful bringing Zirb eggs home for Kael's last day. It might even buy him enough goodwill to avoid explaining why he was out in the pre-dawn hours.

Grasping the door, he looked back at the line of eggs one last time and smirked.

# Chapter 3:
## Destiny

*"Those who walk in the Stars' eternal path may choose the direction they travel, but destiny sees them arrive at the same destination."*
—Starlit Covenant

The city bustled; it seemed everyone was working hard. Massive crates of supplies marked with various tags were loaded onto shuttles. Dangerous, fragile, perishable, and explosive materials were all moved and loaded into their respective zones. Kael stood tall in the afternoon sun, its warm yellow glow glinting on the silver star of his uniform.

His mother and Auctor had come to see him off near the entrance of the recruitment plaza. A pulsating crowd milled around them and chattered, making it impossible to see the radiant plaza and its golden statues.

"This is as far as we can go, my son."

Kael turned back to look at his family. "I will miss you both."

His mother wrapped her arms around him and hugged him tight. "I love you, come back to us," she whispered.

"I love you, too."

Releasing him, she examined his uniform, teary-eyed, and brushed it straight where it had wrinkled. "My boy, all grown up."

Kael smiled at her before turning to Auctor. "Brother, I will miss you, too. Take care of Mom."

Auctor gave him a thin smile.

Kael hugged his mother one last time before entering the plaza. As he walked away, he turned and waved at his family. "Goodbye! May the Star keep you both well."

"I'll see you soon," Auctor called, as Kael was swallowed by the crowd.

Kael turned back for one last glance, but the crowd pressed in. He came face to face with a large man in a corps uniform.

"Where are you going, recruit?" The man's voice was guttural and intense.

Kael's breath caught in his throat, causing him to stutter. "I-I was going to see my brother."

"The time for family has passed, recruit. Fall in with the rest."

"Yes, sir." Kael made his way toward the other recruits, clenching his trembling hands.

Someone nudged him. The recruit next to him nodded toward an officer who had begun speaking. He stood at attention and listened as the officer continued his oration. The man spoke reverently and intensely, each word filled with emotion:

"Recruits, today you stand at the threshold of transformation, ready to embrace honor and the burden of becoming soldiers of God's light. Today is not a day of recognition, it is a day of rebirth. You're no longer individuals bound by fears and failures of the past. You're vessels for divine light, cleansed and made anew by the Star's embrace." The officer waved his arms about as he spoke, like a reverend speaking with passion.

Kael's heart hammered, and he stood tall, looking up at the officer.

"A soldier's purpose is not to endure but to illuminate the path for others. You will face darkness, despair, and unimaginable trials. You're not here to survive, you're here to shine in the face of darkness, to guide others who falter, and to carry forward a beacon of hope and righteousness."

Kael could almost see it—himself as a missionary of the Star, guiding lost souls into a world of hope and life.

"Each soldier is a star unto themselves. Together we form a galaxy of light. Remember this truth as you press forward. Alone, your light is significant; together, we are unstoppable. We are not individuals, we are a constellation, a unified force reflecting the will of the God Ruler." A resonant thud echoed throughout the plaza as the officer slammed his fist on the podium. "Today, you leave behind who you were. Step into a destiny greater than yourself, forged in service to the Star's eternal brilliance. Go forth, and may your light never waver."

Kael couldn't help but let out a cheer. He wasn't alone; every recruit roared along with him, creating a deafening, thunderous chorus. The ground seemed to shake from the sheer force of their collective voices, carrying their shared anticipation and determination outward from the plaza.

The officer at the podium remained steadfast, allowing the recruits' zeal to reverberate and subside before lifting a gloved hand for silence. The sound of their labored breathing and the electric charge of the moment lingered in the air as the boom died down. "You're prepared." The officer's voice was like a sword, sharp and clear. "You're the light meant to shine through the darkness from this day on, so let this be the first roar among many."

Kael's fists were clenched, and his resolve was evident. He was prepared. They all were.

The officer's voice boomed out as he waved at the transport ship. "Stand and claim your future."

Kael sat on the transport and fastened his belt, which felt like a cage and a comfort. On the one hand, it was a guarantee of security; on the other, it was a prison, keeping the anxiety and excitement inside of him.

The ship filled to bursting with recruits, and the doors groaned shut with an affirmative clang. Inky black filled the compartment before the glow of dim yellow lights ignited. A countdown began, and the computer voice sounded, "Sixty seconds." Humming of the engines grew louder as they flamed to life, starting the heating process. The recruits became silent as the voice announced, "Thirty seconds."

A jolt of the ship had Kael grasping the hard metal sides of his seat. The ship tilted up, bearing its nose to the sky as the countdown sounded, "Ten seconds." He shifted in his seat and placed his head against the cushioned rest. "Five seconds." Frantic, he checked his restraint one last time.

A voice rose from across the shuttle. "For the God Ruler!"

"Two, one."

The full force of the engines pushed them upwards. Kael was glued to his seat, unable to lift his head and limbs. Closing his eyes, he focused all his concentration on breathing. His chest was heavy like a boulder was crushing him. Belts dug into his shoulders as they pulled tight, groaning under the strain of gravity.

Minutes were days, then a wave swept through the cabin, pressure eased, and he was weightless. A recruit snatched a coin gliding through the air.

The intercom squawked, and the pilot spoke. "Welcome to space, recruits. Please remain seated, your restraints secured. We will begin maneuvers for escape velocity and transit speed in a moment."

A moment was an understatement. The craft began to accelerate almost as soon as the intercom clicked off, and Kael remained cemented into his seat. He had heard about transit speed before, but he didn't understand how it worked, not really. His knowledge was limited to the base idea: it altered how the ship interacted with normal spacetime, allowing it to cross vast distances in a short amount of time.

The intercom once again clicked. "Recruits, we have established transit speed. Once we arrive, there won't be any time for rest. I suggest you get some while you can."

Kael looked around at the other recruits, his eyebrows scrunched. He had expected signs of further acceleration or changes in how time felt. Everything looked as it had when they'd first achieved weightlessness.

Several others unlatched their harnesses and floated around the cabin, testing the physics of this new sensation. One recruit spun another, and by the time they hit the inner hull, she had become sick and spewed vomit across the compartment, eliciting unified disgust from the entire group.

Intending to heed the pilot's advice, Kael shifted in his seat, finding a comfortable position. There was an odd comfort to being weightless, and he let it ease him from awareness. Other recruits and their activities became muted, dull background noise. Kael smiled. He had started fulfilling his dream and soon would realize what it meant to serve under the Star's light. Hum of the ship's systems, a soothing rhythm that blended with the chatter of the other recruits, lulled him further into his thoughts.

Kael's anticipation of the adventures ahead was palpable as he closed his eyes. No longer confined to his home, now he was part of something greater, a galaxy-spanning purpose, a calling he had yearned for since childhood. His destiny.

He felt a weight lifted from his shoulders, a feeling of shedding the burdens of the past and stepping into the unknown. For the first time, he was free.

# Chapter 4:
## Constellations

*"Many travel different paths among the stars; he gave us constellations so we might find our way."*
—Starlit Covenant

Space was endless, cold, and dark except in the blinding glare of a star's embrace. A ship glided through the void, silent and looming. Floodlights illuminated letters spelling out its name: Radiance.

It was no ordinary capital ship; it was one of six cathedral battleships. Its slender, shining hull was a grand canvas sparkling with a golden glow—the constellations etched on its surface waved like starlight. Like the turrets of a celestial cathedral, towering pylons curved down its length, capped with spheres glowing with soft light. The ship, which rose above all who beheld it, symbolized strength and devotion. But under its glorious appearance, the Radiance had a purpose. Deployed to bring supplies and provide command and control for the ongoing war effort, the massive vessel, many hundreds of meters long, flew toward Xalthryn.

And inside, Captain Junova wasn't where one might have expected her to be. She wasn't on the bridge overseeing operations or on the lower decks managing supplies and landing crews. Instead, she had retreated to her quarters. Modest by design but the largest on the ship, the room was barren despite its size.

She sat at her desk, face ashen, breath shallow. The desk beneath her hands was bare, save for one thing. A holo photo rested there, revealing faces she once knew, frozen in time. Despite their smiles, all she could see now was pain. Death. Every person in the image was gone, obliterated. Junova's gaze lingered on it, the memories as heavy as lead in her chest. She hadn't taken the order easily; disbelief had stricken her when it had come through.

*Insurrection on Corvallion. Secure and eliminate.* Even now, the words echoed in her mind, a haunting reminder she couldn't escape. Friends and family had turned against the Starlit, and he had sent her to restore peace. No, not peace. Submission. Her fists clenched tight, nails biting into her palms, though the sting was distant. It had been a test of loyalty, a cruel affirmation of her faith, one she could not refuse.

Her stomach twisted as nausea set in. Years of loyal service, each promotion a step closer to command, had not prepared her for that moment. She'd reconciled doubts before, brushed them aside as necessary sacrifices for the greater good. But this wasn't something she could deny.

The grav chair bobbed as she pushed away from the desk, its hum echoing her unsteady breath, her thoughts unraveling.

Her fists unclenched, palms stinging from the marks left behind. She knew the price of defiance. If she defied the God Ruler, he would execute her. The Radiance would remain a tool of genocide, its captain another pawn in his endless game.

She took a deep, unsteady breath. Her decision was fragile but resolute. She could dissuade others from revolution, guide them away from insurrection. It would be worth it if she could save even a handful.

Her eyes flicked back to the holo photo on the desk. Those faces were gone, but she would not let their memory be for nothing. Not while she had the power to act.

Monotonous chirping pierced the quiet hum in the room. "Captain, you have an incoming transmission."

She steadied herself before pushing a button on her desk. "I'll take it here."

The device routed the transmission, clicking before falling silent.

"Captain Junova," she said.

"Captain, I'm Commander Hernz, commander of corps forces on Xalthryn. I hear Radiance is coming to provide support."

"Yes, Commander. My crews will start transporting supplies and manpower upon entering a stable orbit."

"Best news I've had in a month."

"I also have orders to establish a training compound. Bringing recruits here and training them on the planet."

"I received those orders as well, and I already have my engineers fortifying a clearing."

"Expect us in two days, Commander."

"With bated breath, Captain."

Coms went silent, and Junova gazed out at the inky black of space.

Time fled all too fast. Radiance was arriving above Xalthryn, and Junova made her way to the bridge. The corridors featured bronze wall panels meant to protect the crew and cover conduits. Alcoves in which statues stood in his likeness were dotted throughout the ship, placed to optimize worship.

On deck after deck, the crew hurried about performing tasks before their imminent arrival. Stepping into a hypertube, Junova pushed a button and was whisked away through the bowels of the ship. She stepped onto the bridge, where officers and crew saluted her before returning to work.

The primary bridge was embedded on the dorsal side of the ship, near its middle. Stations were displayed on the port and starboard sides; these controlled and monitored every part of Radiance and a seven-hundred-million-kilometer spherical radius around her. An elevated walkway separated the sides, allowing officers to monitor many displays at once, while a statue of the God Ruler stood at the end as a reminder: *he sees all and none escapes his reach.*

After receiving a status update, she walked to the viewport, needing to see this world herself. These people lived in shadow, not knowing the warmth of the Star's embrace. At least, that was what the Star had told her, but now doubt and curiosity crept in. Touching her jacket pocket, where she kept her photo, she thought again of her friends and family, silenced forever. Her eyes drifted toward the planet that lay before her.

Xalthryn glowed blue-green, the cyan grasslands shimmering under the faint light of its distant star. Wisps of white mist pooled in the valleys, their soft haze contrasting with the dark streaks of angry mountains. The planet's surface appeared alive, its strange colors shifting with the Star's light, as if breathing beneath its thin veil of atmosphere.

A distant voice was calling her name, beckoning her. The ambience around her ebbed, and there was nothing save for Xalthryn and herself. Her ship was a breath of light, and the world below was a breath of mist.

"Captain."

She remained enthralled, unable to look away. Her inner voice attempted to respond, but its sound was as distant as the voice calling her from upon the bridge.

"Captain!" the voice called again, and this time a hand grasped her shoulder. Reality rushed back, drawing her away from Xalthryn. "We are on final approach. Your orders?"

Junova turned to face her officer, shaking off the strangeness that had overtaken her. "Commence transfer into orbit." Approaching navigation, she examined the screens. "What's our status?"

Astronav Liora was busy inputting and correcting calculations. "Smooth sailing, Captain. Nothing unusual about this planet's gravity well, and no extraneous space debris."

"Very well, Astronav. What orbit parameters are we expecting?"

Liora frowned at her display. "We are looking at a stable circular orbit eight hundred kilometers above the surface at seven thousand eight hundred and ninety-three meters a second. Orbital period around Xalthryn will be one hour and forty minutes."

Liora had been assigned to the Radiance a year prior and showed excellent technical expertise and intuition for being twenty years old. Junova smiled at the drawings stuck around the edges of her console. They were constellations of every star system she'd been to since joining her crew.

After checking the numbers and making adjustments, Liora bit her lip as Radiance settled into orbit. Xalthryn's gravity could be felt pulling against the ship's grav plating, creating an unusual diagonal pull.

The ship's massive presence loomed over the planet below. Junova let out a breath, relaxing her shoulders. No matter how often they brought Radiance into orbit, it made her anxious. Mistakes, even small ones, could be fatal for a large ship.

"Excellent work."

Liora grinned. "Thanks, Captain. Do you think I might visit the surface?"

"We will be busy down there. But I think we could find use for an extra pilot."

Nodding, Liora turned back to her controls.

Junova pressed a button on the nav console. "Crew, orbit established. Launch landing craft."

Yellow warning lights reflected on the windows, casting fractured shadows on the bridge. Grinding vibrations pulsed through the decking, indicating the opening of the hangar doors. Junova watched from the viewport as numerous small crafts emerged from the hangars and descended toward the surface below. Each one vanished into the clouds like an unanswered prayer.

# Chapter 5:
## Blinded

*"If a person finds themselves blinded, they should ensure they stand in the light and their eyes are open."*
—Shepard of the Covenant

Kael's fingers, gripping the arms of his seat, turned white. Lights flickered, and the shuttle shuddered in the turbulent atmosphere. It plummeted toward the surface of Xalthryn. Sweat rolled down his face; he could taste the salt of it on his lips. Deafening groans and pops came from the hull as the atmosphere heated the shuttle. Still, Kael held onto his seat, reminding himself to breathe.

*I can do this. Pilots do this every day. It's safe.* Those few minutes felt like years. A jolt sent him reeling against the restraints, which dug into his shoulders. He grimaced. The shuttle leveled, and the turbulence subsided. Releasing the hold on his seat, Kael's fingers ached.

Static hissed from the intercom, and the pilot spoke. "Welcome to Xalthryn, recruits."

The rest of the flight was calm compared to their arrival. The landing gear wailed as it protruded from the shuttle, and there was a resounding thud as it came to a rest on a landing pad.

Kael exited the shuttle onto this new world. Bright blue light from the sun's pinprick was a sharp contrast to the shuttle's dim yellow lights. Kael held up his hand, protecting his eyes while they adjusted. Light caught his arm, casting a spectral shade he didn't recognize as his own. The sky was a painting of cyan and turquoise hues mixed with wisps of white and gray clouds, nothing like the sky back home.

Blue light made his vision off-color, as if he were viewing the world through a filter. Cyan grass rippled in the breeze, and trees with broad silvery leaves and black trunks sprouted from the ground.

Breathing in through his nose, Kael tried to sense the smells of this world but was bombarded by thick and humid air. Taking another breath was more manageable, though it was like breathing liquid. Yet, there was no urge to cough up the watery air.

Infantry stood at attention, waiting. One by one, they fell out of line and picked a recruit. Kael's guide was a tall, broad-shouldered man whose appearance was kind, though he wasn't. After a brief introduction, he clarified Kael wasn't to ask questions. His pace was quick and deliberate, and Kael struggled to keep up. They walked along streets named after heroes of the corps; Kael recognized a few as he ran to keep up. The streets were lined with sharp white lights, barracks, a mess hall, and an infirmary. The buildings were low and symmetrical, plastic and metal melded into rectangles. Overhangs attached to buildings held statues of God waiting for the penitent. Even the trees were trimmed into squares.

HQ rose before him, and Kael was guided to a large group of recruits assembled in front of the building. His guide left and added himself to the ranks of soldiers surrounding the area.

Recruits nearby were murmuring to one another as several individuals walked out onto the second-floor balcony of HQ. A man with a commanding voice shouted, "Recruits! Form ranks and attend."

The recruits stumbled around Kael, trying to form a cohesive line, while Kael examined the three individuals on the balcony. They wore different uniforms.

The loud man wore the same uniform as the guides, a drab blue color resembling that of Xalthryn's grass. Behind the loud man was a tall, middle-aged man in a gray uniform adorned with several medals and ribbons. His face bore a scar traveling from his right cheek over his nose and ending on his left. He looked battle-hardened, and his stare was empty. The other individual on the balcony was a woman who appeared to be some years older than Kael. She wore a black uniform with a radiant white star on her left shoulder and five pins upon the right collar of her shirt that looked like golden stars glinting in the blue stars light.

The three watched from the balcony as the recruits worked out something resembling order. Then the woman stepped forward, examining and scrutinizing each recruit. Kael stood frozen, trying not to make a sound. Even a breath could have broken the silence around him.

"Welcome," the woman said. "I, Captain Junova, have been tasked with your training. You will be the first trained here on Xalthryn. We expect you to set the standard high."

Pointing at the tall man behind her, she continued. "This is Commander Hernz. He is the corps authority on Xalthryn. His orders come from God, and you will treat them as such. You have all made an honorable dedication to the Star. I bring a message from our great ruler, addressed to you." She held out a roll of yellowed paper, like all Starlit decrees were written upon. "It is a special privilege to receive guidance from God."

She went on to read from the paper. "Recruits, distinguished soldiers, and officers of Xalthryn. Your self-proclaimed ruler and god addresses you as I've addressed no other. I had wished to see Xalthryn join the Star and see their path lit. However, I am not immortal, I am passing my throne on to my son, Solovian. These are my last decrees." Junova stopped reading for a moment and looked back at Hernz.

Daring a glance around, Kael saw the other recruits looked unsettled and nervous.

After Junova and Hernz conversed, she returned her attention to the recruits and continued reading. "For years, I allowed the people of Xalthryn to live in peace. My envoys spent decades living with the Starless, forming a relationship of mutual benefit. However, time has abandoned myself and Xalthryn.

"My first decree. The Starlit Corps will attempt to negotiate with Xalthryn's leaders. Help them see they are in danger.

"My second decree. Recruits, train well and train hard. As the inevitable comes to pass, your life may depend on it. Never forget this admonition. Give your hand to those in darkness, lead them into the light.

"I quote from the Covenant, 'Light reveals and blinds in equal measure, a wise man may see the difference.'

"Walk with wisdom, do not become blinded. Those blinded are walking in darkness, unable to see their path."

The entire group stood silent.

Several seconds passed before Junova's uneasy but firm voice cut through the silence like a razor. "Your DEX has been updated with barracks and squad assignments. I suggest you get rest, training begins tomorrow." She turned and disappeared into the building with Hernz.

Recruits began moving about as Kael slipped his DEX from a pocket. The display read *DO I X0 B1 squad one.*

On entering his barracks, he found it housed more than one squad. Forty cots were arranged in a row on the left and right sides of the bunkhouse, leaving a path down the middle.

Each squad had ten recruits, and the Dravian wool blankets on each cot were dyed squad colors: squad four was a pure and unyielding white, three a dominant and aggressive red, two a bright and loud blue, and one a stalwart and true yellow.

Some recruits were introducing themselves to others while the rest had sprawled out in various undignified ways on their bunks.

The muscles in Kael's legs burned as he sat on the edge of his bunk. He couldn't remember a time when he'd felt so heavy. He lay back on the thin, hard mat, which wasn't uncomfortable after the day he'd had.

Kael hadn't considered Xalthryn's days might be longer or shorter. The corps hadn't told him. And sometime during the night, far too early, music blared somewhere in the camp.

Kael turned over and groaned. The music persisted, giving him no choice but to wake. It was a hymn from the Starlit Covenant, though altered. Its reverent tone quickened, its solemnity replaced by the unforgiving cadence of a military march. He didn't know it then, but this would be the first of many mornings it roused him from slumber.

The thin metal door on his bunkhouse clanged open, and lights flickered on. A man entered, his voice booming with an authoritative tone. "God's light is shinin', recruits! What's this, a nursery? Did yer mommas let ye sleep through tae Star's gift? Outta bed! Five minutes! Exercise gear! Nova pace!"

Scrambling to get on his feet, Kael found he could breathe easier, but the air remained alien. One thing hadn't changed: he was still heavy. There was one conclusion: Xalthryn had higher gravity.

Kael and the others dressed and stumbled outside to form, at best, a rank of disoriented and disorganized recruits. The man standing before them was short and stocky. He looked well-rested and was clean-shaven and square-jawed. He glared up and down the ranks of recruits while shaking his head with disgust. "Ye lot move like newborn calves! How did any o' ye skinny-limbed runts survive tae trip 'ere?"

Shivering in the cold, Kael wondered if he should answer. The man paused as if expecting one, but Kael thought better and remained silent.

"Ye might be wondering who I am right aboot now. I am Sergeant Krennak. It means one thing to ye runts—I am yer god until ye prove otherwise!" Taking a step forward, he examined the recruits, his gaze so sharp it might pierce their souls. "I see fear. I see weakness. I see children who'd sooner cry an' cling to their momma's ankles than set foot on this world. But it ends 'ere. Right now."

He let the silence hang in the air before pointing out one recruit. "You! Do ye know why ye're 'ere?" The recruit gave no immediate answer, and Krennak stepped closer, raising his voice. "Are ye deaf, recruit? Answer me!"

"I'm here to fight Starless," the recruit said in a weak voice.

Krennak scoffed, pacing. "Ye are 'ere 'cause ye are nothin'. Not 'cause ye're special, not 'cause ye're strong, but 'cause tae Star demands it. Ye'll see me in yer dreams, I'll tear out yer weakness, forge ye in tae fires o' tae eternal Star, an' hammer ye into unbreakable shards o' light until tae worthy remain."

Turning, he pointed toward the distant launchpad. "What're ye waitin' fer? Ye've got untrodden ground to cover. Run! Nova pace!"

Krennak paced, keeping them in line and moving. Kael lost count of how far he and the others ran during the day. They would run for hours then stop and do push-ups, which Krennak called "taking a break." Then they would run for several more hours. This routine went on for two days: no food, some water, a run, and calisthenics. Krennak made appearances, and his staff of corporals, Ford and Otho, ruled in his absence, keeping Kael and the other recruits hard at work.

Running for days on end wasn't how he'd imagined himself bringing light into the shadow. It was like he was preparing for more ominous work.

Kael swore to himself Krennak must not need sleep and somehow he had been created by God to make his life miserable. In their limited free time after worship, the recruits would talk about how much they hated Krennak and his corporals. One night, the squad planned how they would hide his body if they killed him, though they would never carry out the thought. All knew the consequences of disobeying the Star. Each bunkhouse had a wall display listing the surest way to punishment. Striking or harming a fellow soldier or superior was featured at the top.

On the third day, Kael rose before daybreak as the march blared. He and the others dressed and formed rank for inspection, expecting another day of the same.

Krennak was waiting for them, looking as rested and spry as always. "What a pitiful lot we've got 'ere. D'ye always look like a bunch o' half-starved apes lookin' for mercy? Is that what ye think ye'll get out there? Mercy?" Krennak paced before them, his gaze sharp. "Tae weak beg. Tae weak break. Tae weak die." He stopped, leaning close to the nearest recruit, his voice dropping to a growl. "An' right now, I see corpses wi' breath in their lungs."

Kael tensed, frightened to be the first corpse to move.

Krennak's voice rose again. "But dead men dinne march. So, if ye want to prove me wrong, if ye think ye're worth tae damn rations, then get up. Move!"

So, they did and ran the entire day with Krennak reminding them how worthless they were and how they would die. Kael's whole body hurt. Blisters formed on his heels where his boots rubbed. Each step hammered his feet into the hard dirt, and his joints ached. Sweat soaked his clothes in the hot light of Xalthryn's blue sun.

Stopping them before sunset, Krennak lined them up near the mess tent. "Recruits. Do ye know what time it is?" Krennak paused, staring down the line of recruits. "It wasn't rhetorical. Answer me."

"I don't know what time it is, sir."

Krennak stepped close to Kael, looking him up and down. "Well, one o' ye has a voice. Imagine that, apes that speak. Ye bought yerself tae first pass to eat, recruit. Tae rest ye'll fall in line, ye'll eat last."

It didn't matter what the food was, Kael hadn't ever been this hungry. He ate until he couldn't.

As music rang out the next day and Kael assembled with his squad outside their barracks in the dim glow of morning, Sergeant Krennak stood waiting in front of a table with a rifle on it. A dark gray weapon of polymer furniture that covered it from butt to muzzle in a mixture of hard angles and rounded surfaces.

"Welcome, this will be yer first day o' real trainin'," Krennak said. "What I 'ave 'ere is tae Corps Portable Rifle model eleven forty-four."

Picking the weapon up he demonstrated how to operate, un-jam, and field strip it. It featured a multi-colored holographic reticle for targeting and an ammo counter on the right side where the old brass cased projectile weapons ejected their spent cartridges. Caseless ammunition allowed for the average soldier to carry more and simplified rifle design by not needing an ejection port.

"Tae CPR eleven forty-four will be yer best friend. It will protect ye if ye'll take good care of it. Think o' it as an extension of yerselves—part o' ye. A part that if lost, will mean yer death," the sergeant said.

Over the next two months Kael and the company of recruits learned warfare. From combat at the Urban Tactics Course to military

Skyler R Ostrom

doctrine and corps history in a classroom. It was long grueling days, and Kael was exhausted at the end of each. Over time, he adapted to the environment of Xalthryn and the corps routine, even to the point of being excited to see what they would learn next. Yet through it all, the thought of what might come next made him anxious

# Chapter 6:
## Identity

*"Those without identity exist as those without meaning."*
—Xalthari Warden of Echoes

Light from Hernz's digital pad lit his face against the red glow within the lander. He hadn't said more than three words to Junova since she'd read God's decree. She hadn't known him long, but she knew his kind. A veteran of the corps, his mind shaped for one purpose: war.

It was apparent he didn't expect the Starless to be receptive. Why else come to meet them in full armor? She had done her work. These locals of Xalthryn were not warrior people. Their lives revolved around nature and spoken histories. Hernz's armor would serve to intimidate and remind them of the horrors he was capable of, from its battle-worn exterior to its scarred and disfigured wearer.

Junova had taken a less aggressive approach. No pomp and circumstance; her standard uniform was enough. She still had to see a local, and she attributed a deficit in her training to Hernz. Learning about people and how to communicate with them while not being able to utilize and refine the knowledge left her stomach feeling knotted.

Now, she had the task of delivering an ultimatum: Join us or see your way of life destroyed.

She scowled at Hernz, who paid no mind, his attention still upon his pad. Was he already making battle plans? Devising the eradication of a people? She had been in this position before, sitting across from the vehicle of a resistant people's demise while being expected to change an entire people's culture and way of life. It was a task doomed to fail.

The red light gave way to yellow, indicating ten minutes to arrival. Rubbing her temples, she felt the crushing weight push down on her shoulders and her chest. It hadn't been like this last time. She'd been numb during the previous negotiation, even with all the bloodshed from her failure.

Remembering her picture, she touched her uniform pocket, feeling the familiar edge of the holo frame. "This is why," she muttered to herself. Had the value of a life no meaning to her until it was a life she'd known, touched? Her chest grew tighter at the thought. A few weeks ago, she'd been like Hernz—serving the Star, maintaining order, and eliminating threats to society. Those lives had value, too, but she couldn't see it. She was blinded by her belief that she was doing God's work, that Starlit lives were worth more than Starless lives.

Now, it seemed all life held value. These Starless were sure to refuse, as had the others she'd negotiated with. Death was inevitable. Oh, she would try to sway them, but how could one change the mind of those happy with life? She would have to convince them there was something better, convince them they weren't pleased with their lives as they were now. There wasn't enough time. She would resort to pleading then. What other option did she have?

When she failed and the fighting started, what then? She could try to limit death where the Radiance was concerned. Hernz was another matter. She couldn't interfere with his command. If she did, her life would be forfeit. Though she commanded the Radiance as a fleet captain, Hernz's authority over the sector meant her authority could be revoked. Instantly and lethally. With Hernz being the ranking commander in the sector, Radiance would be under his command. She shuddered at the thought. Him controlling such destructive power could cleanse Xalthryn of every living being in a week, leaving the planet an uninhabitable burning ruin. Unacceptable.

The lander set down with a thud. Hernz had moved to the ramp door, and she hadn't noticed the light change from yellow to green, indicating arrival. She stood behind him as the latch released and the door popped open with a hiss. The ramp extended with a reluctant whine then scraped stone as it came to rest.

Junova peered around Hernz's shoulder through the clearing dust, hoping to glimpse some Xalthari. Her eyes did not meet people; instead, she saw an expansive, cavernous room. Hernz stalked down the ramp, giving her a clearer image of where she was. She stepped onto the landing ramp, and the roof above her closed like a great stone jaw clamping shut. Hernz was unfazed, uninterested. He'd been here before, she remembered.

Light emanated from circular disks spaced along the walls. The stone floor stretched along the empty room, meeting the dome-like walls in a gentle curve. Junova realized the room was constructed with no corners or edges, nothing like her ship, which had sharp angles and crevices everywhere.

Hernz stopped between two light disks and stared at the wall. Junova followed suit, her eyebrow raised. It looked like any other wall section: tall, seamless, and carved from ancient stone.

"Hernz, why are we staring at a wall?"

Hernz glanced at her. "These heretics do things in their own time. No sense of import or urgency as we see it. Wait. They will come."

She frowned. It seemed Hernz wasn't in the mood to answer simple questions. Being a military commander, she'd have thought he could at least provide clear and concise communication.

It hadn't been enough for him to ignore her requests to meet the locals or impart even a sliver of his knowledge about them so she could do her job—he had to avoid her, and when she did get him to speak, to say only, *Wait. They will come.* She clenched her fists, nails biting into her palms. Her teeth pressed against each other as she tightened her jaw.

A deep, resonant groan vibrated from somewhere beneath her feet followed by a low rumble through her boots. Her eyes darted around. The shaking stopped, and a low clanging came from within the wall before them. The air shifted as the solid rock began to move.

The wall split, not in halves or along any visible seam, but in a mass of spirals. Once indistinguishable, giant columns began to twist apart, each one a perfect helix of interwoven stone. Coiling in a slow, deliberate motion, they unwound.

As the spirals unraveled, lines of pulsing magenta glowed like blood coursing through veins. It looked alive, like the heartbeat of something ancient. The grand columns settled with a final whisper of stone against stone, leaving behind a passage where solid rock had once stood.

For a moment, the air was heavier. In all her travels, all the worlds she'd been to, never had she experienced something so impossible. Had someone opened the door for them, or had it chosen to let them pass? Hernz had said, *In their own time.* Was it the Xalthari's time, or was it something more?

She stepped through the once-wall. The air was cool, like it was temperature-controlled, unlike the previous space, in which she had felt as though she was standing in sunlight. The stone passageway soon gave way to modern angular construction. And while maintaining its rounded aesthetic, the walls appeared constructed out of a dark gray alloy.

She let her fingers glide across the metallic surface, which was cool to the touch. They whispered across its smooth surface like they were skating on ice. Although the wall looked to be the same material the floor was made of, their boots maintained their purchase on the latter, losing no friction against the smooth metal.

Hernz stalked ahead, paying no heed to the strangeness of this place. She didn't imagine he would've been the slightest bit curious even if this were his first visit. Quickening her pace, she made to keep up with Hernz. There had been several turns now, and it wouldn't do to get lost.

Having yet to see anyone in this place weighed upon her mind. The Xalthari knew to expect them, and yet they'd sent no escort. It was as if they didn't care or else thought they didn't need to send one. The latter was more worrisome than the former. It didn't settle well in her military-trained mind. If they didn't require an escort, what manner of security watched them now? Her eyes darted around the wall of the curved passage in front and behind her. Nothing.

The light dimmed then flickered out as they walked along, shrouding the hallway in black. Returning her attention forward, she saw a door. It was large, as large as the passageway, and made of the same smooth alloy. The latch looked familiar and worked like a hatch aboard the Radiance.

Hernz swung the door open and stepped through it to a small room. Dust hung in the air, lit by small amber orbs attached to wall fixtures, as did a scent of old paper and something loamy, like there were damp roots under the floorboards. Dark wooden chairs surrounded a scarred table with a bent leg while several desks overflowed with books and half-full mugs.

A man sat at a long desk with open texts in front of him. His back was turned, and he waved them in with a hand over his shoulder, making no effort to see his guests.

"Come in, please seat yourselves," he said in the common tongue. He spoke it well, though his accent was strange to Junova.

A gentle wave of relief swept through her; at least she didn't have to translate everything from common to Vekhara. She didn't have much time to learn more than a few words.

Taking a chair in his grasp, Hernz slid it across the floor. It groaned in complaint as he sat on it. Pointing to another chair, he motioned for Junova to do the same. Once she'd seated herself, the man turned to face them. He was black haired, dark skinned, and wore brownish-green garb that was loose fitting and appeared informal to Junova. A tattoo with a small creature that looked like a long haired rat was inked onto a visible part of his right shoulder.

"It is rare to receive people like yourselves, from stars." He glanced upward as he spoke. "Commander Hernz, long since we last spoke. Do stars still watch over your people?" His voice carried a rhythm unlike the clipped precision of the common tongue. Words rolled smoothly and steadily, each syllable deliberate, like stones shaped by a river. There was a depth to his tone, an unhurried patience, its sound softened enough to seamlessly blend his words. Yet, beneath the calm cadence, there was a weight, like he spoke with the wisdom of generations.

Hernz looked unsettled. Shifting in his chair, he returned an obligatory emotionless smile. "The Star's light always guides us." Waving his hand toward her, he continued. "This is Junova. She captains a ship traveling between stars. She brings a message."

It was Junova's turn to look uncomfortable. Knowing what she had to do and saying it were two different matters. The room shrank around her. Hernz and the Xalthari were like giants next to her, a child among men.

An odd but warm smile spread across the man's face, and his eyes glistened with curiosity. "To meet a person from other stars is my privilege. Vashar, I am called."

Returning his smile, she gave a polite nod. "Vashar, vethar shokai."

His smile transformed to a full grin. "Junova, khorai vethar. Star people have never spoken my language before."

Junova's brows bunched. "Not even the envoys?"

Shaking his head with apparent sadness, Vashar sighed. "Vekhara, every envoy refused to speak. It is beyond my understanding."

Her mind buzzed. How could you be an envoy to an entire people yet refuse to speak their language? Of course, the common tongue would need to be taught, but so much would be lost by not learning their tongue, their ways. It was starting to look to her like the Xalthari were never meant to be indoctrinated. Had the son of God had his eyes on Xalthryn long ago?

Junova tapped a foot in irritation as she smiled at Vashar. "Those times are gone, Vashar. I have come to ask you to join the Star."

"It is of no concern to us."

Doing her best not to frown, Junova kept a straight face. "His eyes are set on Xalthryn. If your people don't join the Starlit, your lives may be forfeit."

He looked thoughtful for a moment, folding his hands across his chest. "Face death, or allow my people to be absorbed. Xalthari have lived on this world since ancient times. Things change, Xalthryn changes, and strangers come down from above." He glanced between Hernz and Junova. "From ancient times forward, Xalthari never changed. What would Junova do in my position?"

The walls pressed in again, and Vashar rose above her like some ancient wise man, calm and principled. Her stomach turned as she prepared her next words. "I would accept the offer, save as many lives as possible."

Vashar smiled. "Ah, tell me then, would it be saving people to strip them of their identity? Saving people by making them slaves to your beliefs?"

Hernz sat quiet, head tilted, looking at Junova sidelong.

All attention was on her. She took a deep breath and thought for a moment. "It might not be ideal, Vashar, but they would be alive. Are your beliefs worth the lives of all your people?"

Vashar seemed to absorb what she said for a moment. "My people have never feared death. What do my people fear? They fear losing wisdom. They fear losing everything defining them." He rubbed his eyes. "To know whether my people value their life over belief, Junova needs to look around." He spread his arms, waving them around the room full of books.

Hernz shot to his feet and pointed at Vashar. "If you and your people refuse to join us, you will all die. I will see to it, Vas."

Vashar sneered at him, rising from his seated position. Even standing, Vashar was three-quarters of Hernz's height, perhaps even a few inches shorter than Junova. He made up for his stature with thick muscle structure and broad, strong shoulders.

Vashar's face screwed up, a frowning, angry sort of mess. "YOU come to my house and insult me, Hernz! I ignored wisdom, letting YOU step foot here. YOU leave this place, never return!" Vashar flung his finger, pointing at the door. He had emphasized *you* every time he'd spoken it as if throwing a vile insult at Hernz.

Hernz's smile lingered, cold and sharp, like that of a vulture waiting for prey to die. Then he turned and walked out.

Junova stood, eyes lowered, and Vashar grabbed her arm. "Make no mistake, Junova. Death holds no finality to my people. They will fight. I will fight."

As she pulled her arm away, he released his grip. She passed through the door without another look. Of course, she'd failed. What other option had there been? Glaring at Hernz's back, she stalked after him. The man had got his war.

# Chapter 7:
## Direction

*"If one follows the Stars' direction, choosing the wrong path is impossible."*
—Shepard of the Covenant

Kael's eyes snapped open, and he leapt from his cot. Sweat ran down his forehead as he rushed to dress. He stumbled toward the door, pulling on his last boot. Outside, Kael stood tall, firm, at attention. Then he blinked. It was dark and quiet. Looking left and right, he saw no one. He relaxed, took a deep breath, and returned to the barracks.

Pike sat on the ground, leaning against the wall. "You have nightmares?"

Kael nodded.

"Me, too."

Pike was a few years older than himself, quiet and strong. His hair was chestnut brown, and his eyes were almost as green as verdant plasma. He spoke with a slow, throaty, lilting drawl, dragging out vowels as if they meant more than the rest of the word.

Sitting next to Pike, Kael stared out into the murky black. "I think of home when I'm awake and dream of Krennak at night."

Scoffing, Pike shook his head. "Damndest thing, ain't it. Can't leave home fast enough, and now it's the only place you wanna be."

Leaning his head back, Kael gazed at the night sky.

Pike chuckled. "I ain't got family to go back to either. Stupid to think of home. You got family?"

"Mother. My father is in the corps."

Pike raised an eyebrow. "Chasing after dad?"

"It was always a dream to follow in his footsteps. It would be good to see him."

Pike stood, dusting himself off. "I hadn't taken you for an idealist. You know there ain't many old soldiers in the corps."

Gazing up at one twinkling star, Kael hesitated. "His payments still come, he must be out there."

Shrugging, Pike offered a hand to Kael. "Maybe. But you ain't gonna find him here."

Taking Pike's hand, Kael pulled himself up. "Yeah, but we can't leave now even if we wanted to. I keep thinking about the decree. Train well, train hard. Your life may depend on it."

Pike frowned. "I don't think we have a choice."

Nodding, Kael walked into the barracks and threw himself into bed. Sleep would be a reprieve from homesickness, as long as he didn't have any more nightmares.

Kael was yanked from bed. He pried his eyes open, and the floor rushed toward his face. He lay for a second, groaning.

"Get to your feet, maggots. Full gear, five minutes. Report to the landing pad. Nova pace." Otho's voice was guttural and angry as he shouted.

Kael dressed, donned full combat gear, and sprinted from the barracks. His breath steamed in the cold morning air as he ran. Several recruits were in front and behind him as they ran for the pad. Panting, Kael slid to a stop. His heart sank.

Krennak was looking at his watch, shaking his head. "Do ye 'ave no sense o' time? Five minutes dinne mean three, five, or eight minutes late. I dinne know how ye expect to win a war if'n ye're late." Krennak pointed out beyond the facility walls. "Yer enemy will never be late. He won't wait fer ye. He'll use yer weaknesses against ye an' show no mercy." Pacing in front of the pad, Krennak eyed the recruits. "If'n we dinne 'ave a schedule to keep, I'd run ye'll across tae compound an' back. One platoon per lander. Mount up."

As squad leader, Kael was first to board. First in, first to fight, last out, the corps hammered it into them until it became instinct. Courage wasn't felt, it was the way you stepped into battle.

The doors whined shut. And with a jolt, the lander lifted straight up, wings unfolding into a V. Inside, the cramped bay rattled, lit with one dim red light. It was built for ten soldiers, not ten plus two corporals who jammed into its seats. The recruits squirmed, trying to find a comfortable position in the mass of bodies.

A roar from the back drowned out the commotion. Everyone froze.

Otho poked his head above the confusion. "Squad leader."

"Here, sir," Kael replied.

"Open the pilot door and create a void."

"Understood, sir."

After he rotated the latch, the door burst open, and Kael fell face-first on the cockpit floor. Twisting himself around, he found himself looking up at the pilot. She sat above him, eyebrows raised and a smirk on her face.

"Found the floor."

It was a young woman, perhaps a year or two older than he was. She had shoulder-length brown hair and hazel eyes. Her complexion was light, and her features were pleasant.

Kael stared up at her for a long moment, a blank expression on his face. "Hello there."

"Hello to you, soldier."

Pulling himself up, he offered his hand in greeting. As her hands were busy controlling the craft, she motioned downward with her head.

"Oh, right, how stupid of me. I'm Kael, and I'm not a soldier, yet."

She chuckled. "Nice to meet you, Kael, not a soldier, yet. I'm Liora, Astronav."

"Astronav? I thought you flew starships."

41

"We do, but they needed pilots for landers, and I volunteered."

Kael smiled. "I feel better knowing we have one of the best pilots in the system."

Liora shot him a wink. "You better believe it."

He could see the treetops whisking by from the cockpit in a fantastic blur of motion. Trees with canopies of dark leaves layered above light green and cyan leaves stretched out before them. Watching Liora work the controls, he studied her movements, trying to learn as much as possible.

Noticing his gaze, she motioned him closer. "Flying interests you?"

"Should it not?"

"Why wouldn't it interest you? It's exciting."

He raised an eyebrow. "Maybe you could teach me."

Chuckling, Liora glanced at her controls. "I assume you know your cardinal directions?"

Kael nodded.

"Good, then you'll need to learn to read the display. See here, it shows our altitude, attitude, speed, and direction."

He studied the display, the controls, and Liora. He pointed. "This control is pitch and roll, and the other is speed and yaw?"

Raising an eyebrow, she smiled. "You're a quick study. Want to fly it?"

Kael shook his head, glancing back at the hatch. "I better not. Wouldn't want to anger the corporals."

She laughed. "I'd rather not have Ford and Otho yelling in my cockpit. Maybe another time."

He nodded. "I'd like that."

"Squad leader."

Kael shuddered. "I have to go." Squeezing back into the crowd, Kael found Otho. "You called, sir?"

The man wore a frown from temple to temple. "Take your position."

"Yes, sir."

Kael wormed his way to the doors. The lander touched ground, and the doors squealed open. Kael marched out and stood at attention, his squad falling around him. The sun peeked over the horizon, and the cold morning started to warm.

Once the other squads had assembled, Ford paced in front of them. "A new cohort of recruits is arriving today. We thought you'd like to celebrate with a twenty-kilometer run." He grinned. "Make sure you're back in time for their arrival. You will be required to be in full dress uniform."

Ford and Otho boarded the one remaining lander and disappeared into the horizon.

Kael and Pike's squad paced their run together. The sun started to beat down upon them, and his uniform soaked with sweat, rubbing in all the wrong places. They were the second and third squads to arrive at their barracks.

Otho stood, frowning. "What in God's great universe have you underdeveloped, unsightly swine gotten yourselves into?" He stepped closer, shaking his head. "Is this filth any way to represent the corps? Drop and give me fifty." Counting, he circled them like a vulture waiting for its prey to die.

Once fifty push-ups were complete, they stood at attention.

Otho stared in disapproval. "If you're not clean and presentable by the time those recruits arrive, the entire platoon will be punished." Stepping closer, he paced in front of them. "It will be your responsibility to bring them up to speed. You will have until God's temper. This is your opportunity to prove you have what it takes to be here. Dismissed."

To say the scene was controlled chaos would've been an understatement. It was absolute chaos. Uniforms flew as recruits scrambled to shower, slipping and tripping over one another. None were willing to risk being late for arrivals and the consequences that would follow.

One undignified hour later, Kael stood at the landing pad with his squad, cleaned, shined, and pressed.

"We're the only platoon here," a recruit murmured.

Kael whispered to Pike, "We must be on someone's bad side."

Pike smiled as the shuttle burst through the clouds, engines roaring. "Maybe we're that good."

Hot, dry wind from the shuttle exhaust buffeted Kael as the shuttle came to rest. The doors opened with a hiss of air and whining hinges. He watched as the recruits filed out. It had already been two months, and the new recruits looked soft and undisciplined. Several shuttles landed, offloading and taking off.

His thoughts drifted across the stars to the little house, a quaint but fruitful garden, Mother, and brother.

An elbow in the side pulled him right back down to Xalthryn. "This one looks like you," Pike said, pointing.

Stepping onto the planet was a tall young man whom Kael recognized. "Auctor."

Pike raised an eyebrow. "You know him?"

"He's my brother."

"Brother? Ain't it a surprise."

They watched in silence while the remaining recruits stepped onto the planet.

Kael wanted to know how Auctor had enlisted in the corps. The why was obvious, he thought. Auctor had always wanted to stay by his side.

Over the next month Kael and his platoon was kept busy bringing the new recruits up to speed on everything they had learned so far. He wanted to confront Auctor but had no opportunity with over two hundred new recruits he had to help train. He bided his time, working hard to keep up with both the new recruits' training and his own.

# Chapter 8:
## Choice

*"Ensure the path of light prevails in your choice."*
—Starlit Covenant

Junova glared at the green circle of Xalthryn. It was like a cyan jewel in a sea of black in the depths of which the occasional star twinkled. She could see why someone might want this place for its beauty, yet the Star didn't make a habit of capturing things for beauty or whims. Whatever he wanted, he had been patient for a time. Turning from the window, she paced across the charcoal floor of her quarters.

With God relinquishing his throne and Solovian taking his father's place, it seemed Xalthryn was out of time. Much of his forces were committed here. Negotiations with the Xalthari were nonexistent after Hernz's insult to Vashar. She had managed to speak with Vashar since, but to no avail. The man had demanded an apology from Hernz for insulting him, to which Hernz had spat at the ground and refused.

In Vekhara, it was an insult to shorten the name of another. Reducing a name to a single-syllable, three-letter word was the worst possible insult. The shortening of the name dishonored the person and their family heritage and wasn't taken well among their people. Junova didn't understand Vashar's reasoning, but she decided it would be best to avoid insulting him anymore if she wanted peace with his people.

"Peace." She scoffed. Hernz had done everything he could to remove all hope of peace with the Xalthari. Junova had received word Justice was on its way. In a year, its fusion power could be brought to bear against Xalthryn and its inhabitants. She took a deep breath, her shoulders tense with stress. She knew the captain of Justice well; he might be sympathetic to her cause. She stared back down at the planet below. Its misty valleys and dark jagged mountains arced slowly and peacefully as the Radiance orbited it.

The Xalthari would not lie down and submit. It would be a bloody battle. Their resistance would start a countdown for Justice, and her crew would not delay delivering judgment upon the planet.

She frowned. If the Xalthari weren't subdued, Justice would be called upon. "A year," she whispered. That was how long she had to find a resolution, to stop the Xalthari or Justice.

Feeling weak, she sank onto her grav chair, which bobbed under her weight. Laying her head back, she removed the holographic photo from her shirt pocket. Its edges were cool and smooth. As it flickered to life, smiling faces appeared. They stared at her, into her; they'd be alive now if not for her.

Loyalty, duty, honor—what fruits had these traits borne her? A destroyed home, people she loved dead, and guilt. She tried to touch one of the faces on the photo, but her finger passed through the image, and light distorted around it. The stray photons tingled against her skin, and she winced.

"As real as they are now," she muttered.

She would never see, touch, or speak to them again. Clenching her fist, her nails bit into her palm, and her hand went numb.

How could they rebel? How could they put her in a position to do such terrible things? Junova threw the photo. It hit the bronze wall and clattered to the ground, its image distorted. A tear fell from her cheek, making a small dark spot on her uniform.

"We all have a choice," she whispered.

She had been trying to make a difference, controlling events when possible. Lifting her head, she peered out at Xalthryn set against the darkness. Perhaps it wasn't enough. Her conscience had been pricking her, and she hadn't given in to its voice.

Looking down again at the distorted and flickering photo, she picked it up. Part of the image was static, and several faces, a blend of light and dark photons, were damaged. It could never display them again.

*Even now I hurt them.*

Running her fingers alongside the frame, she powered it off and put the photo back into her pocket. The glow of Xalthryn and its moons was ever present at her window. She touched the transparent alloy, cold and smooth against her palms. She had to stop. The violence had to stop. She took a deep breath and hardened her resolve. There was much work to be done and little time to do it.

# Chapter 9:
## Gamble

*"Be careful what you wager; a gamble may cost everything."*
—Starlit Covenant

After flinging open the door to the barracks, Kael stalked in and found Auctor lying in a bunk. "Auctor, why are you here?"

Frowning, Auctor sat up. "Is that any way to greet your brother? I traveled from home to be here."

"Don't change the subject, you know what I meant."

Auctor's frown faded into a devious smirk. "It was easy." He waved a hand. "Change a few records, get a couple of signatures, and here I am. Eighteen and enlisted."

Now Kael frowned. "What if they find out?"

"The official record says I'm eighteen. The corps can't know unless someone rats me out."

Sighing, Kael rubbed his face. "I'm sorry. This place hasn't been what I expected."

"It does have a less-than-idealistic appearance."

Sitting next to Auctor, Kael laughed. "It's more than appearance. You shouldn't have come."

Putting his arm around Kael, Auctor looked at him sideways. "Sounds like you need me to look out for you."

Kael's shoulders sank as he gave Auctor a weak smile. "It's good to see you, brother. Any familiar face here is a blessing."

"There's the brother I came to find."

"Tell me, how is Mother?"

Auctor shrugged. "She was well last I saw. You know our mother."

"Does she know you left?"

"How cold do you think I am? I left her a letter explaining everything."

Ford burst through the barracks door. "Recruits. Get your milk-drinking, diaper-wearing bodies to the landing pad. Nova pace."

Kael scrambled to his feet, heart pounding, and sprinted out. He joined his squad at the pad and stood at attention, trying to slow his breathing.

Krennak stood rigid, his frown ever-present. Once all companies were in attendance, he began to pace. "Every day until now has been child's play. Ye've survived tae hammer. Those o' ye that dinne survive 'ave found a new home at Eesbex. Now ye'll face tae final test. All yer skills 'ave been forged in tae fire and hammered into dull shards." Krennak's gaze met Kael's eye. "This is God's temper. Where ye will be polished from dull excuses o' recruits into soldiers, ye will be bright shards o' light to challenge any shadow."

Krennak clasped his hands behind his back. "Ye will be out there fer one week, by yerselves. Platoon against platoon. Otho will provide each platoon leader wi' a brief an' a map o' tae area." He took a rifle from Ford and held it out. "These are identical to tae ones ye've been practicing wi'. They are loaded wi' marking tags. If ye are hit wi' one, ye're dead, out o' battle." Handing back the rifle, he stepped closer to the recruits. "Each one o' ye will be issued one upon arrival at yer designated landing zone." Staring right at Kael again, Krennak's eyes narrowed. "Dinne fail me, recruits. Now get yerselves into those landers. Nova pace."

Kael boarded the lander, sat next to the cockpit door, and leaned his head against the wall. Sound rumbled from the lander's twin engines as it lifted off. He rubbed his trembling hands together, taking a deep breath. Krennak had made him platoon leader for the test—not a responsibility Kael wanted. Not one he felt comfortable undertaking. Though, what choice did he have?

A thumping sounded against the cockpit door. He opened it and peered inside. A familiar voice met his ears. "Hello, soldier. I haven't seen you in a while."

His heart thumped. "Liora, I'm not—"

She spoke over him. "Not a soldier yet. How could I forget?" She smirked.

Kael's chest tightened, and feeling rushed in like a great tsunami. His mind froze.

"Void got your tongue?"

He hesitated. "I'm preoccupied with the test today."

"Yes, God's temper. This one will be harder than mine."

"Yours?" He gawked. "You took the test?"

She frowned as if trying to look hurt. "Ship crew aren't exempt, I'll have you know." A slight smile returned to the corner of her mouth.

Kael pulled himself through the hatchway and shut it behind him. "What can you tell me about it?"

Looking shocked again, she placed a hand on her chest. "Me? Help you cheat?"

"Not cheating, giving a friend some help. What can I expect?"

On returning her attention to flying, she was quiet for a moment. "There's not much to tell. You'll know your objectives and the conditions. The best advice I could give would be, watch your back out there."

Kael released a breath, and his shoulders slumped. "I had hoped for something more tangible."

"You're being tested on everything you've learned in training. What could be more tangible? Did you expect an easy victory? Because there's no such thing." She gazed down at him for a moment. "Almost all will graduate at the end. How well your platoon and its leaders perform will affect where you're assigned."

Slouching against the cabin wall, he stared off somewhere distant. "Is the corps everything you thought it would be?"

Liora watched her controls, lips pursed. "I wanted to explore, see the galaxy. I've been to eleven worlds. It wouldn't have happened if I had never joined the corps."

"Eleven worlds? I can't imagine."

"Why do you ask?"

Kael glanced at her for a moment, wringing his hands. "My father is in the corps. I can't remember a day when joining up wasn't my dream. I always thought I'd save people by the thousands by bringing them into Starlight. Now I'm here, and it's not what I expected." He crossed his arms. "It's unrelenting, brutal, and merciless. I was naive to think it would be any different."

"Did you think war would be merciful?"

"No, but I thought...I don't know. It would feel like it meant something."

"It doesn't?"

He rubbed a hand across his face. "Feels like I'm part of something bigger but not in the way I imagined. More like I'm a cog in something I don't understand."

Liora tapped a few buttons, correcting a heading error. "I think that's how most people feel."

"I don't know. Auctor, Pike, and the others are made for this."

Liora leaned back, watching him from the corner of her eye. "You weren't?"

Kael's jaw tightened. "I thought I was."

She gazed ahead for a long moment. "You? Naive? No, I refuse to believe it."

Kael huffed. "Don't mock me."

She lifted a hand. "I wouldn't dare."

"You already did."

Her smirk lingered as she turned back to the controls. "How about this? You win the test, and I'll show you something that'll remind you of why you dreamed of seeing the stars in the first place."

Kael raised an eyebrow. "What, a map of all eleven worlds you've been to?"

She grinned. "That, and a little something else. You'll see."

"What do you get if I lose?"

Liora's grin widened, a playful glint in her eyes. "Oh, that's the fun part." She tapped a finger against her chin. "Let's see...how about you owe me a favor of my choosing?"

Kael scoffed. "A favor? Sounds suspicious."

She shrugged. "Think of it as a gamble. Win, and you get a reward. Lose, and I get to call in a favor whenever I see fit."

Kael's eyes narrowed, weighing the cost of his following words. "And what kind of favor are we talking about?"

Liora smirked, leaning back in her seat. "That's for me to decide in the future."

"I feel like I'm walking into a trap."

"Then you better not lose." She winked before turning back to the controls.

Kael exhaled, staring ahead through the cabin glass. He wasn't sure if he was more intrigued by her secret or wary of whatever she had in mind. Either way, there was no turning back now.

A light on Liora's panel flashed. "We are ten out. You'd better get ready to win our little bet."

Kael opened the hatch and climbed back through it, pausing to say over his shoulder, "Don't worry, I'll be back to collect my winnings."

Her voice followed him as he shut the hatch. "I'll be waiting."

Standing on the landing deck, the vibration of the engines pulsated through his boots. He made his way to the lander's rear, took up his position, and held onto the grab rail, steadying himself. He glanced toward the cockpit, the corners of his mouth pulling up.

Pike clapped him on the shoulder, taking position on the opposite side of the ramp door. "You ready?"

Drawing in a slow breath, Kael nodded. "Ready to win."

Pike grinned ear to ear. "Ready to win."

# Chapter 10:
## Temper

*"Those who refuse to follow light and insist on living in shadow;
those Starless will witness God's Temper."*
—Starlit Covenant


Odd-looking green and orange little birds flitted between the trees, their song unlike anything back home. The damp ground dulled the crunching leaves under his feet. Breathing reminded him of his first days on Xalthryn; the air was thicker than at HQ.

Checking the rifle he'd been given, Kael slid out the magazine. Little yellow tags with short but sharp prongs on one end rested inside of it. He shuddered; they looked like they would hurt. After sliding the magazine home with a click, he smacked the bottom to ensure it was seated.

Looking down the sights of the blue-green training weapon felt identical to looking down the sights of the combat rifles he fired at the range. A plain red dot sat in a small holographic sight. He checked his safety was engaged, pulled back the charging handle, and let it snap forward.

He turned to his squad leaders. "Anything useful?"

Pike looked over the infrared map he was studying. "Not much. No large animals to take. The lake could have fish, but the infrared reflection makes it hard to see."

Hands on her hips, Qenni frowned. "So, we eat plants?"

"Looks like it." Ordan scratched his head. "Hunting will be dangerous without real weapons and noisy. Trapping might work."

Grumbling, Pike threw his hands up. "Trapping rats won't feed us all. Ain't gonna happen."

Auctor pointed at the map. "We have to take the supply cache."

"It'll be dangerous." Kael pursed his lips. "It might be our only chance, though." He held up the map. "We know the lake is north and the river is east. Auctor, take your squad and scout along the river. Report any activity, don't engage."

Auctor nodded then stalked off toward his squad.

"Ordan, take your squad north and scout the supply cache. We will move north behind Ordan and wait for his report."

Kael's eyes settled on Auctor as he moved his squad out.

Finding the river was child's play. It burbled and rushed over rocks fifty meters away. Looking upon the cold water flowing by, he held up a fist, and the squad slowed behind him. He directed them left and right, and they spread out, taking cover.

Auctor scanned the opposite bank. It was too quiet. There were no insects, no birds. A bush rustled. A recruit emerged on the far side, followed by an entire platoon. They were moving toward Kael. He smiled and rallied his squad.

Moving his squad north, Auctor found a bend in the river. He spread out his squad, setting up his ambush. Sight lines. Kill zones. It was too easy.

Flicking on his transmitter, he relayed his position to Kael.

Kael echoed his previous orders. "Observe and report."

Frowning, Auctor switched off the transmitter and readied his weapon. And after waiting a significant amount of time, there was no sign of the enemy platoon.

Standing, he rallied his squad. "I think they got around us. We're going north to rendezvous with Kael."

He ran, squad in tow, ducking under branches, snaking between trees. After checking the time again, he spotted a track. He skidded to a knee. Tracks. Northbound. Heavy traffic.

He powered on his transmitter and keyed the mic. "Kael."

"Is that you, Auctor? We've been trying—"

"No time. There is a platoon headed your way from the south. Maybe an hour out."

Silence. "Understood. Get here as fast as you can."

Switching off the transmitter, Auctor sprinted north.

The sun was low, and twilight settled on the jungle. Trees blended together, and vines snagged his arms and legs as he ran. The footfalls of his squad behind him never faltered, never slowed. Wind flowed through his hair, and twigs pulled at his uniform, scratching his exposed skin.

A tremendous crack echoed through the trees. Sliding to a stop, Auctor flung himself onto the carpet of leaves and brush. A group of silver creatures skittered from the bushes, one of the rat like critters running across Auctors back causing him to squirm.

*Dirty little rodents,* he thought.

But was distracted from frowning at the retreating rats as more weapons fire sounded ahead, maybe a few hundred meters. Nothing hit or landed near him.

Getting to his feet, he motioned the squad forward. Low and slow, they made their way toward the supply cache. He moved to cover as a pause in the weapons fire allowed silence to take the jungle. Scanning his surroundings, listening for any sign, he remained still.

A shape bounded out of the brush into a clearing, followed by several others. They spread out and started firing toward the cache. More shots rang out, and a tag buzzed over Auctor's head. Another tag struck a recruit in the clearing, and he screamed and thudded against the ground, writhing in pain.

Another recruit was struck in the neck and fell, gurgling and shaking. Auctor fired, striking someone in the back. The recruit tried to reach behind himself and fell, grunting in pain. His squad joined his attack, and after a short exchange, silence fell again.

Auctor's heart pounded, his fingers trembled, and a smile crept across his face. The sun had vanished beyond the horizon, and moonlight cast beams through the trees. He crawled forward to the recruits. Silhouettes of hard-lined shapes were visible in the clearing.

More weapons fire rang out. The tags left glowing blue streaks in the air as they zipped back and forth across the clearing. Pulling the magazine from his rifle, he counted the rounds. He slid it home with a click and prepared to move his squad again.

The enemy, circling the clearing, was lit by shafts of moonlight. Auctor signaled his squad to spread out. Opening fire, he emptied his weapon into the darkness.

As the firing stopped, a calm settled upon the jungle. The recruits on the ground moaned and cried out in agony. A tap on the shoulder alerted him to a problem. One of his squad had been shot. She lay sprawled out on the ground, muscles tensed but silent. He stared down at her, frowning.

Throwing his weapon down, he sneered at her. "Are you trying to make me look bad? Can any of you do anything without making a star wreck out of it?"

Auctor stomped off as his squad stared in silence.

Pike sat against a crate, chewing a piece of jerky. Blue rays of sunlight filtered through the canopies overhead. Hearing a crunch, he raised his rifle. Auctor came strolling out of the jungle, followed by his squad.

"Where have you been?"

Auctor smiled. "Making your life easier."

Pike jumped to his feet. "We tried to get you on comms for hours."

"I was too close to the enemy, couldn't risk it."

"Too close? We were fighting half the night."

Auctor glared at him. "Where do you think I was? Out there fighting, lying in the dirt."

"You could've found a way."

Auctor waved a hand in dismissal.

"Kael gives the orders here," Pike reminded. "You forgot the part about reporting."

"That's enough, Pike, I think he understands," said Kael.

Frowning at Kael, Pike stalked over to a pile of recovered magazines lying on the ground. Crouching, he started removing tags and consolidating them to make full magazines.

Footsteps came up behind him. "When will the platoon be prepared to march?"

Tossing an empty magazine aside, Pike sank back into the thick mats of dead leaves. "Within the hour. Why did you let him off?"

"I didn't," Kael replied. "I also have to consider keeping our platoon from falling apart. We can't be fighting each other."

Pike nodded. "What do you make of our chances?"

"Expecting the worst, we are outnumbered two to one."

After examining a tag he found, Pike tossed it aside. "Spent." Pulling himself upright, he smiled at Kael. "They don't know what we know."

Taking the last bite of jerky, Kael clapped Pike on the shoulder. "Right. Rally the platoon, we have a lot of ground to cover. Nova pace."

"Four days in this rotten jungle. I'm sick of it."

"Oh, it's not bad." Qenni grinned. "Don't you like seeing a thousand identical trees?"

Kael shook his head. "I'd rather eat nutrient blocks than see another tree."

Qenni curled her lips in disgust. "Those things taste awful."

"I don't know," Ordan said. "I kind of like them."

She glared at him. "Of course, you would. You'll eat dirt and call it gourmet."

Ordan was tall and thin; his hair was bright blonde and cut to a flat top. He was never picky, always followed orders, and didn't complain, though he liked giving Qenni a hard time. Kael thought maybe he liked her, but there was no real evidence to support his suspicion. Though watching such a short, wiry, red-haired woman scowling up at a tower of a man like Ordan was comical. He shook his head and ignored their banter.

Kael stared at the canopies. They were thicker now, and only a few shafts of sunlight made it through. He breathed deep, and air filled his lungs. It was no longer thick and stifling but filled him with energy, motivating him to keep going.

Auctor appeared next to him. "We're almost there. Another hour at most."

"Any sign of the other platoons?"

"None. But my squad is looking."

"That's good. Let me know if you see anything. And, Auctor, don't give away our position."

Auctor stalked off. "I'm not an idiot, brother."

Ordan glanced at Pike. "Hey, what do you think of blocks?"

"They ain't bad. I wouldn't want to eat them every day, though."

"See, they aren't bad."

Qenni shook her head. "You can keep them."

Kael pushed forward, sweat dripping from his forehead. They needed to make good time.

Nearing the primary objective, Auctor was waiting with his squad.

"Report?" Kael asked.

"One platoon," Auctor replied. "They're low on manpower, it looks like they've been fighting."

Kael stared off into the trees for a long moment. "Qenni, take your squad and flank left. Ordan, you take the right flank. Pike and Auctor, with me. Attack on my signal. And coordinate with each other, I don't want friendly fire." He watched Ordan and Qenni move out their squads.

"Why spread us out?" Pike asked.

Kael met Pike's eyes. "If another platoon is out there, we won't be easy to flank."

Auctor chuckled. "The platoon holding the objective will be confused. Being shot at from two sides."

"Right."

Moving into position, Kael could see the defending recruits. They looked nervous. He flicked on his transmitter and gave the order to attack.

A hail of weapons fire erupted around the defenders, dropping several in the first few seconds. More fell, screaming in agony.

Kael's ears rang with the sound and smells of burnt propellant hanging in the air, smokey and metallic. As the few remaining recruits dropped their weapons and surrendered, he could taste the bitter sulfur permeating the clearing.

Kael eyed the surrendering recruits. "Who's your leader?"

One pointed a shaky finger at another surrendering recruit.

"You. Do you know if there's another platoon out here?" Kael asked.

She blinked at Kael. "We took the objective from another platoon two days ago."

Kael took a deep breath, and his shoulders dropped. "We did it."

Pike clapped him on the shoulder. "What do you want to do with them?"

"We've won. Let's march them to the landing zone."

Nodding, Pike pointed at their prisoners. "Let's get moving."

Kael helped the recruits who had been shot get to their feet, still in pain. It would be a long walk to the landing zone. But they had done it; he had won, they had won—both God's temper and his bet with Liora.

# Chapter 11:
## Comrades

*"Starlit and Starless are all comrades here."*
—Warden of Eesbex

The landing zone became visible through the thick matted jungle underbrush as Kael hacked away at the vines and broad-leafed plants. He could see one prominent figure, Krennak standing rigid and unmoving, his hands clasped behind his back. His eyes were fixed upon the incoming recruits as if they were lasers.

Krennak didn't often lose his temper, but Kael had come to know the signs indicating he was teetering upon the precipice of rage. He imagined waves of seething rage emanating from Krennak, enveloping everyone in his path, a destructive force no one could withstand. Feeling a lump in his throat, Kael knew there was no avoiding the imminent tongue-lashing.

When the last recruit stepped foot in the clearing, Krennak ordered everyone to form ranks at attention except the recruit prisoners. Those, he lined up to the side, at attention, facing the jungle. He stood scowling several paces in front of Kael and his squad leaders. The veins on his forehead bulged like tension cables, and his face was flushed, not with rage but with sheer unrelenting force. His voice tore through the air like a shock-wave, raw with authority, demanding obedience without hesitation.

"Which one o' ye canne tell me how tae lot o' ye black-hole-brained, dust-eating, voidborn scum turned this exercise into a star wreck?"

No one spoke. Kael knew this was a time to remain silent; nothing they said would be correct.

Krennak stepped closer, putting himself right in their faces. "Nae, ye canne tell me," he said in a calm voice before screaming, "'cause none of ye 'ave tae slightest clue what I'm talking aboot, do ye? Do ye need an invitation to follow orders? Answer me!"

In unison, Kael and the others replied, "No, Drill Sergeant."

Krennak scoffed. "O' course, ye don't. Not one o' ye 'ave any sense. If tae enemy doesn't kill ye first, I might!" He pointed at the backs of the prisoner recruits. "Each an' every one o' ye would be dead right now if these were Starless. They don't care ye showed them mercy. Each an' every one o' tae godless savages would kill ye given tae chance. Ye canne risk taking prisoners. They hinder ye progress an' make time fer their friends to find an' kill each an' every one o' ye." Readying a training rifle, he walked behind the prisoners. "Ye prisoners, on yer knees!"

One by one, each of the eleven prisoner recruits reluctantly dropped to their knees. Krennak stopped behind the first recruit, aimed between her shoulder blades, and fired. As the tag planted itself into her back, she convulsed from the electric shock and fell to the ground, screaming in pain.

Kael recoiled. He blinked hard, trying to wish away this nightmare, but it was no dream.

Krennak turned to face Kael and the other squad leaders. "This is how ye deal wi' prisoners. As leaders, it is yer responsibility to lead by example. If ye canne handle a few prisoners, ye canne expect yer squads to do tae same. Now tae five o' ye, execute tae lot o' them."

Kael looked at Pike, and there was an unspoken unease between them. Neither relished the idea of killing prisoners, even if it was an exercise. What choice did they have? In unison, they stepped forward, taking position. Kael looked for a way out, but there was none. Racking his brain provided one answer—those words, spoken by God: *Train well, train hard. Your life may depend on it.*

Krennak stepped in front of them. "Wait. Barzi, this is yer platoon?"

Her voice came weakly. "Yes, sir."

"Get off tae ground. Give her a rifle. Yer going to execute them fer not fighting to tae last."

Hesitating, she took the rifle and stood next to Kael. He could see her hands trembling.

This was training, and none would be killed. If they had fought to the last, they would not be faced with this choice. Kael was the last to prepare his rifle. Taking aim, they prepared to fire. He closed his eyes, his heart racing, and fired his weapon.

It was over as fast as it had begun. Recruits on the ground writhed in pain, screaming, no longer prisoners but comrades. Krennak ordered they be taken care of with the other exercise casualties.

Barzi was on her knees, crying, her rifle beside her. Kael wanted to help but didn't dare move.

"There has been a serious failure in leadership," Krennak spat. "Discipline wasn't maintained."

Sweat running down his brow, Kael feared what Krennak would say next.

"This recruit has failed tae corps, her platoon, and herself. Barzi, ye are excommunicated from God's corps."

She dropped to the ground, screaming, pleading for mercy. Corporal Otho grabbed her by the arms, restrained her, and pulled her into a lander. She cried the entire way, thrashing against the corporal's grasp.

Krennak walked between the recruits and the doomed recruit. "Let this be a lesson to ye. She will live out her days at Eesbex, locked away in tae frozen fortress, mining ice. Tae rest o' ye get yer gear and load up. Nova pace."

Kael had stood there. Stood there and done nothing. He'd watched her beg and watched them drag her away like she was nothing. He could still hear her sobs, see her face. And he had done nothing.

He picked up his gear and ran to the nearest lander. He sat down near the cockpit, his fingers grasping the edges of his seat, turning white. His breath came hard and fast. This was the corps. And maybe this was what he had signed up for.

# Chapter 12:
## Purpose

*"The path set before you may not be obvious, but trust in his purpose."*
—Starlit Covenant

Specks of dust floated, carefree, in the rays of sunlight filtering through the window. Kael rolled over, pulling his blanket over his head. His eyes snapped open, and throwing his blanket off, leapt to his feet, and began to dress. Pulling his pants on, he caught a foot in one leg and crashed to the floor with a thud. He moaned.

"What are you doing? Did you hurt yourself?" Pike stood looking down at him, grinning from ear to ear, and muffled laughter came from others nearby. Pike stretched out a hand in aid.

"My pride." Kael grabbed Pike's hand, lifting himself upright. "What are you doing here?"

Pike looked confused for a moment, eyebrow raised, then he chuckled. "I'm here to become a soldier in the corps. You must've hit your head. I would've hoped it would knock sense into that brain of yours, but it appears you lost what little you had."

"No, I meant to say, why is Krennak not threatening to launch me into a black hole?"

"Ah. In Krennak's words, 'Since God's temper wasn't a total failure an' ye managed to capture tae objective, I've decided to give ye'll a day o' rest. Don't think ye live in luxury now, tae real thing starts tomorrow.' Since you were so tired, we figured on letting you sleep."

Sinking onto his cot, Kael let out a sigh. "That was almost a month ago. Why now?"

Pike shrugged. "I figure they want to give us a day to get ready for whatever is happening tomorrow. I doubt Krennak is rewarding us for anything."

"What are your plans?" Kael asked.

Pike glanced over his shoulder, eyeing his squad. "There was some discussion about that. The popular choice was going out to flaunt our day off in front of the losers."

Kael winced. "I'd rather go for a walk."

"Can I join you? I ain't excited about watching the soft skins anyway."

Kael nodded.

"Where do you want to go?"

Kael looked at the shaft of sunlight. "Urban Tactics Course. It's a pleasant walk."

On the road to the UTC, Kael looked out at the flat landscape. Long, thick cyan blades poked up in clumps along the road's edge. Grass was the one bit of nature weaseling its way back into the compound.

"You ain't talkative today," Pike observed.

Kael glanced over at him. "I've been thinking."

They walked a few more steps in silence. "You want to talk about it?"

"How do you feel about god's temper?" Kael asked.

Pike shrugged. "We handed the other platoons a beating."

Kael slowed. "That's not what I was asking."

Pike stared off at the horizon, lips pursed. "I know. I keep telling myself it's training, but if they expect us to show no mercy here, I can't imagine what it'll be like after."

Kael frowned. "The exercise was one thing, they could fight back. But I keep seeing myself pull the trigger. Those screams of pain and convulsions. I don't think I'll ever forget that."

"If we didn't, we'd be like Barzi."

Kael shivered. "Is this what you expected from training, shooting people in the back, executing them?"

"I ain't seen a thing I did expect." Pike spit. "Maybe they are preparing us for the worst."

"Maybe. It feels like God contradicts himself."

Halting, Pike glared at him, his mouth open. "Explain yourself."

Kael took a deep breath. "During his decree, he said stretch out a hand, but then he told us to train hard. Train to execute people?"

Pike let out a sigh. "He ain't contradicting himself. I think he wants us to try and help these Starless of Xalthryn but also prepare for the worst. If everything goes supernova, wouldn't you want to be prepared?"

"Have the skills and not need them versus needing them and not having them." Kael kicked at a rock and clenched his fist. "I still don't like it. If we are to help, why aren't they teaching us about them?"

Pike shrugged. "I couldn't say. Before we came here, we knew Starless existed, but we didn't know anything about them. Maybe the corps doesn't want us to know."

Kael looked out at the horizon again. The great wall of the compound sat like an old palisade, holding the barbarians at bay. Washed-out blue light from the sun shone against the flat side of it. "Maybe. It feels wrong. Like we are training for one purpose." Closing his eyes, he took a ragged breath. "Even if it was training, it opened my eyes. I won't execute people in cold blood. It's not who I am."

Pike clapped him on the shoulder. "Don't worry so much. We're done with training and with Krennak. It has to get better."

Kael gave Pike an unconvinced smile. "I hope so." He looked out toward the UTC, its giant buildings growing out of the ground like out-of-place mountains. At least he didn't have to train there anymore.

# Chapter 13:
## Slaughter

*"The meaning of slaughter is relative. For example, if I were to kill you, some may say I slaughtered you, but if I were to kill everyone present, almost all would call it a slaughter."*
—Shepard of the Covenant

Breath steaming, Kael held his DEX card. The cool metal card read, *D1 I XO Squad Zero.* He was a soldier now and assigned to a squad. Slipping his DEX into a zippered pocket, he stood at attention.

The sun hadn't crested over the horizon, and every platoon was present in the HQ courtyard. They'd assembled before muster, before corporals or Krennak had come to rouse them from sleep.

He balled his trembling hands. Were they trembling from excitement, reluctance, or the cold? He wasn't sure. Looking around, he caught Pike smiling at him.

As muster blared from the speakers around the compound, Xalthryn's sun edged above the horizon, lighting the recruits' backs with a soft blue glow. Shortly afterward, Krennak, followed by his cadre of corporals, marched up the street and into the courtyard. Scowling at the assembled recruits, he and his men stood before them.

"Ye think ye lot are somethin' special dinne ye? Arrivin' before meself?" His scowl melted away, replaced by a grin from ear to ear. "Ye 'ave surprised me fer once. I've hammered ye into shape, an' ye 'ave been tempered into soldiers o' tae Star."

Something about Krennak's smile was cold and predatory, making Kael's skin crawl. He had a sudden urge to step back, but he held his ground.

Krennak spun on his left heel and paced as he had many times before. "There won't be any ceremony, no celebration. Ye are soldiers in tae corps now. Yer responsibility to uphold tae Starlit Covenant is paramount." Snapping his boots together, he turned around. "Lads, tae time has come, an' our orders are written in stone. We are to meet tae enemy in glorious battle, carryin' tae word o' Starlight to these heretics." Grunting, he cleared his throat. "Platoons! Get yer gear, an' get yer asses to launch! One hour, nova pace!"

The lander filled with the usual red glow and hum of the engines. Kael and his squad sat in silence, and the prospect of actual combat and real danger loomed over them like a wildcat waiting to pounce on its prey. The nearness of it was sobering. Even the veteran troops they'd been integrated with sat motionless, staring into nothing.

Kael was thankful he wasn't a platoon leader now. Leading people into battle wasn't something he wanted. Kael, Auctor, Pike, Qenni, and Ordan had been brought in as replacements for Zero Squad. Zero had lost half their squad on another world before shipping out to Xalthryn.

Zero's squad leader was a tough no-nonsense woman. Alandra had two rules: keep your head down and always obey her orders. The first made enough sense to Kael: you can't get shot if you keep your head down. As for the second, he thought obeying orders would be a given, not optional.

Shuddering as it vectored to a new heading, the lander's light turned yellow. "Ten minutes then," Kael muttered to himself. Hand still shaking, he checked his weapon one last time. It didn't need to be checked, but it gave him something other than the impending battle to focus on. Breathing rough and clenching his teeth, he focused on his weapon check.

He could die out there; they could all die when the ramp dropped. "Don't think about it. Focus on the mission." He ignored the fact that he was checking his weapon for the third time.

Auctor elbowed him in the side. "Stop playing with your weapon. It makes you look scared."

Kael rested it on his lap. "I am scared."

Auctor scowled as a voice came over their earpiece radios.

"All squads, touchdown in thirty and counting. Twenty-nine, twenty-eight...."

Auctor turned his attention to his weapon. "I've got your back, don't do anything stupid."

"Twenty-four, twenty-three...."

A corner of Kael's mouth edged upward. "Thanks, I'll try." Nudging Pike, Kael tried and failed to give him a reassuring smile that was really more for his own reassurance.

Pike winked back at him. "Ain't got nothin' to worry about. We made it through Krennak, after all."

"Sixteen, fifteen...."

"Right," Kael said, adjusting the clasps on his rigging. "Like training."

"Ten...."

Everyone stood. Pike checked his weapon and charged a round.

Kael stood shoulder to shoulder with Auctor and Pike, and while neither were battle-hardened, he trusted them. Having someone you could trust was essential in battle. His new squad was another matter, though. How could you trust someone with your life whom you'd met an hour ago?

"Five, four...."

Everyone turned to face the door.

"Two...."

The lander jolted as it touched solid ground.

"All platoons, go, go, go, nova pace!"

The door opened, and the ramp extended. Blinding blue light filled the compartment, and there was a thunderous cry as the veterans around him shouted at the top of their lungs. Joining his voice to theirs, Kael charged into the fray.

Taking cover alongside the squad behind anything he could find —trees, rocks, deployable barriers—Kael ran with Zero toward their objective. Alandra shouted orders, watched for the enemy, and kept an eye on her squad.

Kael ducked behind a barrier with Gatlin, the squad sergeant, as projectiles whistled overhead in a furious hailstorm. Gatlin looked at Kael and grinned. "This is nothing, kid, you should've been there when we torched Hytow." He shot over the barrier a few times before looking. "Clear enough, let's move."

Kael scrambled out of cover, frantic, searching for his next hiding spot. A large mossy rock sat about twenty meters away, and he sprinted for it. About a hundred meters ahead, robed men were scurrying between trees and rocks, shooting in his direction.

Running, stumbling, and almost falling, Kael threw himself behind the moss covered boulder. Breathing hard, he looked back the way he'd come. People were lying on the ground amidst the lawn of cyan grass—bodies, he realized. They sprawled out like some artist's idea of a macabre scene, emotions frozen on their faces: fear, anger, pain, surprise.

There was familiar shouting; Auctor was advancing with more soldiers. They were pushing hard, and some Starless gave up their positions to move back. Kael lost sight of them behind a stand of black-trunked trees.

He jumped as two men threw themselves behind the rock after an explosion. One landed face up, eyes staring at the sky. Dead. The other groaned, and Kael rolled him over. "Pike!"

Opening his eyes, Pike looked around. "I feel terrible."

Putting his field-med training to use, Kael performed a quick exam. "There are no broken bones and a few scratches. I can't say for your insides, though."

Pike tried to sit up on his elbows but fell back to the ground. "I ain't getting up, the whole world is spinning."

*Crack.* A projectile struck the edge of the rock then skittered out of control, keening off into the distance. Dust and shards of broken rock pelted Kael and Pike. He had to get Pike out of here. No one was around to help; the nearest soldiers had disappeared now. Frantic, he pushed off the ground and grabbed Pike. "I'm going to carry you out of here."

Pike nodded as Kael strained, struggling to lift him onto his shoulders.

After getting a good hold on Pike, Kael started back toward the landers. As he stepped out, a whistle blew.

"Retreat," Pike groaned.

Kael ran as fast as he could. Soldiers passed him by as they ran for the landers. A voice called, "Keep going, kid, we've got your back."

Glancing back, Kael saw a group of soldiers heading right for him. It was Gatlin, Alandra, Auctor, and a few others from Zero. Through the confusion, he could also see the Xalthari advancing, now in a full sprint toward the remaining corps forces.

Eyes widening, he pushed himself harder. He had to move faster. It was the one way they would make it out alive. Rounding a patch of thick brush, he slowed, gawking at the open field before him. The landers were gone. Blackened circles made by the engines in the blue-green grass remained.

Kael stumbled to his knees. The hope of escape, which had welled in his chest, was gone, leaving nothing but emptiness.

Pike groaned. "What's wrong?"

"They're gone, they left us."

Someone pulled at his arm. "Come on, kid, no time to rest."

Gatlin hoisted him to his feet and helped him along. Ducking behind a boulder, Zero and a mix of other soldiers took positions, returning fire and setting up barriers on their flanks.

Gatlin helped set down Pike. "Rest easy, soldier," he said, winking at Pike. "We've got it from here." Gatlin yanked Kael down by the elbow. They sat on the ground, backs resting against a barrier. "Alright, kid, we hold them here."

Nodding, Kael got himself up on one knee and fired his weapon over the barrier. The power of it was familiar, like in training. As he shot and reloaded, his mind drifted away from the battlefield to his home and his mother, her smile, and safety. Sweat ran into his eyes, and he wiped it off with his sleeve. What an idealistic fool he had been. A few months ago, he'd been home, safe, and sure of his future. Now, he was scared and at real risk of dying.

The words of the God Ruler flashed through his mind. *Train well and train hard, your life may depend upon it.* He understood the meaning now, and he had trained hard, but his training felt insufficient at this moment. He was trapped by the enemy with no hope of escape.

He wanted to run, but where? No matter which way he went, death would be waiting. Looking around frantically, he spotted Auctor, his face a hard line, shooting and shooting. He didn't look scared at all. Kael grasped the cool metal of his rifle tighter and kept firing over the barricade.

"Lander incoming, one minute," someone shouted.

Kael's heart pounded harder. There was hope after all. A slight warmth crept back into the abyss of his chest. He even almost smiled at the news. He would live.

Unable to see the enemy, he kept shooting. He had to keep them back, keep them away until rescue arrived.

A soldier near him leaped back, tearing at his helmet, screaming. Blood trickled and then gushed down the side of his head and out of his nose. A medic went to his side, and, upon removing his helmet, the soldier went limp, blood pooling on the ground under him. Tossing the blood soaked helmet aside, the medic returned to his other wounded men.

Kael's face turned ghost white, the final bits of his new reality snapping into place. The metallic smell of blood mixed with burnt rifle propellant in the air sent his stomach turning.

An explosion rang out, and several soldiers flew through the air. Kael hunched over, trying to protect himself from the raining debris.

"Where is the lander?" someone shouted.

At least he wasn't alone in being ready to leave this nightmare. At least someone else was asking the right questions.

"There it is!" another voice said.

A lander circled overhead, black against the odd green sky. Its weapons were deployed and fired with a deafening ratcheting sound. Kael peeked out from behind his barrier to see trees torn and men running. A projectile caught a man in the torso, and his body seemed to explode. Legs flew one way, head and shoulders the other.

He looked away, nausea returning to his stomach. Someone was shouting a rally call, and soldiers moved toward the lander as its ramp extended. Kael crawled to Pike, and Gatlin helped Kael carry him on board. As the lander lifted off, Kael slumped against the wall, sliding down until he hit the floor.

His whole body was heavy, and everything hurt. He leaned against the wall, watching the tangled mess of men and women trying to help the injured. The wounded themselves lay strewn across the deck, writing and grunting, and a muffled yell occasionally emerged from the chaos.

Kael sat and watched. He was empty. Sounds ebbed, and bodies melded in a heaping mass of coppery blood and burnt clothes.

Nothing happening mattered. It was like he had left his emotions back on the battlefield, another victim among the dead, a casualty of war.

Someone was standing in front of him. Blinking, he tried to see the face through the light's red glare. It was Auctor. He was saying something, but Kael couldn't hear him. Auctor bent over and grabbed him by his uniform, hauling him up. It looked like he was yelling something, but Kael still couldn't hear him.

Auctor shook him by his shoulders, and Kael blinked again. Looking around, he remembered where he was and what he had been doing. Auctor's voice was louder now, though it was distant. "Can you hear me? Have you been shot?"

Kael shook his head. "I...I'm okay."

"Can you stand?"

Checking his footing, Kael nodded. "Yes, I think so."

Auctor smirked. "See, I told you I'd have your back."

"Yeah. Thanks." Kael gawked at the mess of blood and uniforms cut or torn off wounded soldiers. "Pike. How is he?"

"Alive, last I saw. He didn't look bad." Auctor threw himself down on a seat. "Who knew war was so tiring. It was a rush, though, wasn't it?"

"I don't know if that's the word I'd use for it."

Auctor closed his eyes and lay back, smiling. Kael slumped into a seat next to his brother, and he stared at an empty spot on the opposite side. How many weren't coming back from this slaughter?

# Chapter 14:
## Trajectory

*"If a path is unsuitable, perhaps a different trajectory is needed."*
—Xalthari Warden of Echoes

"Hold him down, I can't work while he's thrashing."

"I'm trying. Nurse, come help me."

Someone shouted something he couldn't understand, and his arms and legs were held down. The world was black. Pike tried to scream, but no sound came out. His heart raced, and he struggled harder.

"Hold still, son, we are trying to help you."

He didn't believe what they were saying and strained against the hands holding him down. "I ain't gonna let you torture me," he tried to yell, but still no sound came from his throat.

Pain stabbed into his leg. It burned and tore at him, causing him to lurch on the cold hardness he lay on.

"I got it out. Where's the nurse?"

Running footsteps approached. "Here is the syringe, doctor."

Something jabbed into his arm. Using the last of his strength, he tried to worm free, reeling and pulling, but the drug took effect. Sounds grew distant, his body light and weak, and every other sensation faded into nothingness.

Sitting in a chair, his gaze transfixed upon Commander Hernz's door, Kael listened to the shouting beyond it. "Unacceptable losses," a voice said, to which another replied, "They are better prepared than we knew."

The heated conversation continued for several more minutes before the company captain, Ispan, was thrown out of Hernz's office. The man straightened his uniform and walked out looking every bit the proud corps soldier.

Hernz stood in the doorway. His face was of a man furious and troubled. His eyebrows were in a great frown, and his jaw was clenched so tightly Kael could see his muscles bulging from his neck. "Kael Vallen?"

Shooting to his feet, Kael saluted. "Yes, sir."

"Come in." Hernz turned and sat at his desk.

Closing the door behind himself, Kael stood at attention. To his surprise, the commander's office looked like every other officer's.

"You're wondering why you're here?"

"Yes, sir."

"At ease, Kael." Hernz smiled. "Have a seat." After Kael took a seat, Hernz continued. "Your sergeant, Alandra, speaks well of you. On your first little outing, you managed to get yourself home and save a fellow soldier. I want to commend you."

Kael winced. "Sir, I...I was scared. I don't know how I made it out alive. I ran."

"Look, son." Hernz's voice had softened. Looking out his window, he sighed. "We've all been there. Our first battle is one we are not to forget. I remember every fight I've been in. Fear comes with the territory, it keeps us from being too overconfident, too brazen. It can be a healthy reminder we aren't invincible. The key is learning to use it, don't let it take over."

With his mouth half gaping, Kael blinked at Hernz. "You were afraid?"

Hernz huffed a laugh. "Oh, yes, on more than one occasion. Keep fighting, Kael, and remember what you're fighting for."

"Yes, sir."

Leaving the command building, Kael made his way to the infirmary. There, he found Pike stretched out on a cot unconscious, a nurse changing a bandage. "How is he?"

After glancing sideways at Kael, the nurse continued her work. "He will live."

Taking a stool and sitting, Kael let out a sigh of relief.

"I heard you're the one who carried him to safety," she said, wrapping Pike's arm. "You must be courageous."

It seemed everyone wanted to congratulate him and say he had done well yesterday, but it wasn't how he felt. He had run and cowered in the face of danger. If not for the squad, he wouldn't have made it. It was they who had been brave, not he. He shook with the truth of it and clenched his jaw at his cowardice.

"It was nothing. I was doing my job."

The nurse winced at his words before standing. "You both made it out alive. That's more than most can say." She stalked off, letting the door slam as she left the room.

She had a point. Many had died yesterday. Yet many of those he knew had made it out alive when the odds had been against them. He put his face in his hands, rubbing his forehead. He had no answers, but something about it was wrong.

Pike groaned.

Kael straightened, looking at Pike.

Groaning again, Pike opened his eyes. "I feel terrible."

Unable to help himself, Kael smiled. "You look alright to me."

"Now I know you're lying."

"The nurse said you're in good shape."

Huffing a laugh, Pike groaned more and held himself. "Don't make me laugh, it hurts." After a moment, Pike looked at Kael. "How'd I get out of there? The last thing I remember...I'm not sure."

Kael looked at the floor. "You were hit with an explosive. I was close by and carried you back."

"I suppose I owe you my thanks then."

Kael wrung his hands. "I don't know how we did it. When the retreat sounded, I was carrying you, and I ran. So many bodies. When I saw the LZ, the landers, they had left us." Kael's breath caught in his throat, and he closed his eyes to hold back his tears. "I thought no one would save us. Then my squad and Auctor came. We held our ground until a lander came." He rocked back and forth on his stool. "Pike, I thought we would die. And I was too scared to move, to fight."

Pike grunted and rolled over to face Kael. "It was bad. I was scared, too. Heck, I'm still scared. Being afraid doesn't make you a coward, quitting does. We'll get back out there, and we'll fight. We'll fight for the Star, avenge our defeat, and end these Starless." Pike sucked in a breath of air and rolled back. "I'd better take it easy."

"I'll let you get some sleep." Kael got up and walked to the door, grasping its cool, rigid handle.

Then Pike spoke. "Whatever you think of yourself, without you, I would've died yesterday."

Sunlight warmed Auctor as he sat with his legs up on a barrel outside the infirmary. He had been waiting for Kael. Of course, he could've gone in, but he didn't see the need.

Pike was worth saving, he was a decent fighter, but not as good as Auctor was. His brother was always selfless, and it figured he'd risk his life for another.

Kael stalked out of the infirmary looking upset about something.

"I've been looking for you."

Kael frowned. "Looks like you've found me."

"What's got you in a mood?"

Sitting down next to him, Kael sighed. "I'm sorry, Auctor. My mind is still on yesterday."

"Yesterday?" Auctor smiled. "It was eye-opening."

"Yeah, and now everyone says I'm brave for saving Pike. But I don't feel brave."

Grabbing Kael by the back of the neck, Auctor shook his head. "You, brave? No, you were being yourself, brother. You've always put others' needs before your own."

Looking sidelong at Auctor, Kael huffed a laugh. "You always know how to make me feel better."

"Ah, that's one of my many talents."

A silence settled between them for a moment, then Kael spoke. "Why were you looking for me, anyway?"

"Oh, that. Someone said you were moping around, so I decided to check on you. Make sure you're not giving up on me."

Kael looked down. "I'm not giving up. It's not like I could if I wanted to. You know, consequences and all."

Lips curling up, Auctor gave a little smirk. "I wouldn't be forging any documents to follow you there."

"I suppose not."

Hopping up, Auctor clapped Kael on the shoulder. "Don't pay attention to what they tell you. Come to me, and I'll set you straight."

Smiling, Kael nodded. "Thanks, Auctor. I can always count on you."

A young man rounded a corner of the infirmary and stopped in front of Auctor, breathing hard. "I have a message for Vallen."

"I'm Vallen," both brothers replied.

Frowning in brief irritation, Auctor looked the man up and down with contempt. "Which Vallen are you looking for?"

Still bent over trying to catch his breath, the man wheezed, "There's more than one of you?"

Auctor scoffed. "You idiot."

"Right, sorry, sir. I'm looking for Kael Vallen."

"That's me."

After getting his breathing under control, the man looked at Kael. "I've been told to have you report to landing pad A. Nova pace, sir."

"Alright," Auctor said, waving a hand in dismissal. "Now leave us be."

"Yes, sir." The man scurried off.

"What was all that about?"

Auctor rolled his eyes. "I don't know, but I never want to see that rat again." Auctor noticed Kael looked put off but decided he wasn't interested in asking why. "You better go find out what they want."

"Yeah."

The landing pad was deserted apart from a singular transport shuttle. As he approached it, the engines hissed and smoked; they were still hot from entry. Kael peeked inside and was greeted by a voice, and a familiar one at that.

"Hello, soldier."

Liora. His heart jumped, and he stumbled inside the transport. A faint giggle came from somewhere inside.

"Don't fall. I wouldn't want to take you to the infirmary before I show you your prize."

Kael raised an eyebrow. "Prize? That's right, our little bet. I was beginning to wonder if you had forgotten."

Slinking down from the open cockpit door, Liora grinned. "No, I would never. A bet is a bet, and you won."

Sliding into a seat and trying not to appear nervous and excited at the same time, Kael gave a polite smile. "I can't wait. What is it?"

Wiggling her finger at him, she shook her head. "Be patient, there will be plenty of time for that. First things first, I need a co-pilot." She climbed back up into the cockpit, waving for him to follow.

"A co-pilot? You don't mean for me—"

"Of course, who else?"

Swallowing a lump in his throat, Kael went to the front of the transport and into the cockpit.

Liora was already seated, flicking switches and poking at buttons. "Sit here." She pointed at the chair next to hers.

Taking his seat, Kael looked at the controls sprawled out in front of him. He recognized a few similar displays from the landers, but most were alien to him. "What do I need to do?"

Liora spun around and looked at him with a little knowing smile. She pointed out several displays and controls and gave him brief explanations of their functions. Once satisfied Kael had enough informa-tion, she turned and initiated launch.

From the air, much higher than the landers flew, Kael watched Xalthryn move below them. It seemed less violent and more beautiful.

"Can you see the trajectory I've plotted?"

Kael tried to remember which display she had referenced. Seeing it, his face went slack. She had plotted a course into orbit. "I see it."

"Good. The controls are yours."

His mouth went dry, and his heart drummed in his chest. "I can't fly this thing into space!"

Liora spun around in her seat to face him. "Where's your sense of adventure, Kael? I thought you wanted to learn more. Am I wrong?"

She had a point, he had been eager to learn. But jumping into the deep end was madness.

"I do want to learn. I didn't think I'd be doing this my first time." His eyes darted between the controls and readouts, as he tried to un-derstand what she had told him.

Liora grinned. "Sometimes you have to take a leap of faith and do a thing. Even when you don't feel ready." She steadied his arm. "Take the controls and make a smooth, steady pull. Follow the guidelines here and here. You'll be fine."

Kael worked the controls, and Liora watched, smiling all the while. Once the turbulence started, he gripped the controls like they were a rope and he was hanging from a mountainside. Sweat glistened on his forehead, and his palms were sweaty and slick on the controls.

A few moments later, they were through. They were in space. It was a lifetime to Kael, each moment vivid and wrought with terror. But now, the rough ride was smooth, and he could breathe easy knowing he had done it. Liora had set him up, but he had done it.

Unable to wipe the grin from his face, he jumped up. "That was...." He was at a loss for words. "I did it."

Still smiling, Liora turned back to her controls. "I knew you could. It's nerve-racking the first time, but flying these smaller ships is a breeze. Now imagine piloting that." She pointed out into space.

Squinting, Kael looked out into the black. He could make out the outline of something, and it was getting bigger. His eyes widened, as he realized what he was looking at: Radiance.

"It's bigger than I imagined. You pilot that?"

Glancing back, she huffed a laugh. "Yes." She brought the shuttle alongside the massive dreadnought and flew along its length.

Kael stared wide-eyed, mouth half open, in awe. "I can see why you wanted to show me this. It's like nothing I've ever seen."

"Are you ready to see what you've won?"

Kael blinked at her. "This isn't it?"

Liora looked him up and down, one eyebrow raised. "Not unless you're afraid."

Feeling a smile overtake him, Kael shook his head. "Who's afraid?"

She winked at him. "That's my soldier."

Radiance was as grand on the inside as it was outside. Liora led him through halls and hypertubes until they stood at the door to her quarters.

They were a stark contrast to the clean corridors. Papers with numbers and scribbles were strewn across a table, and little notes with what looked like constellations drawn on them were scattered about.

He wasn't sure why, but he had expected her to be more organized than this. Yet, it wasn't important now he was thinking about it. She was a fantastic pilot, intelligent and witty, and not so bad to look at.

She cleared some space on a chair for him to sit and went around the room, activating emitters on each wall. Taking a seat next to him, she clicked a button on a remote.

Light beamed from the emitters, and soon the room was transformed into a garden of green grass, flowers, trees, and even birds flitting in the background. Kael stuck out a hand, and a bird flew right through it, the light distorting as it passed over his hand.

"I've never seen anything like this."

"Mm, this is one of the planets I've visited. This is better than maps, wouldn't you say?"

He gawked at the detail of the once room turned garden and nodded. "Yeah."

Then the image shifted, distorting, and they were on a series of cliffs overlooking gigantic violet waterfalls. The sky was star-bright, and three moons hung above the vista.

"You've been here, too?"

"Mhm. This one is my favorite. I love to sit and listen to the rushing water under the tranquil skies." Liora jumped up and shuffled through a stack of notes on the half-hidden table. "I almost forgot. Ah, here they are." She sat and showed him two small pieces of paper. "I want you to have these." Handing him one, she asked, "Do you recognize this?"

Examining the piece, Kael smiled. "This is my constellation, the star I'm from. How did you know?"

"A girl never tells her secrets." She laughed. "This one is my constellation, and this is my star. So you can always find me."

After studying the constellation, Kael slipped it into his zippered pocket. "I'll keep it with me, always."

Smiling, Liora bent over cupping her hands in the little stream running across the floor. Light flowed around in distorted waves, filling her hands with nothing more than photons. Captured light rejoined the flow as she pulled her hands up.

"It reminds me of a river back home," Liora chuckled. "It was real though."

"What's your home world's name?" Kael asked.

Rubbing her hands as if expecting them to be wet, she glanced up at him. "Obralon. It's a beautiful world. Not as beautiful as this," Liora shrugged. "But, it's home. There's no place quite the same."

Kael stared off into the projected sky. "No, there isn't."

"What are you thinking about?" Liora asked, resting a hand on his arm.

"My father. The last time I saw him," Kael looked down, then tried to smile. "It was the day he left to join the Corps. We sat on our front porch as the frost glistened in the morning light. I was so excited, I wanted to know everything—answers he didn't have. I still don't know where he is."

"I could ask the Captain."

"No," Kael said, shaking his head. "I'm not sure I'm ready to know." After a brief pause, he looked at Liora. "What about your family?"

Sliding closer, she took Kael's hand in hers. "Just a normal family, really. Mom, dad, sister. My dad was always busy so mom raised the two of us. Until I was old enough to help, then he wanted me to work with him."

"And you didn't want to?" Kael asked.

She shook her head. "It was all office work and politics. I couldn't stand it."

"Politics?" Kael asked, raising a brow. "What was his work?"

Liora sighed. "His official title would be Governor Veltrin. Governor Walleck Veltrin of Obralon," She said, waving her other hand in front of them.

Kael stared at her in surprise. "Your father is a planetary governor?"

She nodded.

"Liora," Kael said. "You could have gone anywhere, done anything. You didn't need to join the corps to visit other worlds. Why?"

"Why?" she repeated. "Because, if I went by any other means, I'd always be Governor Veltrin's daughter. Now I'm an Astronav, I never would've got to pilot a ship like Radiance otherwise. And only you and Junova know about Governor Veltrin's daughter."

"I think I understand," Kael said. Then giving her a smirk, he continued. "Imagine if everyone knew you were Governor Veltrin's daughter. Oh the rumors," Kael scoffed. "Did you see her take that common soldier from some insignificant planet to her quarters?"

"Scandalous," Liora said, letting her mouth hang agape. "I don't know how my father will ever recover."

They laughed together.

She rested her head on his shoulder. "Let's listen to the water for a while."

Kael slipped his arm around her waist and leaned his head against hers. "I'd like that."

The distant rush of the falls faded behind the warmth they shared, and for a little while, the world was quiet.

# Chapter 15:
## Path

*"Once again, his chosen have been forged for a path of light."*
—Corps Commander

"She had a grand constellation!" Ordan said, tossing his cards on the table. "How does she always have what she needs?"

Sighing, Kael flung his cards down on the dark plastic table. He regretted playing now, but it was too late for second chances. Sergeant Alandra was a blonde-haired, blue-eyed independent sort. She was twenty-eight years old, and when she wasn't cheating the squad out of their money, she was lifting weights or running.

Frowning, he pushed off the flimsy table and walked to his cot.

Sunlight filtered in through the open door, and a gentle but thick breeze blew through the musty barracks.

The sergeant's voice scraped at his nerves like sandpaper. "Done already?"

He shook his head. "I don't have anything left."

Giggling, she smiled at him. "I could loan you some money."

Kael frowned at her. "Not a chance."

Alandra waved a dismissive hand. "Have it your way."

Ordan glared at Alandra, stabbing his finger at the cards on the table. "Deal the cards."

Trying to look hurt, she placed a hand on her chest. "Be patient. I'll give you a chance to win your money back."

Sitting back and staring at specks of dust floating in the air, Kael thought about Liora. He had never met a woman like her. The girls back home were interested in the usual things: fashion, money, and stagnation. Back home, they didn't want to leave their cozy front rooms and explore the front yard, not to mention other worlds.

Liora was adventurous, confident, and intelligent. She dared him to face the unknown, yet somehow, he remained certain the choice was his. She made him forget about the horrors of battle.

He'd gotten the chance to speak with her many times over the last few months, yet that night on Radiance was different. Kael's cheeks heated and he glanced around, looking to see if anyone noticed. They hadn't. He shared a part of himself with Liora he'd not had with anyone else, and it left Kael conflicted. On one hand he needed to see her again, touch her again. Feel her warmth, hear her voice, see the light in her eyes.

Yet on the other hand, this was the corps. Could he have a chance at a relationship here? Getting to know her, see where she lives, a governors daughter—Kael wasn't sure why she liked him. Of all the choices she had—he shook the thought out. At the thought of not seeing her again, a nagging feeling of emptiness welled in his chest, and his heart pounded in his ears. It drowned out the noise of people arguing in the room.

Whatever this feeling growing in him was, Kael had to see it through. He had to tell Liora how he felt.

Sergeant Alandra shot to her feet, knocking several pads off the table. "Attention, officer in the house!"

Captain Ispan strode in with his aide close behind. "Zero Squad. You and your platoon will report to mission control at oh four hundred tomorrow. We are getting revenge for our black-eye soldiers. As you were."

The door swung shut with a click, and no one spoke. The gentle breeze brushed against the window frame above him, and there was a squeak of breath through Ordan's bent nose.

Alandra blinked then started grabbing her winnings. "Everyone move. I want you all to be ready for tomorrow. Nova pace."

Kael lingered a moment in hesitation. He had known the moment when they would be sent to fight again would come. The last week of trying to forget his first battle was washed away in a few words. Now it was all he could think about. Pike was still in the infirmary and would be out of combat.

He wished he could be home, see his mother, and know everything was right in the galaxy. Yet, dread of the coming battle overshadowed the glimmer of home, crushing his hopes and dreams and stamping out all his foolish notions. Sitting up, he planted his feet on the floor. He had been silly to think joining the corps would be anything more than kill or be killed. Those naive ideas of being a missionary among the stars and guiding lost souls into light were all children's fantasies.

Kael began prepping his kit, checking the buckles and tugging the straps. This place was anything but a child's dream. Auctor had been right, he should've stayed home, and now he had his brother entangled in his delusion. He should've realized it on day one, but he'd maintained his idiotic convictions, hoping the training would be precautionary. It was time to leave his conceptions behind and embrace his chosen life.

His resolve hardened, and he remembered God's words: *Train well and train hard, it may save your life one day.* Kael slotted the magazines into his vest after checking they were loaded.

Getting up, he found Auctor sprawled out on his cot, looking bored. "I need to talk."

Auctor sat up and raised an eyebrow. "About what?"

Kael sat next to his brother. "I need to apologize. You tried to tell me joining the corps was ridiculous, but I was ignorant and went anyway."

Auctor chuckled. "You were stupid."

Grimacing, Kael looked sideways at Auctor. "Do you remember how I used to get you out of trouble when we were children?"

"How could I forget?"

"Now I think the roles have reversed. You tried to keep me from getting into trouble and followed me right into the heart of it when I didn't listen."

Auctor grinned. "I couldn't let you go. Besides, you'd never survive here without me."

"I'm beginning to believe that. I never imagined it could be like this."

"You're going to have to change, Kael," Auctor rasped, waving a hand at the room full of soldiers. "This is war, not some group of traveling proselytes."

Kael sucked in a breath. "I'm not sure I'll ever agree with killing." He paused and looked at Auctor for a moment. "I'll do what's necessary to survive, and when this is all over, we can go home."

"Hey, you lovebirds, are you done wasting the Star's gift?" Alandra stood above them, hands on her hips. "Out front with the rest. Nova pace."

Outside, the sun cast its usual blanket of blue across the compound. It had been intriguing when Kael had first arrived on Xalthryn, but now it reminded him of where he was. Alandra worked them hard during afternoon exercise, stopping long enough to complete afternoon worship.

Kael's legs wobbled when he sat down with his tray of food. His legs were aching, but his stomach's protest was more intense, and the food was hot.

"They served this for breakfast!" Qenni's voice squeaked. "I can't eat the same meal twice in one day." She shoved away the tray.

Qenni was eighteen, like Kael, but he was convinced she'd missed some years of growing up. A short, plain-looking girl with red hair and brown eyes, she could always be counted on to complain even if there was nothing to complain about.

Ordan had sat across from her. "Can I have it?"

She waved a hand. "Help yourself."

He grabbed the tray and dumped it onto his own, food splattering.

Qenni curled her lips in disgust. "You will eat anything, won't you?"

Mouth full of food, Ordan nodded. "Mhm."

Gatlin sat next to Kael, shaking his head. "Qenni refusing to eat again?"

Auctor walked up, and Kael tapped a spot on the table he had saved for him while leaning over to Gatlin. "Looks like it."

"Alandra is not going to like that."

Huffing a laugh, Kael stabbed a piece of food. "I don't know how she does it."

Alandra walked in, standing over the table. "Qenni, I know you didn't eat your food. I can see it right there. No one gave Ordan a double portion."

Auctor paused mid-chew. "Another argument? Why can't she eat the food they give her?"

"Sergeant, I can't eat the same thing every day. I joined the corps to see new places and eat exotic foods not reprocessed nutrients."

"The corps isn't a culinary travel agency, Qenni. I can't understand why Krennak let you through training."

The commotion did nothing to stop Ordan from eating, even when the others stopped to listen.

Kael nudged Gatlin. "Why doesn't Alandra order her to eat?"

"Do you think she'd listen?"

"Not a chance," Auctor said.

"Exactly, my boy, and Alandra has a perfect record as squad leader. She's not about to escalate something like this to the captain."

"Now I know why Krennak recommended you for my squad, he knew you'd be a pain in my backside. If you're not going to eat, return to the barracks," Alandra ordered.

Sliding her legs out from the bench, Qenni shot to her feet. Before she could storm out, Gatlin caught her by the arm and handed her something.

Pretending not to notice, Kael went about eating his food.

Alandra wasn't so generous. "Why do you insist on pampering her?"

Gatlin shrugged his shoulders. "She's a good fighter. Besides, I don't want her stabbing me in the back."

"Her family disowned her for joining the corps." Everyone looked at Ordan. "That's what I heard."

Alandra shook her head. "Still, it's no excuse to act like a spoiled child. She's going to have to learn some hard lessons."

Almost choking on a piece of food, Auctor coughed and laughed.

Gatlin looked at him, frowning. "You think it's funny?"

Auctor cleared his throat. "You think she's going to learn any lessons? This morning, she asked me how to get to the mess. It's a wonder she remembers how to fight."

Now Alandra was frowning. "Keep making jokes, and I'll make her your responsibility."

Everyone returned to eating in silence.

"As you know, we are short a few soldiers. Pike will return to us but not until after tomorrow, leaving us with six for our mission. I want you all looking out for each other, no injuries or dying."

Nodding in agreement, Gatlin looked up. "We are God's chosen, forged by his light to carry his will across the cosmos."

Ordan bowed his head. "As the Star lights the path he has provided."

"As the Star lights the path," they all echoed.

"Most of all," Alandra continued, "I want you to make them pay for our comrades, make them pay for the crimes of all Starless." After slamming her fist on the table, she stalked out.

Mouth half open, Kael stared at the empty doorway. "What was that about?"

Gatlin sighed. "She has her reasons. It would be best if she told you."

"You can't leave it at that," Ordan said. "Now you got us curious."

Looking sidelong at Ordan, Kael frowned. "Gatlin's right, it's not his place to tell us."

Getting up from the table, Gatlin shook his head. "You're not going to hear it from me. I suggest you kids get some rest before tomorrow."

# Chapter 16:
## Nothing

*"Beware the darkness of shadow and the cool seductions of its embrace, for they bring nothing but pain."*
—Starlit Covenant

Kael had never been inside the war room, with its glowing wall-sized displays and central holoprojector. It was displaying a map of someplace on Xalthryn.

All of Zero was there, excluding Pike, of course. A woman wearing a dark uniform stepped in, and Kael recognized the captain from his first day on this hostile planet. Her name was Junova, he recalled. She stopped in front of the holographic map and faced the squad.

"Good morning. Due to the outstanding records of your leaders," she looked at Alandra and Gatlin, "and the bravery of your squad," she looked right at Kael, making him uncomfortable, "Zero has been chosen to take on a special role in the upcoming mission."

Pointing at a spot on the floating map, she continued. "This is your target." As she touched the spot, the map zoomed in and displayed a large building. "Intelligence has reported a Xalthari base of operation at this location. You're to take it, capture any Xalthari leaders, and find any information which may help us."

Leaning forward, Ordan snorted. "Doesn't look like much."

Alandra smacked him across the head, frowning. "Keep your mouth shut."

Spreading her hands wide, Junova expanded the map view. "You're right, it doesn't look like much. Yet, I have come to realize making yourself look less than you are is a good way to fool your enemy." Circling the projector, she looked at Kael then the rest of Zero. "We will land a company here to draw the enemy away and engage them until you complete your mission. May the Star guide you."

As they filed out of the room, Junova pointed and said, "Wait, not you." They all stopped and followed her finger, which was pointing right at Kael. "The rest of you can go."

After looking back with suspicion, Auctor stepped out of the room, followed by Ordan, who winked at Kael.

Frowning, he turned to face the captain as the door clicked shut. He stood straight and tense. He couldn't imagine why she would want to speak with him unless he had caused offense, but if this were the case, shouldn't Ordan be standing here instead? Maybe she thought he had been the one to open his mouth; it was dark in here, after all. Kael held his place, unmoving, fists clenched tight behind his back.

Moving around the circle of the protruding floor projector, Junova walked right up to him until she was almost in his face. Her eyes met his, and she gazed at him for a long moment. A sudden need to look away tugged at him, and he fought the urge.

Her eyes were inquisitive and examining. It was as if they pierced every part of him and knew his every thought and secret. Then she smiled at him, a warm and inviting smile.

"I heard you carried one of your squad-mates out of combat. Commander Hernz said it was quite heroic."

He relaxed a little.

Now circling him, she looked him up and down as if measuring him. "There's also the matter of my Astronav."

Kael's heart thudded in his chest.

Leaning against the projector, Junova raised an eyebrow. "Care to explain yourself?"

"Erm...." He shifted his weight to one foot and back to both. "I don't know how."

"You don't know? Well then, I think I can fill in some blanks for you." Pushing off the device, she took a deep breath. "For starters, I'd say you care a great deal for other people. It was evident in your rescue of a man you'd known for a few months at the time, during your first fight, no less. Most are lucky to survive their first encounter with an enemy. Do I hit the mark?"

Uncomfortable, Kael tried to relax his muscles. "Yes, captain. I would say you're correct."

Junova continued. "Now we come to Liora. My Astronav has been pursued by many in the corps. All ignored, all turned away. Yet, she lets you walk right into her life as if you belong there. She speaks of you as if you've been old friends. As her captain, it is my place to protect my crew and their best interests. So, I ask you, Kael, are you going to hurt the best navigator in the fleet?"

He had no idea Liora had been such a topic among many within the corps, but now that he thought about it, he could understand why. The idea of her talking about him made him feel light, as if he could float away. It was an odd feeling, a satisfying feeling.

"I couldn't say why she decided to let me in. The first time we met, she was open and happy, and I didn't do anything. Liora is different. I've never met anyone like her. I would never hurt her."

Junova frowned and pursed her lips. "Tell me, what do you think of our campaign here on Xalthryn?"

Kael raised an eyebrow. "It's not my place to say, Captain."

"Don't give me that. I asked you a question. How do you feel about what we are doing to the Xalthari?"

"Does the captain want my honest opinion?"

Shaking her head, Junova huffed a laugh. "I asked the question, didn't I?"

"Well, erm, yes, Captain. I don't like it, sir. Ehm, ma'am, I mean. I was expecting something quite different when I joined the corps. Killing the Starless wasn't part of my fantasies. I wanted to help them, guide them to the Star." Kael swallowed. "But I see how naive I was. It was foolish to believe it could be otherwise."

Her eyes narrowed. "Foolish, perhaps. If you were faced with an opportunity to let your enemy live, to show mercy, not knowing if the same enemy would try to kill you later, would you do it?"

Hesitating, Kael shifted his weight again. "Yes, Captain, I think I would."

She smiled, looking quite satisfied. "Well, Kael, you and I may have more in common than I thought. What if I told you there may be a way to end the war, saving thousands of lives in the process?"

"I'd ask why we aren't doing that."

"You would be prudent in asking, my young friend. Our esteemed Commander Hernz likes what he does too much. He doesn't care for life the same way you or I might." She straightened up, tugging at her uniform. "For now, I would have you gauge whether your platoon has like-minded people. And come back alive, Liora does like you."

The recognizable scent of flowers mixed with a thick, stifling haze hung in the air. Weapons fire sounded in the distance, and Zero Squad moved low and slow. Going by the rule of threes, Kael had been grouped with Auctor and Gatlin, and Alandra took Ordan and Qenni.

It wasn't the valid rule of three, but they had had to make do. Together, they moved through the mist at the edge of a line of black trunked trees, their limbs hanging low, weighed down by the thick waxy green and silver leaves they bore. He hoped his second engagement with the enemy would be more effortless, but Kael's nerves were raw and made him jittery.

In the fog, they couldn't see ten meters in front of them. Between trying to stay silent and keeping track of enemy movements by sound, it was a wonder Alandra kept her bearings. But she did, and soon, the haze thinned near a huge building. It looked ancient, with ashen vines growing up its sides and chunks of stone missing from its face.

It didn't look like anything of strategic importance to Kael, but you never knew what could be inside. As they moved to an archway resembling an entrance, the weapons fire grew distant. He hoped this meant the Starless were losing. Yet, if they were losing, they might retreat right into them. He couldn't make up his mind what scenario would be worse.

Auctor nudged him. Gatlin had moved up. They caught up to the sergeant as Alandra opened the large wooden doors. Each team entered and took a side of the room.

The room was large, dark, and dingy and consisted of dusty tables and empty bookshelves. Shadows lurked in every corner, and on the far side was a plain, smooth door.

Stacking up on the door, three on either side, they prepared to make entry. The sergeant touched its smooth surface and pushed. Nothing, not even a wiggle. Kael frowned.

Gatlin and Alandra were already busy setting small explosive charges near the hinges. Once done, everyone made space, and the sergeant counted down with his fingers. There was a loud crack followed by Kael's ears ringing. The door was off its hinges, and they advanced through the opening.

Kael wiped sweat from his palms as he stood in the dark, empty room. He readjusted his grip on his rifle as hot and cold air mixed in the doorway.

"Nothing? How could there be nothing?"

Gatlin swept the room with his light. "I don't know, Sergeant, our intel looked good."

Kicking a chair over, Alandra walked through the door. "Tear this place apart, and you still might find something useful. Auctor, come with me, we'll stand guard."

Tables were flipped over, drawers emptied, and walls checked for hollow spots where little things might be hidden. They found nothing; it was just a barren room filled with junk.

Throwing a box in exasperation, Ordan frowned. "I don't want to be out there fighting any more than you, but this was a colossal waste of time."

Qenni thrust a box filled with dusty papers at him. "It would waste less time if you did more work and less complaining."

"This coming from someone who won't eat the same food twice in a day."

"At least I have standards, Ordan. Not like you could understand."

Stabbing his finger hard into the air, Ordan scowled. "It's not my fault I was an outcast. I tried to find work, but no one wants to hire a lowlife."

"Shut up, you two," Gatlin said, ear pressed firmly against the wall. "I think I hear som—"

The room vibrated.

"Take cover!"

Throwing himself down behind a table lying on its side, Kael looked around its edge. The wall Gatlin had stood next to moved back and then dropped down, making a thunderous racket. Shots rang out, causing his ears to ring. Disoriented, he shot back into the darkness where the wall had once been.

Gatlin's voice bellowed, "Retreat!"

Kael tried to get up, but a hailstorm of projectiles hit the thick wooden table, showering him with splinters as they ripped through the wood. Dropping back to the floor, he checked himself for wounds. He was uninjured, but he couldn't be thankful yet. Not until he was out of this mess.

He could see the doorway, perhaps a few steps away, and beyond, safety. The furious shooting had stopped, and someone called his name.

"I'm pinned down."

A few shots peppered the table and the walls around him. He covered his face, protecting it against the rocks and splinters pelting him.

"We've got a plan, you'll know when the time is right."

As he hugged the floor for dear life, there was a thud and the sound of something rolling across the floor.

"*Grenade!*"

He had enough time to cover his ears before it went off. The sound boomed, and his ears rang anyway. The flash of it made him see a giant spot when he blinked, even from behind the table.

Pushing up with all his might, he struggled to his feet. He took two significant steps toward the door when a tremendous blinding flash of white-hot pain coursed through his head. Stumbling, he tried to keep himself upright, but the room spun. He grunted and grasped at the doorway, trying to make himself move. His vision grew darker, and his face thumped onto the hard, cool floor, and then nothing.

# Chapter 17:
## Queen

*"Kings and Queens may have ruled in ancient times, but now is the time of the Gods."*
—God Ruler

Sitting on the bridge was like being a queen, and the crew were her subjects—at least, that was how Junova used to feel. Now, she was an impostor on the throne. She had killed the queen and taken her place, subverting the king's orders at every turn. But she wasn't a queen, and the king was a self-proclaimed god. It seemed ludicrous even to consider disobeying, yet here she was.

The Radiance had been ordered to strike Xalthari targets. An orbital bombardment was a simple matter for the broadside rail cannons mounted on the ship. A cannon fired, and the vibrations reverberated through her chair and the deck under her feet. It used to be a satisfying feeling, but now it knotted her stomach, dragging her back home to those she had murdered.

Still, it didn't change the fact that she was murdering people now, and by the droves. Between the time Junova had received her orders and issued them to her crew, she had altered them, shifting targets away from dense populations to areas with low populations, prioritizing military targets and personnel over casualties.

When Hernz found out, he was sure to be quite angry, maybe even enough to report her to God. But it was a risk she had to take. Hernz's blood-lust had been growing, and she could no longer curb it without risk of discovery.

More vibrations ran through the ship as another cannon fired, and her stomach twisted in response. Putting herself in danger was part of being captain, though this was a new level of peril. Any one of her crew could kill her if they found out and be hailed as the hero who put traitorous Captain Junova in her grave. Yet, it was another risk she had to take.

She had spoken with many trusted crew members and received favorable responses. This wasn't enough to maintain control of the ship if she decided to challenge God, but it was a start, and the number of crew members supportive of her thinking grew every day.

The cannon closest to the bridge fired, and the metal under her feet jolted and trembled like a tectonic quake. It was powerful but brief, then the dull vibrations resumed.

*A few targets left,* she thought, gripping the sides of her chair so tightly her knuckles were turning white.

Liora pushed off from her station and stood with a sudden sharpness. She stalked right up to Junova's side and stopped. Keeping her eyes averted, she took a slow, deep breath. "Can I be excused from the bridge?"

On looking up at Liora, it was clear to Junova something had upset her, though she was hiding it well. "Yes, of course."

Liora stalked off toward the corridors, head down.

"Take command of the bridge," Junova ordered.

Standing from his seat, Reed saluted. "As you command."

Following Liora into the corridors, Junova watched her enter the briefing room. Junova hesitated for a moment, unsure if she should follow or return to the bridge. But she couldn't leave her like this. She padded into the room and sat next to Liora at the table. "Liora, what's wrong?"

Removing her hands from her face, Liora looked at Junova, watery-eyed and sullen. "Why are our hearts such fragile things?"

Taking a sharp breath in, Junova clenched her jaw. It was the boy, it had to be. Had she misjudged him? "I wish I had answers for you, my dear, but the heart is vast and complex. We may never know why or how it chooses those we care for." Taking Liora's hand in hers, she continued. "Over time, the pain will lessen. I'll always be here for you."

Wrapping her arms around Junova, Liora squeezed her tight. "Thank you. I still can't believe it. I thought everything would be fine, but he's not going to come back." She sobbed into Junova's shoulder, the pair locked in an embrace.

Junova pushed Liora back with gentle ease and looked into her eyes. "What happened to him? Why's he not coming back?"

Liora tried to compose herself by brushing the hair from her face and swallowing hard. "The report came in. Kael's squad returned." She paused for a moment. "Without him. He's missing, presumed dead." Her voice sounded hollow, as if a piece of her was gone.

Junova blinked. She had assumed wrong; he wasn't a liar. Her face was hot, and she looked down, unable to meet Liora's eyes. "If he's alive, I'll find him." She finally met Liora's eyes with her own, which were now filled with determination. "I'll find him and bring him back. We'll bring him back."

Liora hugged her again. "Thank you." Her voice sounded renewed as if a small glimmer of hope warmed its tone.

"Of course, my dear. Take all the time you need. The bridge will still be here when you're ready."

Liora nodded, wiping a tear from her cheek.

Junova smiled at Liora as she got up and walked out, the door hissing shut behind her.

Stopping in the corridor, Junova leaned back against the wall. Her breath came fast, and her stomach churned. The pain spread throughout her head, from her temples down the back of her neck. She rubbed the sides of her head, trying to alleviate the discomfort.

It was no use. There were too many problems to juggle now: Hernz, Xalthari, God, her crew, Justice growing ever closer, and now a missing soldier.

He was one of a thousand missing men and women, and yet, this soldier was more important than the others. How ironic.

The intermittent vibrations had stopped; the bombardment was completed. Now, all she could do was wait. If Hernz wasn't pleased, it wouldn't take long to find out. Until then, she had work to do.

# Chapter 18:
## Regret, Guilt, Anguish, and an Itch

*"Regret, guilt, anguish. These are but the beginning of what those sent here feel."*
—Warden of Eesbex

Gripping the edges of his cot, Pike tried to resist the urge to scratch his leg. If he slid his fingers under the bandage, he could alleviate the itch, but the last time he'd given in, it'd reopened his wound. The doctor had frowned at him, given him a stern speech, and restitched it with no pain medication. If he had to ride this itch into his insanity, he wouldn't scratch his leg.

What if he gave it a tickle? It could help. The itch beckoned him, seducing his fingers from their iron grip, first one releasing and then another. He told himself to stop, but his fingers moved of their own will, creeping closer to the bandage, to relief. His middle finger touched its edge, which was fibrous and rough. Losing the will to fight the craving, his finger snaked under the bandage, reaching.

A violent crash made him jump as the bunkhouse door cracked against the wall. Auctor stormed in, threw down his gear, and flung over his cot. His shoulders moved with his breath, and his eyes flashed with rage. While Pike lay still and silent, Auctor turned back to the door and thundered toward it only to have Alandra block his path.

"Get out of my way," he growled.

Alandra gripped his arm and tried to restrain him. Auctor twisted, pulling his arm away. She snatched him with her other hand, stopping him from leaving. Roaring, he yanked himself around and butted the back of his head right into her face, knocking her flat on her back.

Pike scrambled to his feet and ran to her side, his leg aching. He looked out the door, but Auctor was nowhere to be seen. He helped Alandra to her feet. Blood was running from her now crooked nose. He handed her a towel, and she held her nose and sat down.

"What was that?"

Grimacing from the pain, the sergeant leaned back. "Today...it wasn't a good day. I should've let him go."

Furrowing his brows, Pike sat down. "Let him go? Ain't you gonna do something about that?" He pointed at her nose.

She huffed a dull laugh. "If I ran to the captain every time I fought with a soldier, I'd have no squad. Besides, he has cause."

"Ain't never seen reason to attack a superior. Let's get you to the infirmary."

She blew bloody snot from her nose and adjusted the towel. "No infirmary. I'll be fine."

Resigning himself, Pike shook his head. "You ain't told me yet, what happened?"

"We lost Kael."

Pike's eyes widened, and he let out a sharp breath. "He's dead?"

"We were forced to retreat. I don't know."

A sudden lump in his throat made him swallow, and his jaw ached from clenching. "We have to find out."

Putting a hand on his shoulder, Alandra looked him in the eyes. "I received word, Captain Junova is doing all she can. There's nothing for us to do but wait."

Pike pushed himself upright until he was standing. "You think I'm gonna sit here and wait?"

"That's what we are going to do, soldier. I won't lose anyone else on some fool's errand."

"Sergeant, we have to do something."

Frowning, Alandra stood face to face with him. "You want something to do? Ensure Auctor doesn't leave the compound, and when he cools off, bring him back."

Pike sighed and hobbled out into the harsh blue sunlight.

Finding Auctor in the compound would be like finding a single blade of grass in a field, and after what Auctor had done to Alandra, Pike wasn't so sure he wanted to see him. He found himself near the Urban Tactics Course. Recruits were training, and Krennak's all-too-familiar voice was shouting at some poor soul.

Still favoring his leg, he made his way into the course, and finding himself a good spot to sit and watch, climbed a ladder onto a flat roof near the recruits. Krennak looked at him and gave an almost imperceptible nod, trying not to break his hard exterior. Pike didn't like the man.

A gentle breeze carried a cool reprieve from the hot sun. Pike took a deep breath and looked up at the sky with its wisps of odd clouds back-lit by the blue-green sky. His mind drifted as Krennak shouted some speech at the recruits. He could imagine how Auctor must feel, at least to a degree. Breath caught in his throat, and he clenched his jaw. It was painful to think about. Almost every day since, he had been trying to forget his childhood, hoping he wouldn't relive it in dreams night after night.

The cavity of his chest was hollow, devoid of love, family, and everything good. Memories flooded back, and he trembled with the remembered fear and anger. How he had escaped that fateful day seemed like luck, but he knew otherwise. Luck was an excuse ignorant people used to comfort themselves. He'd joined the corps with a hope of escape—a hope he could leave the past dead and buried.

Then he'd met Kael, a friend among fools who understood without knowing and cared without judging. Pike's head sank, and he took a deep, ragged breath.

"And now who's an unknown?"

How stupid he had been for letting himself care for someone again. He had known it would lead to more pain, and yet, he'd gone and done it anyway.

One of the recruits below discharged his weapon, the tag hitting the woman next to him in the leg. The crack made Pike jump, heart pounding, ready to find cover. Krennak's voice echoed between the houses and down the streets as he screamed at the boy. Pike rubbed his face. He thought of how much easier things had been in training. No one had died during training.

"And we thought it was bad," he muttered.

No. Opening his heart and caring about those idiots in his squad was the actual punishment. Nothing good lasted forever. He had forgotten this truth. It had to stop before he could be hurt any further. Being a soldier was his job, and soldiers didn't allow themselves to be weak. He worked his fingers, now sore from balling into fists.

Krennak set the recruits off on some task, his corporals spurring them along. Taking a deep breath, Pike lingered on the feeling of air filling his lungs, his chest expanding. It was as if all his cares left him with this breath blown out of him, carried away in the breeze. The march of boots on concrete faded away, and the sun's warmth caressed his face. It would have been easier for him to shut himself off from others if it weren't for his itch.

"Soldier?"

Pike jerked around, catching his leg on the roof's edge, but managed to stumble to his feet. "Sergeant." He snapped to attention.

"At ease, lad. I saw ye up 'ere lookin' troubled an' thought ye might wanna talk."

Relaxing a little, Pike looked down. "I needed to think, sir."

"'Ave a seat," Krennak said as he sat where Pike had been. "I heard aboot yer squadmate."

"It's not hopeful."

"Never is, lad. This is war, people die. Good people."

Getting comfortable on the ledge, Pike wondered at Krennak. The man had never spoken to him without shouting, cursing, or demeaning him. Now, he was different, almost human. "You don't ever get used to it, do you?"

"No. An officer once told me to hope ye never get used to it 'cause it means ye lost somethin' important. Somethin' in 'ere," he said, pointing at his chest.

"Think there's anything to it?"

"Aye, pain is a harsh teacher, but a teacher nonetheless."

A cool breeze ran through Pike's hair and brought with it the distant rhythm of a corps cadence. Staring at his feet, Pike sighed. "What if the pain is trying to teach you not to care?"

Silent for a long moment, Krennak gazed out at the mock city. "I'd say yer hearin' what ye want to hear."

"Maybe I am. Perhaps I'd rather not feel the pain of losing anyone else."

"Avoidin' tae pain bottles it up, keeps it down in yer gut. If ye dinne face it, it'll consume ye. Then ye won't be tae only one to suffer, ye'll hurt tae ones around ye, too."

Getting to his feet, Pike frowned at Krennak. Sergeant or not, this conversation had gone too far and become too personal. Who was this man to tell him who he would hurt, how he would behave?

The sun bore down on him, hot and relentless. Mixed with the heat rising in his chest, it became oppressive, weighing him down, trying to subdue his will to fight.

He stabbed his finger toward Krennak, driven by his anger. "What do you know about pain? About suffering? Did you watch your entire family murdered before your eyes? Don't preach to me about pain, you know nothing of the torment my life has been. The devastation of losing those you care about most. Regret, guilt, and anguish, and when life gives a glimmer of hope, it's ripped away without mercy. A complete decimation of any hint at having something good."

He could see Krennak's jaw muscles working, but the man said nothing and looked at the empty buildings. Shaking with rage and sorrow, Pike's legs went weak, and he collapsed to his knees. Tears ran down his contorted face. He struck the rooftop once then again, not to punish it but to feel something. His fists shook. His voice caught in his throat, somewhere between a curse and a sob.

"Ye may be right, lad. I may not understand what ye feel," Krennak said as he stood. "But it dinne mean I'm wrong now. Does it?" He climbed off the roof, leaving Pike to his fury.

# Chapter 19:
## Question

*"When faced with evidence, is it wrong to question a belief?"*
—Xalthari Warden of Echoes

Pain radiated from the back of his head in waves. Kael tried to move, but his arms were restrained. He was sitting in a chair, his hands resting on its arms. Even his feet were anchored to the seat. The sharp edges of the cool metal dug into his wrists.

Eyes snapping open, Kael reeled, fighting against the restraints. The last thing he remembered was running. He had been running from an ambush. Now, darkness enveloped him. A weak trace of light was coming from the edges of what appeared to be a closed door. It wasn't enough for him to make out the room around him.

Echoes of his ragged breath sounded short and sharp in the black. Muffled voices came from beyond the door, speaking a language he didn't understand. Pulling against the restraints, he tested their strength. No use. There wasn't even a wiggle to suggest they might come loose. The room smelled of stale dampness, and the drip-drip of water sounded somewhere behind him.

Metallic scraping came from the door as it was unbolted, and its hinges groaned as it swung open to reveal a dark silhouette, the outline of a short figure with stout features. A man's voice resonated in the small space.

"Vashar, I am called. I have questions." On the wave of his hand, a small girl brought over a table and set a bowl upon it. "First, food."

He lit a small plasma lantern and closed the door, the bolt sliding shut behind him. After hanging the lantern from a hook in the ceiling, he unlocked Kael's shackles. He moved the table close enough for Kael to reach the bowl then sat cross-legged on the floor in front of him.

"It is unappealing?" the man asked.

Studying the man, Kael's stomach protested in hunger. Yet, he could not allow himself to eat the enemy's food. No matter how much he didn't like what the corps was doing to these people, they were still Starless, heretics to the Star. Perhaps they would poison or drug him. He blinked at the man then looked down at his hands. His wrists were cut and crusted with dried blood. Reaching for the back of his head, he touched a rough cloth bandage. His scalp was tender underneath it.

Pointing at Kael, the man smiled. "It will heal."

The room was indeed small, made of smooth-cut brownish-gray stone. His pounding head raced with questions. Where was his squad? Were they alive? He looked at the man motionless on the floor, his shining black eyes glinting in the light. Kael hesitated at those eyes, so different from any he'd seen. His stomach insisted he eat. Looking down at the bowl, he saw it was filled with a dark liquid and various vegetation native to Xalthryn.

"No trick, it is quite good."

Shoulders slouching, Kael sighed. By the Star, he was hungry, and it smelled hearty. The bowl reminded him of home, picking vegetables in the garden. Helping his mother prepare a stew. It had been months since he had eaten anything other than corps rations. It couldn't hurt to eat a little. If he was ever going to escape, he needed his strength.

Reaching out, he took the bowl in his unsteady hands, warm to the touch. He sipped at first, tasted the contents, then drank the liquid. Rich and flavorful, it tasted of savory spices and salt with a hint of something pungent like the garlic he used to grow back home. On finishing, he set the bowl down to find the man had not moved; he sat there, watching.

"Satisfactory?"

Kael gave a slight nod, still wary of his captor.

"There is no trust between us, I perceive this. I would have that change."

Clenching his jaw, Kael looked down. This was the enemy, his enemy. Yet, they had not killed him. Instead, they had treated his wound, fed him, and spoken of trust. The pounding in his head worsened, making it hard to think. "What do you want?"

"Ah, what do I want? Answers to questions."

"What questions?"

Switching how he crossed his legs, the man gave a sharp nod. "Star soldiers, what numbers do they arrive in?"

Frowning, Kael bit down harder, jaw muscles aching. It was information he couldn't give, not even if he knew it. He could guess, but why would he give the Starless any information? "I don't know," he said through gritted teeth.

The man stroked his beard, furrowing his brow. "What number of battles?"

Hesitating for a moment, Kael wondered if he should lie. "Two."

"Ah, no fountain of knowledge here. What is your name, Star-born?"

What interest could this heretic have in his name? These were brutal people. Krennak had said they wouldn't have mercy. They must have wanted something more from him. This had to be some tactic to get what he wanted. Kael remained still, hands grasping the chair. He was set in his resolve; there would be no more answers.

The man waited without a hint of movement while Kael wondered if he'd ever leave. Neither seemed willing to break the silence. The gentle water drip still sounded behind him. After some time, the man stood and brushed the dust from himself. And after picking his lantern from the hook, knocked at the door. The same small girl opened it and took out the bowl and table.

Looking back once more before shutting the door, the man sighed. "Food will come every day. Speak to this child to deliver a message." He turned, and the door slammed shut, leaving Kael in utter darkness.

There were two significant problems. The shackles on his legs were locked tight, and the one around his waist was out of reach. He couldn't get through the door even if he got free of this chair. What was on the other side? A group of Starless ready to capture or kill him?

Resting his face in his palms, he screamed. If this was a nightmare, he needed to wake up. Where was the music he woke to every day, the signal marking the end of this cursed dream and the return of safety? Nowhere, it seemed. He was awake. This was real. Captured by the enemy with no hope of escape.

As his new routine had become, the girl brought vegetable stew, waited for him to eat, and left with the empty bowl. She never spoke to him, not even when he tried to ask her name. Her dark brown eyes watched, silent and inexpressive.

The man hadn't returned to speak with him, and Kael wondered if he ever would. Perhaps he would rot here forever if he never told the child he wished to talk to his captor. His body hurt from being confined to a seated position for days now, and the reek of feces and urine was becoming unbearable.

Perhaps he'd get used to the odor, he thought. A foolish thought. He should talk. It was a matter of the right words to his small keeper. It wasn't like he knew anything that would be of value to these heretics anyway. What was the harm? His shoulders couldn't droop any lower. The will to fight had left a day, maybe three days ago. He couldn't remember.

One day, after picking up his emptied bowl, the girl opened the massive door with a grating sound.

"Wait," his voice cracked.

Halting in the doorway, she looked back at him with those same scrutinizing eyes, giving nothing away.

"I...I want to talk."

Hesitating a moment, her eyes filled with the slightest hint of empathy, which was washed away by her veneer of indifference. Then she was gone, and the room resumed its now familiar inky black appearance.

Soon after, the door swung open, and a bright light blinded him. Voices of several people could be heard speaking words he didn't understand. They unbound him from the chair and carried him out, a man under each arm. Kael tried to get his feet under him, but they had no strength. The best he could do was keep them from getting caught on the stairs as they climbed.

They entered a plain brown solid stone room with a small hole in the floor, where they stripped and washed him. After he had dried, they provided clothes for him to wear. Someone took his soiled uniform and headed out of the room. Kael tried to take a step to stop them and stumbled over his weak legs. On being caught by one of his captors, he pointed toward his uniform. The man straightened Kael and gave him a cautious smile.

"Clothes, they will wash," he said in broken speech.

Nodding, Kael gave him the benefit of the doubt. This was an odd turn of events, he had to admit.

When he was shuffled in front of a mirror, Kael scoffed at his appearance. Besides his lighter skin and gray eyes, he might be mistaken for one of these people. He wasn't a vision of a prisoner of war, but he must have been a few short minutes ago.

Getting his legs back, Kael managed to walk without someone holding him up. The strange procession led him through a maze of identical hallways. He couldn't say how they knew their way around without getting lost. Every intersection and corridor looked the same to him.

Stopping, the old man who'd been leading him opened a door at the end of the hall. "Enter."

With the door closing behind him, shuffling footsteps faded as the group moved away down the hall. He was in a dull room, and orbs attached to the walls emitted a warm glow. Someone sat at a table on the far end of the room; it was the man he had spoken with on the first day. On the table sat two heaping plates spilling over with some meat and fresh vegetables. His stomach tightened in anticipation. He hadn't had meat since before leaving home.

Books lined the shelves behind him, stretching from floor to ceiling. Old books. The man waved at Kael. "Come, seat yourself."

Grasping the rough-hewn wooden chair, his fingers touched the wide grain of the wood's growth. It whispered on the smooth stone floor as he pulled it out and creaked when he sat on it.

Pushing one of the plates across the table toward Kael, the man nodded. "Satisfy your hunger, then talk."

Even if Kael looked like a savage gnawing at the bones of his enemies, it didn't matter. He ate the sumptuous white meat until he was full to bursting. Looking at the plate, he regretted he could not finish it all. It wasn't the entire truth; a nagging guilt in his mind reminded him of one thing. These people were supposed to be his enemy. They had captured him, locked him in a dungeon, and left him sitting in his filth for days on end. He expected to be asked question after question about military strategy, troop deployments, when reinforcements would arrive, and so on. But he was asked none of those. The man asked two.

"Vashar, I am called. What is your name, Starborn?"

Wiping the food from his cheeks, Kael closed his eyes. *Maybe he'll go away.* Opening his eyes, he sighed. "I am Kael."

"Kael." Vashar rolled the name around in his mouth as if he were getting the taste of it. "A good name. A single question further." He blinked and looked into Kael's eyes.

His intensity made Kael want to look away, but he gritted his teeth and stared back into the scrutinizing black eyes.

"When divine voices speak, gaze upon them, heretics shaped by shadow. Starborn responds: we have observed heresy abounds. Do Starborn, does Kael, ever ponder what perception emerges when gazes return upon them?"

Kael found himself lost, bewildered, and in a state of indecision. These enemies were anything but what he had been told to expect, yet they hadn't treated him like a friend. Guilt swept through him. He had never stopped to consider what the Xalthari might see when they looked upon him. Did they see a young man caught up in a war he had been too naive to expect, or did they see him as a murderer, a conqueror coming down from the stars on wings of fire to burn them all?

His first night, he found the outer door, and although no guards were present, it had been sealed. And having found no way to open it, he sat down racking his brain for ideas and fell asleep. Vashar found him the next morning and returned him to his room.

Memorizing the corridors was easier than he expected. He had been given freedom to move about in the sanctuary, and Kael wasted no time familiarizing himself with its layout. His uniform had been cleaned and returned, and he wore it at all times. It was a reminder to his captors as much as it was a reminder to himself of where he had come from, whose allegiance he had sworn to follow. At first, the residents of this place had been startled or shied away from him, but now they were used to seeing him roaming about. Some even offered greetings, which he could not understand but accepted.

His room, although plain, contained the necessities. A bed, large enough for one person, and a small cabinet next to that. Waste rooms were centralized and shared by the populace. He lay on his bed, looking up at the brown ceiling and hewn stone floor in his brown room, perhaps a shade darker than the walls. Even the blankets on his bed were brown. These people could learn a thing or two about color. The corps was drab, but they used more than three shades of the same color.

Huffing a laugh, he shook his head. Here he was, a prisoner, thinking about decor. A sudden lump in his throat made him swallow. Reaching into his pocket, he pulled out the paper Liora had given him. Smiling, he unfolded it, memorizing the pattern of stars drawn on the now wrinkled paper. As he put it back, he felt the hard edge of his DEX card, and curiosity urged him to look at it. He slid it out and flipped it over in his palm. The display glowed, and the words struck him like a punch to the chest. *Missing in action.* He winced. At least it didn't say he was dead.

No matter how pleasant these people were to him, they weren't his people, family, and friends. He couldn't leave the building or look out at the world. Yet, no matter how hard he tried, hate for these people wasn't in him.

He rolled onto his side and pulled the blanket over his head. Same shade of brown as everything else. He imagined it was soil he'd buried himself in. No light down here.

Vashar's question burned inside his mind. These were people. They hadn't asked for this. Yet, the Starlit had come—the corps had come—to exterminate them from the face of Xalthryn like they were an infestation of pests, insects to be squashed. All for the purity of the Star's light, to bring the Star to every Starless. To bring light into the shadows.

Kael wasn't sure he knew what that meant anymore. He had been sure before he left home. The idea had sparked in him hopes and dreams of helping people who needed saving—people wanting to be saved. His reality was much different.

Vashar and his people faced extermination, and even though they had been cautious at first, they were now pleasant and inviting. Kael could not say he would have acted the same in their place. It left him with a niggling doubt.

# Chapter 20:
## Hopeful

*"Is it weak to be hopeful, or does it show trust in his plan?"*
—Shepard of the Covenant

They all expected him to sit around, doing nothing. Auctor had been furious the first day, but now his anger was like a pale shadow fading in sunlight. He almost couldn't remember what the rage felt like.

Auctor wasn't as upset about Kael being gone as he was about him getting himself killed. Kael was supposed to be better than that, but his failure made Auctor look like a fool. The thought of not being the best was almost too much for him, and no one else seemed to care.

Tapping his fingers on the table, he paid little attention to the squad yapping and playing cards around him, stuck here inactive because of his brother and holding out hope for a safe return. All this last week had amounted to was unbearable boredom. He wanted action. He needed excitement. Alandra kept telling him it would come, but he watched as other squads went on missions and came back tattered, tired, and missing men.

Everyone else had all the fun, it seemed.

Qenni bumped him on the shoulder, pulling him from his thoughts. "Auctor, why don't you play with us? I need someone new to play against. Ordan cheats."

"I do not! If anyone is cheating, it's Alandra."

"How dare you accuse me of cheating, soldier."

Then they were off arguing again. Auctor almost laughed. Ordan had it right. Alandra was good, even skilled. She cheated every game she played, but the fools never managed to catch her.

Accusations flew back and forth across the table until Gatlin pounded his fists down, bringing the room to silence. "Stop arguing. I'm tired of sitting here and doing nothing productive. We don't even know if the boy is alive."

Everyone turned to look at Auctor as if some insult had been leveled, but he ignored them. Gatlin was right, but Auctor didn't care to involve himself in another unproductive argument. It would lead to the same conclusion they all had, with Alandra telling them they would wait until Junova had news.

Pike sat in the square near HQ and watched little birds flit between trees, cheeping. The squad held out hope and seemed to be making the most of their time off, trying to distract themselves, except Auctor.

Kael's brother hadn't shown any emotion after the first day. Either he was brooding or he didn't care, Pike couldn't tell which, and it bugged him. If you were to care about anyone, wouldn't it be your own family? That was what had taught him such a harsh lesson, but he doubted Auctor had the same teacher.

A thick breeze grazed his cheek and carried the sweetness of new blossoms. This would be a lovely planet to live on if it weren't for the war. It could end soon, and he could stay awhile. Stop running and even build himself a home. He scoffed. Foolish dreams would get him nowhere. Best to leave the future to itself and focus on the now.

Auctor had been right about one thing: getting back into the fight. The captain had conceded to Alandra's wishes to be available if any news came of Kael. But it was a lost hope. One didn't turn up after going down in a fight. Huffing a laugh, Pike looked up at the sky. At least he hadn't fallen too far into the black hole of caring about people.

A young tech stumbled his way out of HQ in a hurry. Catching himself on a support, he looked around, teeth bared, trying to see if anyone was watching. Upon seeing Pike, his face and eyes flashed with embarrassment and excitement. "You," he yelled. "You're part of Zero?"

Pike nodded, frowning at the boy.

The tech ran up and handed him a folded scrap of paper. "Can you make sure your sergeant gets this right away?"

Taking the paper, Pike looked at it. "What's it say?"

The boy was almost giddy, like a schoolchild bouncing in excitement. "They found out where he is, and he's alive."

Pike gaped at the tech, mouth hanging open. It couldn't be, yet there was no doubting the boy's excitement. Pike got to his feet and started toward the barracks.

A few simple words had called into question everything he had considered over this past week. *He's alive.* It was another nightmare getting ready to unfold before his eyes. People he cared about died; they didn't come back from the dead. Not ever. His pace quickened to a jog then a run. Telling himself he wouldn't care and doing it were fast becoming lines he could not define. No matter how hard he had tried this last week to free himself of hurt, he was relieved. He was smiling and happy Kael had been found.

Trying to push down the feelings, he gritted his teeth. Nothing good could come from this. He would lead himself down a path of more pain. Gripping the paper tight in his fist, he thought for a moment perhaps he should lose it, save himself from the internal war he was waging.

Slowing, he looked at the small, crumpled paper in his hand. What would be the harm? They couldn't stay hopeful forever. Soon, everyone would move on. Taking a ragged breath, Pike turned his hand slowly and steadily. It would be easy. He could be free of this attachment, which was making him weak. The message started to shuffle toward the edge of his palm. He swallowed, his mouth dry as a desert.

Pike's mind shifted to Auctor. It was Kael's fate Pike held in his hand now. Auctor's family. Images flashed in his vision; the screams of his own family echoed. Snatching the paper in his fist, he scowled. If he got rid of this note, he wouldn't be any better than the men who had taken his family. No matter how much he wanted to be free and strong, there would be no returning once he became the monster. And it was a price too high to pay.

Auctor frowned as the door swung open, and Pike stumbled in breathing hard, hunched over, hands on his knees. "I have a message," he managed to get out between breaths.

Taking it from Pike's hand, Alandra looked at it, brow furrowed. Her eyes moved back and forth as she read. A smile ran across her face, and her eyes widened. "He's alive. Intel is a bit spotty, he could be in one of three locations."

Pounding his fists on the table, Gatlin sent cards flying everywhere. "This lad might be our good luck charm. Two star wrecks he's lived through now."

Ordan frowned. "We haven't rescued him yet."

"Do you doubt us, son? We'll be strolling outta there arm in arm with the boy. You wait and see."

Alandra looked at Auctor with a grin from ear to ear. They all looked at him. So, he smiled and did what any good brother would do. "When do we leave?"

Holding up a finger, Alandra made for the door. "Don't do anything rash, I have to speak with the captain."

Qenni jumped up and yelled, showing too much excitement and irritating him. "The squad will be back together again. Then we can do some real missions."

Auctor looked sideways at her, frowning. There was some relief he wouldn't be bored yet another day. It was something to do, and he might get a taste of excitement while doing it.

The entire platoon squeezed into the war room, looking like a pack of wide-eyed refugees. Manipulating the map, Junova focused on where the three strongholds were.

She cleared her throat and pointed at one of the green dots. "Intelligence believes with some certainty Kael is being held here. Zero has requested this assignment, and I'm obliged to let them have it."

Everyone in Zero stood a little straighter and smiled.

"The rest of the platoon will handle the remaining two targets. Your captain will fill you in on assignments."

The lights flickered on, blinding her, and the doors opened, revealing Hernz and a few of his staff.

"What in the Star's name has been happening around this place, Captain? First, I found out you've placed one of my platoons on inactive duty, and then I find out they are going on a mission without my order! When were you planning on telling me?" Hernz demanded.

"Perhaps we should talk about this in private, Commander," Junova responded.

"Not a chance, Captain. You've left me in the shadows where my troops are concerned. You will explain this insult at once."

Taking a deep breath, Junova prepared herself. Hernz would be screaming at her before the end. So, she explained the events of the past week in great detail. To her surprise, Hernz listened in silence. When she was done, he asked the platoon if she had omitted any details, which she had not.

"All this to rescue a boy, Captain? That's quite ambitious of you."

Junova smirked. "How do you think I became a ship's captain?"

Hernz's face hardened at that, and he stared at her for a long moment as if to say, *Don't fly too close to the sun with your ambitions.* Then he turned to the platoon. "I'm disappointed in all of you for not coming to me with this. Most of all, your leadership." He paced in front of them. "I have seen the details of your targets. Besides this little rescue, they do have some strategic value. Go on your mission tomorrow and pray to God you do not fail." Hernz stalked to the door, his staff close behind. Before stepping out, he stopped and looked back. "There will be some changes when you return."

Frowning at the closed door, Junova turned to find everyone looking at her. Straightening her uniform, she sighed. "You have your orders."

Saluting, the platoon made its disorganized way out of the cramped space.

This time, she had made a mess of things.

# Chapter 21:
## Shredded

*"A belief shredded, a soul lost, creates a path to find, a world to re-build."*
—Kael, in hindsight

 

Eating with the Xalthari was almost pleasant now. They seemed to be generous and kind people. That was if Kael could overlook his first few days as their guest. He watched children play as he ate in what he assumed was their common room. They scurried about chasing one another and laughing. Two ducked under the table and stomped on Kael's toes as they ran through. He should wear his boots to breakfast from now on.

Vashar entered the room, and despite the man's bearing and power as their leader, they treated him like everyone else. They were one giant family to Kael's eyes.

Placing his bowl across from Kael, Vashar sat. "I would join Kael."

Kael nodded.

"My people, do they welcome?"

"Your people have been kind to me. Though I have not forgotten I am a prisoner here."

Waving a hand in dismissal, Vashar gave a toothy smile. "Is this true? When last does Kael attempt to leave? First night. After, doors were opened."

Kael frowned. Had he been free to leave after the first night? Heat started to well in his cheeks, and his fists clenched tight. Sharply, he stood. He was going to find out.

Vashar smiled and gestured toward the door.

As he stalked down the corridor, Kael's anger rose like a great wave. It washed over him and drove him toward those doors. People smiled at him as he passed, but his focus was a laser.

A horrible grating sound pierced his head. People around him started to scatter, their faces wrought with fear. What sort of weapon was this? Someone grabbed his shoulder.

It was Vashar, by himself and holding no weapon. "Follow me, there's danger."

Vashar ushered him into his room and told him to stay until he returned. The sound was muffled through his door, and the pain in Kael's head subsided. Soon, the sound stopped, and all was quiet. He considered leaving, but Vashar had warned of danger. Kael wished he had been more specific.

He sat on the edge of his bed for two minutes before the building rocked, throwing him onto the floor. Dust lifted from every surface, and stone chips flew from the ceiling and walls. Glancing up, Kael watched the ceiling split apart, and larger stones fell. He tried to cover himself, but they battered him. Pain shot through his legs and back.

A flash of agonizing white light sent him reeling. The room spun, and he wasn't sure where he was anymore. Another sharp pain in his back made him lurch. His hands reached for the source. Another flash of white crossed his vision, and all was dark.

The rocket had hit its mark. A trail of smoke ran through the air from the launcher to its point of impact. He had known it would. No one was better. It left a hole in the building wide enough for a vehicle to fit through. Split tree stumps stood yawning, and blackened leaves settled onto the carpet of charred blue-green grass. Daring a smile at his handiwork, Auctor discarded the empty launcher.

Gatlin gave him a pat on the shoulder. "Good shot, lad. You gave us an entrance and took out the comms tower."

A thin, stale haze hung in the air like smoke lingered after a battle. Irritating little insects flew about, whining as they circled his head. It would be hard to hear the enemy over the incessant racket. Waving his hands about, Auctor tried to scare them off, but their noise-making intensified.

Qenni walked over to him and sprayed something on his face. Some of it got into his mouth. It was pungent-smelling and tasted of chemicals.

Auctor spit, lips curled in disgust. "What in the void is that?"

"It's repellent. Keep the nasties away." She moved on, looking quite satisfied with herself, and Auctor frowned at her back.

Assaulting him without asking, what was she thinking? Though it wasn't important right now, he would remember. He never forgot a slight against him.

The gnats were gone, though.

He checked his rifle—loaded, charged, and safety off. He wasn't acting out of fear. When your life depended on your gear, you checked everything, twice. They encountered no resistance on their way to the gaping hole. As they moved through it, Alandra barked orders, setting them to task. They spread out, covering the area. They encountered nothing—not a single person, no sound. Looking around, Auctor saw it wasn't a building but a perimeter wall he had blown to bits. They were in a massive open space. The grass had been cleared, leaving exposed dirt, and a lone building stood in the center.

Auctor stared expressionless at the building. "Not impressive."

Shaking her head at him, the sergeant huffed a laugh. "Most of it will be underground. Didn't you pay attention in training?"

Auctor frowned. How dare she demean him like that? Why was everyone treating him like an idiot? They were the fools, not him. Auctor stalked ahead, glowering at Alandra's back.

As they took their positions at the door, Auctor noticed Qenni's rifle shaking and a bead of sweat on her forehead. "Scared?"

She nodded, eyes wide.

Smiling, Auctor leaned close. "Don't be. If you shake too much, you might miss."

After setting charges on the door, Ordan moved into position with the rest. Alandra made the count, glaring at each one as if to say, *You better not make a star wreck out of this.* Auctor stared back, expressionless; he would not be the one to foul this up.

After several loud pops, they could pull the door and moved it out with ease. Entering, Auctor took the left side, moving clockwise with Qenni at his back. An ample space sprawled before them, and movable dividers separated some areas from the larger room. He tore down the thin cloth barriers to find empty chairs and tables with hot food.

Gatlin stalked in, glaring around the room like it was a disappointing child. "Where are they?"

Ordan shrugged his shoulders and looked down. "They must be there. Did anyone bring a shovel?"

"Find a way in," Alandra ordered, scowling at him. "Keep an eye out for an ambush, I don't want a repeat of last time."

Giving the nearest wall a weary look, Ordan grimaced. "Right. Don't want any disappearing walls."

Smirking, Auctor began his search. He would find a way, and before these idiots. He had to be the best. He was the best.

"This is taking too long," Pike said through gritted teeth.

Rubbing her head, Qenni paced the room. "You'll get no argument from me. I've never been good at puzzles, and my head hurts."

Think. Where would one hide a secret passage? Scanning the room once more didn't help. They had spent the last half hour moving everything outside, and all they had to show for it was an empty room: no prominent doors, hatches, latches, or buttons.

Brown ceiling tiles of rough hewn stone ran uninterrupted, forming an odd counterclockwise circle spreading out from a central point.

The walls were smooth and flat stone, and there seemed to be nothing strange about them.

Almost everything was a shade of shit brown, except the bright yellow painted patterns on the ceiling and floor tiles. Pike curled his lip in disgust. What if they used shit to color the place? Shaking his head, he decided it couldn't be. The whole place would've reeked of the stuff. The air was musty and stale.

This was turning out to be some rescue mission. He wondered if the other squads were having as much trouble. The other squads may have been full of incompetent fools, too.

Auctor was on his hands and knees examining every millimeter of the floor. Getting down to the floor as well, Pike scrutinized every detail and ran his fingers across every edge and surface. If it were here, they would find it. Kneeling next to him on either side were Gatlin and Ordan.

Stamping her foot, Qenni growled in frustration. "I'm not getting into that filth."

Grasping her shoulder, Sergeant Alandra gave her a stern glare. "The faster you start, the sooner it'll be over."

Qenni tried to pull away, but Alandra held her tight. "I'm not made for dirty work, Sergeant. I can't."

Sweeping Qenni's legs out from under her with a swift kick, the sergeant dropped her to the floor face first. Dust scattered in puffs. Qenni coughed and spit, groaning in pain.

"Oh, since you're down there, you might as well help."

Scowling, Qenni started grubbing around the flooring, cursing under her breath. Ordan looked back and snickered, the sound cut short by a harsh glare from Gatlin. Now they were all down on the grimy floor like beggars looking for precious coins.

Having covered about half the space, Pike's fingers were raw from running over the gritty stone. He stopped for a moment, sitting back on his heels, and looked at his fingers. They were red with irritation and coated in brown dust.

Auctor was focused on a particular tile.

"Did you find something?" Pike asked.

Frowning, Auctor pressed down on the tile with his weight. Nothing happened, and he sat back, his brows drawn. "This is it."

Pike scrambled over, followed by the others. The tile was almost hot, and a low vibration tickled at his fingertips.

"There's something here."

Crowding in, they pressed against Pike's back as he swept his fingers around the edges. He had seen Auctor add weight to no avail, so he would try something else. There were no buttons or movable parts around the edge. Digging his nails into the cracks, he tried to pull it up by the sides. Fingers slipping off, he cradled his sore fingertips. "It ain't moving." Letting out a sharp breath, Pike lay on his back, staring out at nothing particular.

Alandra and Ordan started examining the tile, pushing, pulling, and hitting it with the leg from a broken chair, but nothing happened.

Pike's vision focused on the ceiling above. He frowned, blinking at what he saw. The center of the design met right above the tile Auctor had found. Could've found it sooner, but a lot of good it would've done. They still weren't getting inside. He followed the lines around and around in circles as they flowed out from the central point.

That was it, so obvious he hadn't considered it. Though logic would say it shouldn't work, if the tile up there marked the spot, the design must have been a clue.

Rolling over, Pike pushed his way through the others. "Move, I have an idea." He placed his palm flat on the warm tile and felt a slight trembling beneath it. As he turned his hand counterclockwise, the tile began to rotate. It popped out of the floor with a hiss, rising as it spun.

Watching in fascination, Pike's mouth hung open. Snapping it shut, he scrambled to his feet. They all watched in awe as the metallic screw-like shaft grew from the floor. Strange glowing lines ran along its surface, following the twist like magenta blood coursing through veins as it rose higher. The top of the shaft met the ceiling tile, and it stopped rising. All was still.

Auctor scowled. "Is that it?"

The room seemed to hum now, and the stone floor at the far end rose from below, blasting cool, clean air into the room, exposing a dark angular metal ramp leading down into the unknown.

Kael woke with a start. His head ached, and pain rippled through his body. As he rolled over, stones shifted and fell away. Opening his eyes, he saw the room was dark, and his vision was fuzzy. Light filtered in through the now-missing door to his room, and dust shifted in the light. The air was warm, almost hot; a thick staleness hung in it like mold. It pressed down upon him like a breath from a devil.

Weapons fire boomed, and unfamiliar voices shouted, blending together as they echoed throughout the halls. Where was he? It hurt to think. Managing to get on his feet, he noticed the bed was covered in blocks and its legs were broken; it leaned to the side. It was familiar, as if he'd slept there before. But when?

As he stumbled out into the hall, the sounds of battle grew louder. He approached an intersection in the hallway, and the sounds seemed to come at him from every direction. Looking back and forth down the tunnels, his vision still blurry, Kael couldn't see anything of worth. He would have to pick a direction and hope for the best.

Making his way down the corridor, his head started to clear. He remembered where he was and the danger. His steps grew quicker, his heart racing. For all the sounds of battle, the corridors were empty. No bodies. No guards. The back of his neck prickled; the sense of being watched was stronger than ever. But no one was there. Or was it that no one needed to be?

Weapons fire and shouting continued echoing throughout the halls. It was a matter of time before he found someone. The question was, on whose side would they be? Kael ran past an open door leading to a large room. Seeing something dark lying on the floor, he skidded to a halt. The air was filled with the acrid smell of burnt rifle propellant and the iron smell of blood. He knew before he looked what he would see, but he had to be sure. Peeking around the corner, he saw no movement. Kael's eyes shifted to the heaps of bodies.

He gawked in horror at the scene before him. Women and children lay in pools of dark blood, their faces frozen in fear. One woman still clutched her child, its almost unrecognizable body shredded. Stepping closer, his stomach turned, and his mouth filled with saliva. Kael spat, trying to control the urge to vomit. He looked on in utter dread as he recognized the mangled corpse.

It was her, the girl who had fed him in the prison cell. Turning his head, Kael looked away, eyes clamped shut. To unsee this nightmare would be a blessing he was exempt from. He ran from the room, breathing fast and heavy. Unable to catch his breath, he leaned against the wall and tugged at his collar. The walls seemed to be closing in, confining him, pressing in upon his chest. Sweat beaded and poured down his face. His heart pounded in his ears, his arms and legs began to hurt, and his muscles cramped. Sliding down to the floor, he hugged himself.

Remembering a lesson from training, Kael tried to control his breathing. "In through the nose, out through the mouth."

He kept repeating it over and over, and slowly and surely, his breath became even, and the thumping in his ears lessened. His head still ached, but he could think again. There was a deafening silence in the dead corridors now. No yelling, no rumbling explosives, no life.

The fighting had been fierce, and Auctor was beginning to enjoy himself. He was good at this, being a soldier. The others had proven more valuable in a fight than he had thought they would be. Being in a squad wasn't so bad, even if they were stupid.

Waving a hand, Alandra called them up to the last hallway. If Kael were here, this was where he'd be. She used a small mirror to look around the corner, and there was a volley of weapons fire. It reverberated down the corridors, and Auctor grew a bit deaf, ears ringing.

Gatlin tossed a starburst grenade down the hall. It went off with a pop, and a blinding light lit the wall opposite Auctor. He had no doubts anyone who looked at it would be blind for some time.

Auctor rounded the corner, aiming. Two men were visible right away, and he squeezed the trigger, hitting one twice in the chest, knocking him off his feet with a yelp. He hit the other in the face, and his target made a strange sucking sound before hitting the floor.

Several more came out, but by this time, the rest of the squad was in position and firing. Two rooms were branching off this hallway, and they had cleared one. It had been empty. Auctor hesitated, something close to anticipation tightening in his chest. Was it his brother or more enemies?

Auctor was first to the door, with Qenni and Pike close behind.

Shouldering his weapon, Pike centered himself at the door. "I'll kick it in."

Auctor nodded, and Alandra made the count. Pike bashed the wooden door in on zero with a roaring kick, and they flooded inside. Radio equipment lined the room, and a man startled by their entry fumbled with a weapon, trying to grasp it.

"Put it down!" Alandra ordered.

But he showed no sign of understanding what she was saying. Auctor frowned. He had done all this work to find a quivering imbecile. He was beside himself with anger. How dare his brother not even be here? The heat and rage filled him to bursting, and he roared, causing the man to fall, still clutching his weapon. He had a grip on it now and aimed it toward them.

Auctor shot him between the eyes.

He watched the man slump sideways, mouth still twitching. Weakness deserved nothing less.

Kael wasn't there. Intelligence had been wrong. Pike kicked a loose stone, sending it flying down the corridor. This had been an outpost of some kind. The people here had been fighters, except perhaps the last one. Looking sideways at Auctor, he frowned. They could've taken him alive, maybe learned something.

It seemed to him Auctor was too eager to fight. But he supposed some grew accustomed to killing faster than others. He knew life wasn't easy; few knew it better.

Exiting the building, he smiled to see the lander waiting in the courtyard. At least they didn't have to walk back to the clearing. A long high screech echoed from above and Pike stopped, eyes glued to the sky. Only about fifteen meters up was one of the Red Raptors he'd learned about in basic training. It glided through the air on it two meter wingspan, and the light of the low sun caught its underside showing its brilliant crimson feathers.

They were harmless to humans as was all the wildlife here on Xalthryn. *It must've spotted a silver rat for it to be flying this low,* Pike thought. Rats were the staple of these birds diet, and the raptors only competitor were the Xalthari that also hunted those furry rats. With a flap of its wings it rose and disappeared into the sky.

Liora jumped out of the lander and ran to them.

Pike winced and looked down. "He ain't here."

She ran up to him, smiling. "I know! One of the other teams found him."

Shouts of relief and joy echoed behind him. It hit like a gut punch. He'd given up on Kael. Almost thrown away the message. And now here Liora was, smiling like she'd known it was going to be okay all along.

Pike looked at her in disbelief for a moment, and then he hugged her. When had he gotten so emotional? No matter how hard he tried, somehow, he still found himself caring for others. His arms ached, and his back was sore. He would fight the need to care another day. After all, it was wonderful to have good news.

# Chapter 22:
## Lies, and Surrender

*"Surrendering to the lies of Starless leads to destruction."*
—Shepard of the Covenant

It was dark when he began to wake. The room was cool, and he lay in bed. Kael's eyes flicked open, and he jerked, pushing himself up on his elbows, trying to see where he was. Searing pain shot through his leg, causing him to tense. There was a dim light by a door and a low hum of electronics. Had he lost consciousness again?

Where was he? The last thing he remembered was death. His heart thumped like the recoil of a rifle. Clamping his eyes shut made the feeling worse as images of bodies flashed before his eyelids. Opening his eyes wide, he grimaced. The images had burned themselves into his retinas. He blinked, trying to get his bearings. The room was familiar, but how?

Thinking set his head ablaze with wildfire. He rubbed his temples, and the room spun. Kael lay back, his head resting on a soft pillow. Oh, being in a real bed again was a relief, even with the pain. Every muscle movement or twitch sent shooting pains through his body. He lay as still as he could manage, his chest rising and falling with each breath. It was a comforting rhythm.

Sunlight filtered through a thin window along the edge of the ceiling. It beamed through with hard-cut lines, the air clean and dust-free. A figure sat in a shadowed corner. Kael could make out the outline of armor on one leg. He struggled to push himself up by his elbows when the figure moved.

"Easy, soldier. I wouldn't want you passing out on me."

The man stood, the flat beam of light striking his face.

"Commander," Kael tried to say, but all that came out was a grated, dry sound.

Hernz thumped a fist on the door. A few moments later, a nurse came rushing in. "He's awake," Hernz told her.

The nurse went to Kael's side and gave him some water. Spluttering, he tried to drink as much as he could. The cool water was a balm to his parched throat.

Pulling the cup away, she felt his forehead.

"Thank you," Kael squeaked.

Hernz glowered at the woman. "I need to speak to him. Alone."

Lips pressed into a straight line, she got up and left.

Hernz's boots clomped on the floor as he loomed over Kael like some giant from a children's story, his face flat and unreadable.

Kael felt like a child under the man's harsh gaze, and the walls closed in.

"I need to know everything that happened to you."

Kael tried to nod. "Of course, sir." Kael recounted the events as they had happened. Almost as they had happened.

Hernz sat and listened until Kael was finished. Then the commander leaned forward, hands on his knees, eyes burning holes into Kael soul. "Is that all?"

Licking his lips, Kael looked down, hesitating.

Hernz's eyes narrowed, his jaw muscles working. "Do you doubt God? All of this is for a greater purpose. Beyond you, beyond me. To doubt his guidance is to doubt whether you live now." He stood looming over Kael, glaring down. "Perhaps I have been too forgiving. What haven't you told me?"

Breath catching in his throat, Kael felt smaller under the looming commander. "Nothing, sir," he managed to get out. "I've told you everything."

Bending over, Hernz grabbed both sides of the bed, coming close to Kael's face, eyes wild with fire. "Lies," he whispered. "You will tell me everything." Grabbing Kael's injured leg, he began to twist.

Pain ripped up Kael's leg and shot through his back. Screaming through gritted teeth, Kael tried to push Hernz back, but the man was too strong and Kael too weak from his injuries. He closed his eyes, tears running down his cheeks.

Releasing some pressure from his leg, enough so Kael could speak, Hernz leered at him. "What are you hiding?"

"Nothing...." The pain tore through his body again, worse this time. Kael's arms flailed until he grasped at the sides of his bed, grabbing for anything to squeeze. Chest on fire, he couldn't get a breath. He tried to gasp for air, but nothing came.

"Tell me, boy, before I lose my patience."

Pain easing, Kael caught a breath. "Stop." Body trembling, Kael looked up at Hernz, tears in his eyes. "I felt sorry for them. They don't believe in the Star but aren't bad people. I...I was sad to see them dead."

Letting go of Kael's leg, Hernz smiled. "That's it? That's what you were holding back? I can see it in your eyes, you're easy to read." He scoffed, turning around as if carefree. "Of course, they're not bad people, boy. That's not the point now, is it? They refuse to integrate. They die out of necessity. It's simple. Doesn't matter if they're good or bad."

Face still screwed up in pain, Kael was both relieved and horrified at Hernz's reaction. "Why is it necessary?"

"Because, soldier, there would be chaos among the stars without order. Under the Star's light, God has brought all humanity together under one ideal, one government, one ruler. Can you not admit the genius in it?"

Kael lay limp on the bed, too weak to move. "Before I came here, I might've agreed with you. Now, I question everything I knew."

Shaking his head, Hernz balled his fists. "Was there crime in your world? What about war, inequality? Can you deny his system works?"

"It does work, but without mercy and kindness."

Waving a hand in dismissal, Hernz turned away. "You say mercy and kindness, I say without favoritism, I say without inequality." Snapping his head around, Hernz stared at Kael. "Will you return to your squad, or will I need to remove you?"

Kael swallowed a lump in his throat. "I may not agree, sir, but I swore to serve the Star."

Hernz smirked, clearly pleased Kael held something sacred. "Good. I expect you to be on active duty when the doctor clears you." The door slammed behind him.

Lying his head back, Kael glared at the ceiling. His body trembled. In pain? In anger? In both. If it was possible for a man to garner hate within one conversation, Hernz was a master, a ruthless, crazy, bloodthirsty monster.

How hadn't Kael seen who Hernz was before? Had he been blinded by ideals, by his naivete? He hadn't missed the signs, he'd followed them, even when he'd doubted. He had marched to their rhythm and called it purpose. He'd convinced himself it was right. And now he saw the trail they left: blood and ash.

Wiping the tears from his face, Kael's breaths came ragged, broken. He had grown up being taught the Starless were heretics who needed saving, but now, he knew differently. The Xalthari still needed to be saved, but not from shadow—from the brutal and unrelenting corps. They were murderers; he was a murderer.

A knock came at the door. The nurse poked her head in. "I saw the commander leave. Are you okay?"

He gritted his teeth, debating whether he should say anything. To do so would put her in Hernz's sights, too. Kael sighed. "Yes."

"Good. How about some visitors?"

Kael frowned. "Who?"

"Well, everyone, of course."

The door swung open, and Alandra walked in, followed by Pike, Auctor, Qenni, Gatlin, and Ordan. They were all smiling, all happy. They crowded around him, asking about what had happened.

Well, almost everyone. Auctor sat at the foot of his bed, listening to the commotion of the others.

"I want to hear all about what happened while I was gone," Kael said.

"Of course, lad." Gatlin launched into the story, laying out all the details until the rescue.

Kael listened, smiling.

When his squad left him to rest, Kael lay staring into the shaft of sunlight. It had moved a significant amount since he'd first woken, perhaps a few hours ago.

The nurse returned with a tray containing the usual corps rations and water. "Time to eat."

"I'm not hungry."

"I have medication for you, and you have to eat something."

Kael sighed. He didn't want to eat but didn't have the energy to argue with the nurse. He nodded, and she helped him sit up.

After giving him his medication, she set the tray in front of him, frowning. "I expect you to have eaten when I return."

He looked down at the warm rations on his tray and curled his lip. It had never been good, yet now it looked and smelled even worse. What he had eaten during captivity had been preferable to this. His whole stay with the Xalthari had been preferable to his encounter with Hernz. He scowled at the door. Hernz was the savage, not the Xalthari.

Trying to make the best of his current situation, Kael took a bite. It was bland and tasted of minerals. It was odorless, too. Made to serve its purpose and nothing more, as were all things within the Starlit Corps. Kael drank water to chase the taste of dirt from his mouth. He wondered how he used to eat this every day. How was he going to eat this every day?

The door creaked open, and Junova stepped in.

Eyebrows raised, Kael set his utensil down. "Captain, it's good to see you."

She smiled and pulled a chair up next to his bed. "You've looked better."

Wincing, Kael looked at his bruised arms. "Most of this happened during the rescue."

"So I heard. I spoke with Hernz. I don't know what's come over him. It seems he loses all sense where the Xalthari are concerned."

Looking down, Kael gritted his teeth. He wanted to tell her how he felt. However, trusting her, a career ship captain, could be risky. What if she were no better than Hernz?

Concern flashed across her face, and Junova touched his arm. "What is it?"

Those three simple words were like a key to his floodgates. He told her everything, unable to hold back, raw emotion spilling forth. He told her the people were kind and welcoming after those first few days. He told her how they had treated him and what he had eaten. He told her about Vashar and his question. He told her they had never laid a hand on him in anger or interrogation. Then he told her about the bodies and the child.

She sat motionless, hand across her mouth, listening to every word, every detail. Her eyes glistened as if she might tear up, but nothing came. Kael's own tears flowed as the images hammered him over and over like a sledgehammer driving in a wedge. His fists clenched, his nails bit into his palm, and his breaths came broken and ragged.

"How can we murder them?"

Junova's gaze lowered. He could see her jaw muscles working. "I...I don't know. I tried to stop it before the killing started. Vashar defends his people and who they are at their core. They would rather die than live stripped of their identity." She hesitated a moment. "I can't say I blame them. It might be better to die with your standards intact, a conscience unblemished by compromise, by blind loyalty."

They both sat for a long moment, then Kael asked, "What can we do?"

"I have been trying to reduce casualties by altering plans and bombardments enough, hoping Hernz won't notice. I'm beginning to think it's not enough, yet what more can I do? The commander will waste no time replacing me if I'm found out. He'd put my body on display as a warning."

"We need support."

"That's why I asked you to talk to your squad. If we can slow the killing, maybe get the Xalthari to surrender...." After a pause, she shook her head. "No. It won't work, they won't surrender."

"After my time among them, I don't think they will, either," Kael said. "I can still speak to Zero for you."

"What's the use? We are talking about treason. Becoming heretics, hated by all. We could never win."

Kael pursed his lips, frowning. "We let them die then?"

Looking at the floor, Junova sighed. "No. I've failed before. Spikernatous still burns because of it. I can't let this end the same way."

The nurse popped her head in with her mouth open. "How are you doing with your food? Oh, you have a visitor. I didn't see you, Captain."

Junova stood. "I'm glad you're well, Kael. I must be going."

"Oh, yes, he needs his rest if he's going to get better."

Kael waved a sore hand at Junova as she left, the nurse shuffling around her. "It looks like you ate some. Next time you will need to eat more, you hear?"

He nodded.

"Good, no more visitors today, you need some rest." She slipped through the door, tray rattling.

Left alone with his thoughts, Kael gazed at the slit of a window, through which the sunlight was dimming. Junova had more reservations than he had thought. It was a small comfort to know he wasn't alone, that someone else viewed what they were doing as murder. No, genocide. They were eliminating an entire people, a culture with their own way of life and beliefs. He swallowed a lump in his throat. She had been right, though. What could they do?

# Chapter 23:
## Powerful

*"Power comes in many forms, even a quiet moment carries power-
ful repercussions."*
—Xalthari Warden of Echoes

"Brother, wake up."

Kael opened his eyes. Auctor was sitting across the room, the corner of his lips pulled upward in satisfaction. Pushing past his soreness,
Kael sat up against the head of his bed. "I'm glad you came."

"I couldn't leave you to face your sickbed alone, now could I?"

Huffing a laugh, Kael winced at the pain in his chest. "Doctor says
I'll be out of bed tomorrow."

"How long until you return to duty?"

"A couple of weeks at best."

Auctor's smile faded into a thin line. "I'm worried about you,
brother. What happened to you out there?"

Looking away from Auctor, Kael stared into the sharp ray of light
from the window. "The Xalthari, they weren't what I expected. They're
people like you, like me."

"Of course, they are. Don't you remember all those recruitment
movies you made me watch? Did you expect them to be different?"

Twisting his body, Kael tried to remove pressure from a sore spot. He looked up at Auctor, catching his gaze. "It doesn't matter what I think anymore. I took an oath."

Huffing a stiff laugh, Auctor shook his head. "Oath? A collection of words made to manipulate control over those lesser than yourself."

Looking down, Kael frowned. "I gave my word. You'll forgive me if I don't throw it away without consideration."

"What would you do without your oath?"

There was a long pause.

"That's the difference between us. I fight because of you, Kael. Not because I took some oath. Do you even know what you're fighting for?"

Kael swallowed a lump in his throat. He had been sure of himself and his reasons for joining the corps a few months ago. Auctor was right. Now, he had no idea what he was fighting for. The oath was a convenient way to justify his actions to himself, to further enslave himself to an ideal he didn't agree with anymore, to place himself in relative safety behind the facade of the greater good, to hide from the ever-present fate awaiting those cast out of the corps. The thought of Eesbex made him shudder with cold.

Wetting his lips, he looked Auctor in the eyes. "What other choice do I have?"

A knock came at the door, and Liora stepped in. She looked at the brothers. "I hope I'm not interrupting."

Smiling, Kael waved her in. "No, not at all. Please, come and sit."

Auctor watched her as she sat on the bed next to Kael.

Kael looked at Auctor. "Can we finish our talk later?"

Nodding, Auctor headed for the door, stopping for a moment when he was halfway through. "We all have a choice, brother. Sometimes you need a little push."

After Auctor closed the door, Liora looked at Kael, eyebrows scrunched. "What does he mean?"

Letting out a sigh, Kael looked down at the bed. "We don't always see eye to eye. He thinks you need a reason to fight beyond the oath."

Liora tilted her head. "You don't?"

"I did. But now with everything that's happened, my reason feels wrong."

"What happened to you out there?"

Kael chuckled to himself. How many times had this question been asked in the last few days? Yet, humor aside, it didn't matter. Each time hit as hard as the previous.

He gave Liora a soft, joyless smile. "I saw horrible things. Noncombatants, women, and children murdered. The same women and children who had fed me, greeted me as a friend, accepted me, an enemy, into their lives. I saw the heretics, the Starless, and who they are. They aren't some evil needing to be eliminated. Their crime is standing in God's way, and that's not reason enough to fight."

Liora's eyes were sad, and her lips were drawn into a thin line. She placed her hand on his arm, giving him a gentle squeeze.

Closing his eyes tight, Kael drew in a ragged breath. "My word, the oath, binds me to the corps. If I break it, I die. If I am loyal, at least I survive."

Her jaw worked. "I've never been this close to war. Always up in a ship looking down at a planet, admiring its beauty. It's a funny thing how distance changes a person's perception. Makes morality flexible and blurs the lines of ethics."

Trying to smile, Kael looked up at her. "Sounds like you're the lucky one. Never having to see what I've seen." He huffed a laugh. "I'm envious."

She chuckled. "You should be. When is the doctor going to let you out of here?"

Stretching his sore arm, Kael rubbed at the muscle. "Tomorrow, but I'll be on inactive duty for another week or two. Why?"

"I think you must get off this planet for a while."

He raised an eyebrow. "What do you have in mind?"

Smirking, Liora's eyes glinted. "I don't think the captain would mind an extra soldier on the ship for a few days."

Kael puffed out his cheeks. "I don't know, she runs a tight ship."

Liora shook her head, smiling. "True, but I can convince her."

"Oh, you must be powerful."

After motioning him to slide over, she sat with him on the bed. Kael put his arm around her and winced in a shock of pain. As she rested her head on his shoulder, her gaze met his.

"You have no idea how powerful I am," she whispered.

Feeling her warm breath brush his cheek, his hand trembled, and his heart pounded like a drum in his chest. He pulled her tight, feeling her warmth against him.

"I'm beginning to understand," he murmured.

A ray from the slit window caught her eyes, and they shined with green and gleaming golds among the hazel expanse. Smiling, Kael brushed the hair back from her face and caressed her cheek, taking in her softness, her beauty.

"I've got you," she whispered.

Their lips met in a passionate embrace. The universe reduced to this room, him and her.

# Chapter 24:
## Feverlit

*"We will not stand in their path if they wish to be a zealot of the Star. Yet those who become feverlit may find we are no longer allies."*
—Shepard of the Covenant

Tilting his head back, Gatlin drained the last drops of a strong drink he'd been nursing. "And then we assaulted the Starless stronghold on Spicker...uh, Spikernatous. You should've been there, lad, it was glorious. I fought their leader, Zepante...oh, his name isn't important." He poured himself another glass of the cobalt-blue liquor. "One-on-one, I fought him with my bare hands. Crowded in on either side by Star...Starlit and Starless."

Gatlin took a gulp and slammed his cup down. "The next thing I knew, the heretic pulled a knife and stabbed me right here." He lifted his shirt and pointed to a scar on his stomach. "Seemed like he never heard of a fair fight before, so I kicked him in the globes, droppin' him to his knees. I took the knife from him and rammed it through his neck." Swallowing the last of his drink, he blinked across the room. "Should've seen the look of disbelief on his face." He laughed. "Let it be a lesson to you. Never expect a fair fight."

Fidgeting with the zipper on his shirt, Pike studied Gatlin. "Do you ever get tired of fighting?"

"Me? No. Battles have been my life. Movin' from one war to the next, never seein' the same people. Don't like staying in one place too long. Don't get sentimental, lad, you'll be like me before you know what hit you."

Pike frowned. He didn't like the idea of being like Gatlin. Yes, Gatlin was a good fighter and knew his way around the battlefield, and he was right; it would be easy for Pike to become the jaded old soldier, living from battle to battle, bottle to bottle. He still fought the empty pain in his chest, a desire to isolate himself. Yet, he didn't want to be like Gatlin.

Looking back up to the sergeant, Pike saw Gatlin had passed out, cup in hand. Shaking his head, Pike looked at Ordan, who was scowling at Qenni. They were arguing again. He wondered when they would put aside their bickering and realize Alandra was the real threat.

The door opened, and Pike tensed, ready to spring to attention, when Liora walked in, followed by Kael. Looking at Kael's limp, Pike winced. Yet, it was good to see them both. He found himself overcome by a grin.

Alandra waved them over, patting a seat. "Look who got released. Doctors decide you wouldn't die from fresh air?"

Shaking his head, Kael sat, Liora next to him. "Yeah, but they said I have to take small doses. I'm going with Liora to spend a few days on the Radiance. No danger of fresh air."

Huffing a laugh, Pike scooted down the table, leaving Gatlin to his drunken stupor. "We got you back, and now you're going to leave us? Ain't it some thanks."

Feeling a sharp elbow in his side, Qenni smirked. "Don't you see he wants to spend time alone with Liora?"

There was a pause in conversation, and Pike glanced at Kael to see him looking at Liora sidelong with a sheepish smile.

She chuckled and took his hand in hers. "It's not a secret."

Pike looked down, gritting his teeth. He wished they'd stop. Stop making him care. "I'm happy for you two. At least you found goodness in this mess."

Clapping Pike on the shoulder, Ordan grinned. "Don't discount the rest of us. We aren't all bad."

"No, I suppose not."

Clearing his throat, Kael looked at each of them. "I want to say, thank you. You held out hope for me when I could've been written off as dead. Risked yourselves to find me."

Pike's stomach knotted. He hadn't held out hope. He'd almost thrown away the news of Kael's life. Keeping his hands under the table, Pike clenched his fists. He couldn't look at Kael any longer.

Auctor sat beside him, smiling. "I couldn't let you die." His smile was wrong, but Pike couldn't pinpoint the feeling. He shook it off as his guilt.

"None of us could," Pike added. "Zero wouldn't be the same without you."

Smiling at them, Kael nodded. "That means more than you know." He swallowed. "When I was being held, Vashar asked me a question. One I haven't told anyone else. It's been burning in my head since." He paused for a long moment.

Raising an eyebrow, Alandra pursed her lips. "Are you going to tell us?"

Pike frowned at her. "Give him a minute." His eyes returned to Kael. Liora was giving his hand a light squeeze. He couldn't imagine what must have been running through Kael's mind.

Scowling at Pike, Alandra shook her head. "Then stop talking."

"He asked me this," Kael said, tapping his fingers. "'When divine voices say, look at them, heretics shaped by shadow, the Starlit answer: We have looked, and heresy is all we see.' Then he asked, 'Do we wonder what they see when they look at us?'"

It was quiet for a long moment. They had been taught to look at the Xalthari as the enemy, heretics, savages. Frowning down at the table, Pike tightened his jaw. Were Xalthari more than an enemy?

"What a load of nonsense," spouted Gatlin. "Doesn't matter what they think of us, long as we kill 'em."

Now the whole room was frowning. Qenni pushed off from the table. "Gatlin, you're drunk. No one cares what you think."

The old soldier chuckled and burped. Pike doubted he was the thinking type. Another look into his possible future.

Grabbing Qenni by the shoulder, Ordan urged her to sit. Alandra appeared distant, as if she were in a different world.

Pike gazed at her empty eyes. "Sergeant?"

She blinked, glancing around the room as if she didn't know where she was for a moment. Now everyone was looking at her, and she frowned. "What? Nothing better to look at?"

Shifting in his seat, Kael's brows knotted in worry. "Where were you a moment ago?"

As she shut her eyes, Pike could see Alandra's jaw muscles working. He knew the look all too well. It was pain, carving itself into you and never letting go.

Taking a slow, deep breath, she opened her eyes. "I can't talk about it, not now." Alandra clenched her fists. "What I can tell you—Xalthari are no better than any other Starless scourge I've fought. I've never considered whether they can think like us, and I can't start now."

Fidgeting with a chip left on the table, Ordan stared at his fingers. "What Kael says reminds me of how it was before I was in the corps. I was an outcast, I had no family and no home. None would give me work. I've seen what it's like to live where people view you as less than human. The corps took me in, gave me a place to sleep, food to eat, and all they asked in return was service." He took a breath, his eyes fixed on Kael. "I can't help but think I've become the same as those who treated me as dirt. I saw it before you gave us an inside view of their lives." Ordan's shoulders slumped, and he looked down. "I have family, food, and a dry place to sleep. What they are can't matter. What I am can't matter."

Liora leveled a glare across the room. "Why can't it matter, Ordan? Why can't it matter to any of you? You heard how they treated Kael but didn't hear what Hernz did to him when he returned."

Kael grabbed her arm, looking at her with fear in his eyes.

Leaning forward, Pike caught his gaze. "What is she talking about?"

Kael winced and looked down, releasing Liora.

She grasped his hand tighter and nodded. "The commander interrogated him before he got out of the infirmary. He didn't tell me either. I found out when a doctor came in and asked him why his broken leg needed to be reset when he had done it the day before."

Alandra's eyes widened as she straightened. "He hurt you?"

Kael gave a weak nod.

She slammed her fist on the table. "Has he become feverlit? When did it become standard procedure to torture our own?"

Pike sighed. He guessed she didn't need an answer. They all knew nothing could be done.

Holding a hand over her mouth, Qenni gasped. "He's a monster."

"A monster?" the drunken sergeant asked. "Not a monster. The commanders, an old soldier, rules with a firm hand." Gatlin tried to pour another drink and missed his cup. The foul-smelling alcohol soaked into the cracks on the table. He shrugged his shoulders and drifted off.

Shaking his head, Pike frowned at the old goat. "I don't know how I feel about the Xalthari." He looked at Kael then down at his hands. "If they are people who deserve to live...we are murderers. I can't accept it." Glancing at Gatlin, he wondered if had any choice but to become the calloused veteran who held nothing sacred, or like Hernz, who tortured his soldiers. There had to be something better.

# Chapter 25:
## Emerald

*"A color, a gem, a star. Can an emerald be more than the sum of its parts?"*
—Unknown

Junova tossed the pad and watched as it clattered onto her desk. Hernz had barred her from spearheading operations, and now he'd assigned her crew without consulting her. With a sharp breath, Junova looked out the window. Xalthryn loomed far below.

Hernz had assigned her senior Astronavs to fly landers on a mission tomorrow. After studying the operation parameters, she reassigned her most junior pilots to the mission. Hernz was becoming more unstable by the day, and this proved it to her. His own projected survival rate for corps forces was twelve percent.

Liora would be given the next few days off, so she'd looked at the roster for planetary operations. Good timing was all. She might've lost all her best pilots. She couldn't run a ship without skilled Astronavs. What was Hernz thinking? Was he thinking?

A voice cracked over comms. "Captain, the shuttle is docking."

Junova touched a button on her desk display. "Are the preparations ready?"

"Yes, Captain. We've prepared the starboard viewing deck as per your orders."

Smiling, she looked out at the void. "Good, I'll greet them at the airlock."

Junova entered her Htube and was whisked into the ship. No matter how often she rode the pneumatic tubes, they always amazed her. Blasted through the ship on waves of air, never running into another person, your hair wasn't even a mess when you exited. The grated flight deck rattled under her boots as she was ejected from the tube. Liora and Kael's shuttle had latched onto the docking port. Good, she wasn't late.

She stood smiling, almost as a proud mother would, waiting for the pair to emerge. With a gentle hiss, the airlock door rolled open. Giggling, Liora came stumbling out. Kael followed close behind, grinning like he had gotten away with something.

Upon seeing her, Liora straightened, her smile easing away. "Captain, I didn't expect—"

"Me to welcome my best Astronav and her soldier aboard?"

Putting his arm around Liora's waist, Kael smiled down at her. "Best Astronav, huh?"

Liora opened her mouth as if getting ready to speak when Junova waved a hand at the door. "Would you like to show Kael our ship?"

Eyes flicking with excitement, Liora looked at her. "Can we show him the bridge?"

Laughing, Junova started toward the tubes. "Of course, we can." It took a few moments to reach the bridge in the tubes. Junova watched, smiling at Kael, who stumbled out like a drunkard. "They take some getting used to."

He looked up at her, grinning. "How does it work?"

She shook her head. "I use them, not build them." Scanning her bridge, she observed its staff were all in their positions, hard at work. She couldn't often arrive on the bridge without someone yelling.

"Captain on the bridge!" Reed bellowed.

She sighed—not often at all. "An informal visit, please return to your stations."

Her staff resumed their work, quickly and quietly. Kael was gawking around the bridge, his eyes landing on the great God statue at the front.

"It's there to remind us he's always watching."

Kael's throat bobbed. "Does he?"

Huffing a laugh, Junova shook her head. "No, I don't think he does. It's more warning than active monitoring."

He looked relieved. She couldn't blame him. Who would want God watching you every second? Liora waved and led Kael to her station. Junova observed them talking for a few moments then strolled along the central command platform. It was good to see them both smiling. After her last conversation with Kael, Junova had wondered if he'd ever look happy again. She knew he wasn't. He deserved a reprieve, and she would give it to him.

Stopping above Liora's station, Junova stood on the edge of her platform. "I have a surprise for both of you."

They looked up at her, excited curiosity on their faces.

"Since Kael won't return to duty for several days, I have reassigned all your duties for the next three days, Liora."

Liora grinned from ear to ear. "Thank you, Captain."

"That's not all," Junova continued. "When you're finished here, a surprise will be waiting for you both on the starboard viewing deck. I would join you, but I have work to do." Junova smiled at them. "It's good to see you both smiling."

Turning, Junova marched back to the tubes. Shutting her eyes and listening to the air whisper past her was soothing in an odd way. Her boots hit solid ground, and she was in her quarters. A second of peace, to be spat out into a life of war. She looked again at the planet out her window. A place of beauty. A place of death.

Walking onto the viewing deck, Kael's jaw dropped. It was a massive open space with a gigantic window. The entirety of cyan Xalthryn with its misty valleys was visible, and its two bright gray moons hung like jewels in the void, peeking out from behind their planet.

"It's unbelievable," he said.

Taking his hand, Liora smiled up at him. "Imagine seeing dozens, hundreds, and each one different. Beautiful in its own way."

"I don't think I can. I wonder what Syrelis looks like?"

"You didn't see it?"

He shook his head. "No."

"After this war, we should go see it together."

"I would like that."

Liora pointed while pulling his arm. "Look at that."

Several crew members were dressed in navy jumpsuits and aprons. They stood around a large table laden with covered trays and flowers. He recognized the latter, a common flower often sold to foreign merchants back home. How could they be so fresh?

He offered his arm to her, and they approached the odd setting.

Liora touched the flowers and smelled them. "These are beautiful."

He looked at her and the flowers. His breath caught in his throat, his heart raging. These long-stemmed flowers, which he had never paid much attention to, took on a new light.

Their petals burst forth like star-struck blades, each outlined in black offset with brilliant emerald green. They jetted out of their vase, boldly and sharply, hearts dark and ringed with indigo.

Liora smiled back at him, her eyes contrasting with the vibrant colors. Both were more stunning than Kael had ever noticed before. She raised an eyebrow. "What?"

He blinked, taking in a quick, ragged breath. "I uh...I can't believe these flowers are here. We call them Emerald Stars."

"From your home?"

Nodding, he smiled.

She pulled one out and threaded it through her hair above her right ear. "An entire section of Radiance is dedicated to growing plants. The botanists grow flowers and other plants to supplement food and oxygen production."

A couple members of the crew had moved around the large table and were standing on the far side next to a much smaller table with two chairs.

Kael looked at one. "For us?"

The man nodded.

Now seated, the lights dimmed, and the soft glow of Xalthryn bathed the room in a twilight blue. Liora gazed out at the void, and Kael watched her for a moment. He smiled, thinking of the day he had fallen face-first on the floor. Her first words to him had been, *Found the floor.* Three simple words and a chance meeting had led him here, with her.

His heart still pounded like a drum, and his palms were slick with sweat. Plates were placed in front of them. Looking down, he saw vegetables.

"You have vegetables?"

"Fruit, too."

His mouth salivated. "Fruit?" He turned his head to look at the crew serving him, and a plate of fruit was placed in front of him. He blinked at it, dumbfounded. "We're eating Nblocks, and you have real food?"

She shrugged. "Not all of us. I get this food once a month because of my rank. Some don't get any. There's not enough for everyone." Looking down at her plate and then his, she frowned. "Junova gave up her rations so we could have this meal."

Kael's eyes softened. "She must care a great deal for you."

"Don't exclude yourself, soldier."

Kael picked up a piece of red fruit and took in the sweet, delicate aroma. Crunchy outside and soft inside, it hit him with sweetness and a hint of saltiness. As he savored the juices, Liora watched him, smirking. He raised an eyebrow.

Stabbing a vegetable with her utensil, she examined it. "It makes me happy to see you enjoying yourself." She crunched into her food. "It's not gone, you know. The war. It feels good to pretend it doesn't exist, even for a few days."

She looked worried, so he smiled. "I don't know what I did to deserve someone like you."

"You didn't," she said. "I chose you, and now you're mine." She took another crisp bite, smirking.

"That's how it is. You had this planned all along, didn't you?"

"Oh, yes, I organized everything. From joining the corps and meeting me until your rescue, when I could spring the trap when you were most vulnerable."

He shook his head, looking out at Xalthryn. "It is a beautiful planet." Swallowing a lump in his throat, he smiled at the flower in her hair. There was nothing else to do. It was a perfect moment. Nothing he could say would make it any better. Time seemed to slow, his breath steady and smooth, his heart thumping, reliable as an old friend. She blinked, and it was an eternity waiting for her eyes to open again so he could see their gleaming colors. Then it was over, and everything moved as it always had. He blinked and ate his food.

When they finished eating, the moons moved out of view, to the other side of Xalthryn. Staring at the dark mountain ridges, Kael winced. "It's almost hard to believe there's a war raging among the beauty."

Standing next to him, Liora rested her head on his arm. "Doesn't feel real from here."

"No. I understand how you felt."

She gripped his arm tighter. "Me, too."

He looked at her. "What now? Do we dance?"

She chuckled. "By the stars, no."

"That's a relief, I can't dance."

They stood there for a long moment, staring at the planet. The crew behind them moved the last table out, and the door hissed closed.

Looking into her eyes, Kael bit his lip. His breath came quick, and he tried to smooth out his breathing. She beamed up at him; her throat bobbed. His eyes shifted between her eyes and lips as he moved closer.

Their lips met. Her breath was warm on his cheek. Kael grasped her neck and waist, pulling her into him. An involuntary growl came from deep in his throat as her lips parted. His controlled, slow breath came ragged, and his heart thundered in his chest. As they parted, he gazed into her eyes.

With a gentle smile on her face, Liora touched his hair. "What now?" she whispered.

He pulled her closer still, his hand resting on the small of her back. "I'm yours, aren't I?

# Chapter 26:
## Abyss

*"The Abyss is not a place we choose to go, yet it can be inevitable."*
—God Ruler

A knock at the door startled Junova. Who on the ship wouldn't use the chime?

"Come in."

Kael stepped through the door, messed up as if he'd just woken, looking nervous. "Captain, have you spoken to Liora?"

"No," she said, pausing a moment. "Why?"

His eyes darted around the room, and his head lowered. "When I woke this morning, she was gone. There was a note." He handed it to her.

Frowning at the paper, she read. *Last-minute order. I have to fly. I have a surprise for you. See you tonight.*

Drawing in a sharp breath of air, Junova glared at her pad. This was Hernz's doing. Checking a few rosters, she found the changes. Liora had been reassigned to active duty. Why her?

She turned to face Kael, the heat giving way to a dark fog creeping into her mind. "Someone reassigned her." The words came out hollow. "I didn't know. It has to be Hernz."

He sighed and looked out the window. "If only she told me. Now all I can do is wait." Looking at Junova, he tried to smile. "Could I get a shuttle? At least I can be there when she returns."

Giving him an insincere half-smile, Junova tapped on her display. "It will be ready for you."

Kael hesitated a moment before turning to leave. "Thank you."

Alone in her quarters, Junova glowered at the planet below. Its clouds were thin wisps stretched across its skies. Hernz, the treacherous old zealot, what was he thinking? This time he'd gone too far.

As he stepped off the lander and onto solid ground, Kael didn't expect to be glad to return to the compound. It was an odd feeling, almost like returning home—if home was crawling with soldiers and a tyrant commander.

There was quite a bustle of activity, and he figured he'd find Zero. They'd know what it was about, and then he could slip into the war room and watch the mission unfold.

Alandra had three soldiers lined up in front of the barracks. He heard part of what she was saying as he approached. "Rule number two, my word is law. Understand?"

Replacements. It had been so long he'd forgotten they needed any. They had been down three since the first battle.

Auctor was the first to see him coming and smiled. How long had it been since he'd seen Auctor smile? It didn't take long for the rest to notice, and he was met with joyful and confused faces.

Clapping him on the shoulder, Gatlin grinned. "Couldn't stay away?"

"I wanted to know what the excitement is, but now I see."

Alandra glared at the replacements. "Let me introduce you to our newest friends." She pointed them out one at a time. "Rody, Mya, and Elim."

They looked young, which was strange to him, as he was still eighteen. Kael leaned close to Pike. "Is this how we looked?"

Pike smiled, looking at him sideways. "We looked worse." He paused. "Where is Liora?"

Hearing her name made his heart flutter, and Kael took a slow breath. "She got a last-second flight assignment for the mission today."

Pike looked worried. "At least you got us to keep you company." He pointed over his shoulder and continued, "Alandra is going to put those soft-skins through the paces."

Glancing over Pike's shoulder, Kael winced. "I'd rather not, I've seen enough corps etiquette to last a lifetime."

Auctor stalked over and put his arm around Kael's shoulders, grinning.

Pike raised an eyebrow. "Are you this excited to see replacements?"

"Them?" Auctor frowned. "Can't I be happy to see my brother getting better? He'll be back in action soon. I can't wait."

It was odd, Auctor showing this much affection. Kael couldn't think of a time since they'd arrived on Xalthryn that Auctor had looked happy. Perhaps he was adapting to his new life?

Shaking his head, Kael huffed a laugh. "At least someone is happy."

Then, as quick as he'd come, Auctor was off, headed into the barracks. Frowning after him, Pike sighed. "Your brother is a bit off."

A brief heat rose in Kael's neck, the kind you get when you're getting ready to defend family. Then it ended. "He's always been this way. Not quite like anyone else."

Pike nodded. "That's one way to put it." He looked at Kael with earnest eyes. "I've seen him in action. Killing comes easy for him."

"He does have to be the best," Kael agreed. "I imagine he applies the same logic to war." He thought for a moment. "I understand your concern. I don't know how to reach him. He won't talk about his emotions."

Shoulders dropping, Pike looked at the sky. "Maybe I'm looking too hard."

Huffing a laugh, Kael shook his head. "No. You care."

Pike tensed at his words, eyes fixed on the blue-green sky. "Ain't it a sight?" After a moment's silence, Pike looked at him. "Where to?"

"The war room. I'm going to check on Liora."

"I'll go with you. Nothing exciting about replacements anyway."

The corps highway, as they'd come to call the main road, was crawling with activity. Replacements had finished training, and fresh faces were being marched around, their instructors yelling. One of the voices stood out to Kael. Krennak. He tensed at the cadence and accent as the man bellowed. He kept his eyes forward and tried not to catch the instructor's gaze. But the instructor halted his recruits, and he smiled once he'd turned away from them.

Pike saluted then waved. "Morning, Sergeant."

"A fine one it is at that, soldier."

Kael's mind reeled. Pike and Krennak on speaking terms?

Krennak smiled at Kael and saluted. "Ye're Kael, right? Never forgot a name yet."

Returning the salute, Kael stood at attention. "Yes, sir."

"Ye dinne 'ave to be formal wi' me anymore, lad. All tae yellin', it's fer show. Teachin' tae young an' impressionable how to survive in tae corps." Krennak whipped around and glared at his platoon of recruits. "Did I hear one o' ye make a sound?"

They snapped to attention, eyes filled with panic.

Krennak turned back to Kael. "Nothin' to it. Good to see ye two still livin'." He marched over to the recruits, shouting new obscenities.

Kael stared at Krennak as he walked away. "I'd have never thought Krennak would be...."

"Nice," Pike finished.

"Yeah."

"I was shocked the first time, too. Then he gave me advice."

Kael frowned. "He remind you how to clean your weapon?"

Pike stopped. "No. He reminded me there's more to life than running from your problems. You have to face them to overcome them." He started walking again. "I didn't believe him at the time. Then things started to change, and...let's say I haven't accepted it, but I'm trying."

Kael sighed. "That's all we can do, right?"

Ahead of them stood the HQ. The building towered out of the ground like a testament to God's authority. It was all white plastic and metal, unlike the charcoal and bronze of Radiance or the gold of his statues. Kael had been here many times before, yet this time was different. This visit had a meaningful weight. It wasn't orders or another mission briefing for the corps bringing him here; he was here for Liora, for himself.

They slipped unnoticed into the darkened war room, where operators were busy at their stations. The operators murmured into their headsets, filling the room with incomprehensible babble. Hernz was nowhere to be seen—a relief.

Pike pointed at a display across the room. "That's monitoring the landers."

Moving around the room, Kael caught glimpses of the other screens. Several squads were engaged with an army of Xalthari, four times their number. It was madness. Even during his first battle, they'd been outnumbered two to one.

As Kael moved into the center of the room, Pike tried to stop him, but the operators were too busy to notice. The projector in the center hummed, glowing bright against the dim room. It showed the entire battle view, with gold dots representing corps troops and black dots representing Starless troops.

As Pike approached him, Kael swallowed a lump in his throat. The entire company in the zone was outnumbered, not four to one. Nine to one. His heart sank. Liora was flying in this disaster?

As he got a clear view of the flight monitors, it was clear there weren't enough landers for an entire company. It didn't make sense. It was as if they were being thrown to the slaughter, and the man cutting their throats hadn't even come to watch.

He could see the individual lander IDs but not the pilot names. A comms light lit up, and a man's voice came through. "Taking heavy fire...." There was some static. "Enemy.... Anti-air...." Then silence.

Looking sidelong at Pike, Kael winced. "When did they get AA?"

Pike shook his head. He frowned and looked back at the displays.

His knuckles hurting, Kael worked his fingers. He had been clenching his fists since they'd entered the room. He watched a light blink out on the flight screen. It was the lander that had sent the warning about AA. His eyes darted, trying to find anything to give him a clue where Liora was.

An operator behind him raised his voice. "Get your troops out of there, Captain, we're pulling you out."

Kael looked back to see Pike staring at the projector map. It was bad. Almost half of the corps forces had been lost since he'd last looked. Landers were on a fast approach to an LZ nearby.

Pike was shaking his head, hand covering his mouth. "It's a slaughter."

Turning back to the flight monitors, Kael moved closer. He had to find her. Another lander's signal indicator went dark. He blinked. It wasn't her. Kael was close enough to see the pilot IDs and had her lander clocked. Pike's hand rested on his shoulder, but his focus was unbreakable.

That one little blip. A dot on a screen was his entire existence. Another transmission came through.

"All landers confirming pickup. They're on the way home."

Good news. He wanted to breathe easier, to relax, but there was still one problem: anti-air. He watched as another lander flashed from existence. The operator scrambled, pressing buttons and murmuring into his headset. Confirmation tones came back across the speakers.

His eyes stung, and he wiped the sweat from his face. His jaw ached from clenching, and his knuckles were still sore from balling his fists. Pike's hand was tight on his shoulder. He couldn't hear over the sound of his heart thundering.

Then a voice. Her voice. He refocused on the display.

"Command?"

Kael couldn't quite make out what the operator said.

"Command, I've loaded past capacity to bring as many home as possible."

He was standing right behind the operator now, his eyes fixed on the comms light, on the moving dot of her lander. He blinked. Another lander had gone down.

"Command, it's looking bad out here. My wingman blew. I'm getting multiple lock-on signals."

Kael listened to the operator. "Confirmed lander three, lower altitude, use evasive maneuvers."

The confirmation signal came through. His breaths were slow and ragged. Kael realized the entire room was silent. Glancing around, he saw every operator was away from their station, watching the terrible scene play out. No one cared that they were there. All eyes were on the remaining two landers.

Her comms signal lit up. "Command." Her voice sounded worried and panicked. Kael grasped the back of the operator's chair with an iron grip. Time slowed; an eternity passed before she continued her transmission.

The words came slowly and precisely, as if she were standing right next to him. "Confirmed lock on and launch. Too heavy for effective evasion."

There was a finality in her tone. A sound he never wanted to hear. The sound of devastation.

"I always wanted to be among the stars."

A pause.

"Find a soldier named Kael. Tell him…. Tell him I…."

Then silence.

He watched as the light flickered for a moment and went out. Kael yanked the headset off the operator and screamed into the mic, "LI-ORA!"

Static, then nothing.

Pike tried to catch him as he fell to the ground. Not so much as a pain shot through him when he landed. Numb. Everything was numb. Was this real? No, it had to be a nightmare. Had to be. But it wasn't. He'd watched the last hour of her life unfold in front of him like some game. Dots moving on a screen. He needed it to be someone's fault.

Hernz, the God Ruler, himself. Anything to make sense of it. But blame scattered like ash in his hands.

His vision moved as someone picked him up. Pike was carrying him outside. The cyan sky loomed overhead. The greens in the clouds reminded him of the Emerald Star, like the one she'd placed in her hair the night before. He remembered how she'd smiled when she'd tucked it behind her ear. Like it was nothing. Like it didn't mean anything. But it had. It had meant she was still here, and now she wasn't.

His breath came in gasps as pain radiated through him. Slowing, Pike looked down at him. Kael grabbed at his chest. He had a gaping wound where his heart used to be. Pike's mouth was moving, but his voice sounded distant, as if he were far away.

A few more steps under the blue-green glow, and it all came rushing in.

"Kael! Stay with me, I'm taking you to the infirmary."

Kael shook his head. "No," he tried to say, but it came out as a whisper.

Pike slowed more and frowned down at him.

"No infirmary," Kael managed.

Nodding, Pike turned and ran.

It was a strange thing knowing she was gone. Surreal. He was empty. He'd lost a part of himself, an important part, and his chest burned with the crushing void growing there.

Pike sat him against a tree. He was numb, unable to move. Sitting next to him, Pike remained silent. Nothing was needed besides the reassuring arm he put around Kael's shoulders. That simple communication broke down the walls holding all the pressure in. He cried out in despair as his heart was ripped from his chest, leaving a cold yawning hole in its place. Pike held him close as the tightness in his chest and convulsions made him gasp for breath between sobs. Light filtered through his tears, and the world stretched and collapsed like matter drawn into a black hole. There was no war, no planet, only the abyss. And Pike, his last solace in a universe of silence.

# Chapter 27:
## Phenomenon

*"Identity is a phenomenon in which a person either knows them-selves or finds themselves."*
—Xalthari Warden of Echoes

Sitting on the edge of his cot, Kael stared into the shaft of sunlight. He hadn't noticed the phenomenon since the day in the infirmary with Liora. He closed his eyes and rubbed at their soreness. There were so many little details he'd never paid attention to that reminded him of her. It was like navigating a bed of hot coals; no matter which way you turned, they were always there waiting to burn you.

A shadow came across his face. It was Pike. "We're ready."

Nodding, Kael took a deep breath, looking around the barracks one last time. Alandra and Ordan had stayed to see them off. On the sergeant's advice, they'd decided Gatlin shouldn't know. Qenni had volunteered to keep him and the replacements occupied and away from the barracks.

Kael hadn't expected Alandra to be so accepting of his decision. Her past didn't allow her to join them, yet she had been supportive, even admitting what the corps was doing here was wrong.

He lifted himself from his cot, and Auctor and Pike joined him at the door. Auctor had a grim little smile; it was half pleased, half solemn. Kael tried to smile at the two staying behind but found himself unable to.

Pike saluted the pair and rubbed at his eye. "Dust," he muttered, and with a sharp breath, he stalked out.

Taking a ragged breath, Kael saluted the pair. Ordan saluted back.

Alandra hesitated a moment then wrapped her arms around him, squeezing him tight. "I would say may the Star's light guide you, but it feels inappropriate now." She stepped back, a smile on her face. "I know I'll see you again."

"Thank you." Kael bit his tongue, using the pain to keep from crying. He saluted them both again then turned away.

It was a dim morning on Xalthryn. Heavy mist obscured the ever-present blue light, leaving a grim, hazy glow. It was a long walk to the perimeter wall, but now Kael's worries about being stopped faded. Until they arrived at the final barrier, the haze would give them cover.

It had been over a week since the day his heart had been ripped from his chest and replaced with a hollow imitation. Whatever was in there now, it was crushing his soul.

They walked without speaking a word. Kael listened to their footsteps as they walked from grass to roadway, the soft crunch replaced by light taps on the hard surface. It was good to be moving toward something better, away from this nightmarish place. The corps, Hernz, and God all left a sour taste in his mouth, making his stomach turn.

Junova had given him the coordinates of a Xalthari scout she had located. It was their best hope to contact Vashar. Hernz had blocked all communications not sent with a corps transponder, so communication with the Xalthari was impossible. Junova assured him she would help in any way, short of leaving her post. He didn't like it, but the alternative would leave the Radiance under Hernz's control. She wasn't staying because of loyalty but because she had to.

Kael focused on the rhythm of his breathing. At least he still had this steady comfort in a world already ruined.

After a sharp sniff, Pike cleared his throat. "Good day for this."

Auctor grinned. "Why do you think I chose it?"

"I still think breaking into the weather station was a crazy idea."

"Weather being classified information is crazy."

"Seems the commander is making everything classified."

Chuckling, Auctor shook his head. "Except the waste."

Pike huffed a laugh. "Ain't it the truth?"

"What do you think, brother?"

Kael stared at Auctor for a moment. "I think I'm done with this place. And Hernz. God's ideals be ash."

Closing his mouth tight, Pike looked away.

Auctor's smile went limp. "You'll get no argument from me, not this time. I never believed in the corps."

Kael gritted his teeth. "I know. Still, thank you."

Auctor's grin did not quite reach his eyes. "This is the best decision you've ever made." He looked forward and muttered, "I will be here for it."

"Ain't going anywhere myself," Pike said.

Fighting the sudden urge him to cry, Kael tried to smile. "Thank you both."

Instructors' voices echoed in the distance, carried through the complex on the soft breeze.

"What would Krennak think of us now?" Kael asked.

"I don't know," Pike muttered. "Though I suspect he'd be more understanding than you'd think."

"Who cares what this old loudmouth thinks? Let him rot here, training new fodder for God," Auctor said.

Kael sighed. "Every new soldier he trains will be an enemy to us."

"Let them come," Auctor said. "I'll be ready."

Pike huffed a laugh. "That makes one of us."

Squinting, Kael could make out the security checkpoint through the haze. The perimeter lay before them. He swallowed hard, the gravity of what they were doing settling on him like a boulder. Stopping, he looked at his companions. "This is it. After this, there's no going back."

"What are we waiting for?" Auctor asked.

"It ain't like we spent much time here," Pike said.

"Kael said it himself," Auctor replied. "God's ideals be ash. There's nothing for us here."

"He's right," Kael said, looking back into the mist. "There's nothing for us here."

"I know. I hate leaving them behind," Pike said.

"They have to find their path. We can't choose for them."

Auctor started toward the checkpoint. "Let's find the scout."

Four soldiers and one sergeant staffed the checkpoint. The sergeant was rough-looking and addressed them with a guttural voice. "State your business?"

Kael stepped forward. "A patrol, sir. There's been word of heretic scouts nearby."

Eyes narrowing, the sergeant waved at one of his men. "Haven't received orders here about a patrol."

Kael smiled. "Must be an oversight, with replacements and recruits arriving."

The sergeant scoffed. "Not the first one this week either. My job is keeping these savages out. So, if you're going out to find them before they attack my checkpoint, I'd say you're doing me a favor." Waving a hand at his men, he flopped onto his chair. "Let them through. They're doing God's work."

A wave of relief swept through Kael. "Thank you, sir."

The three saluted. Quickly and quietly, they left the corps behind them. Kael didn't look back. Not once. The corps was done with him, and he had nothing left for the corps.

# Chapter 28:
## Sledgehammer

*"When ice forms around the bulkheads, we shatter it with the sledgehammer."*
—Warden of Eesbex

Pike gawked when they met the Xalthari scout, a strong and ugly young woman. She led them to the edge of a sheer cliff and along a narrow descending path until they arrived at a yawning cave in the rock.

Auctor was smirking. Pike wished he knew what that smirk meant. He kept one hand on his rifle while the other tapped a nervous rhythm on its grip. He had the feeling they weren't alone, yet there was no place a person could hide. Skin on his arms bristled, like his body knew something his eyes didn't. Yet, the cave behind and in front was silent, empty. The Xalthari led the trio deeper into the dark, the cave walls giving way to man-made stone. Brown. Why was it always brown?

His gaze lingered on Kael's back, and Pike drew a slow breath. He understood losing loved ones and family. Yet, he knew this was different. To lose the woman you loved to this war, for nothing more than a madman's bloodlust—it was soul-shattering. His emotions ran raw and unpredictable. And he hated himself for caring and kicked himself for hating. Healing wasn't getting any easier, but he was trying.

They passed through a large stone door into an enormous room in which a crowd boiled and chattered. People passed food around, several offering him a curious-looking mushroom. When he reached out for one, the scout smacked his hand, eyes wide with shock. She shook her head and pointed across the great room.

He scowled back at her. "I only wanted to look at it."

But she didn't understand and left him to brood.

"Best if we don't eat anything until we know it's safe," Kael said.

"You spent a week with them, don't you know?" Pike asked.

Kael turned and followed the scout. "Never saw mushrooms."

Auctor chuckled as he stalked by. "Don't die on us."

Snugging a strap on his harness, Pike started after them, frowning. "I wasn't going to eat it," he muttered.

The scout led them into a dim room and left, shutting the door behind her. The room was cool and smelled of old books. No wonder; the walls were lined with brown, dusty books, floor to ceiling. A central table with several chairs held stacks of books, and a Xalthari sat writing at the table's head.

Kael stepped forward. "Vashar, I'm glad you're alive. We have come to speak with you."

As the man looked up, his middle-aged face came into view. Pike wasn't sure what he had expected, but it wasn't this sturdy, dark-skinned, wise-looking man.

Vashar eyed the three of them. "Kael, we both live. Your friends?"

"Yes, my brother Auctor and Pike."

"Welcome to my home. Come rest." He waved a hand at the open chairs.

Taking a seat, Pike looked around. "What is this place?"

"This room is my work. I write records in books. Identity of Xalthari."

Pike blinked at the rows of books. All this was their entire history?

Auctor's eyes settled on Vashar. "Books? Can't use data pads?"

Vashar smiled. "We have technology. Some history is stored there, though my people value written history. It is sacred." Setting down his writing pen, Vashar's smile vanished. "Coming to my home, what is your motive?"

Taking a deep breath, Kael stared into the void for a moment. "We have seen what God represents, what the corps does to people who resist. They...They don't deserve our loyalty. We want to help you." Kael's voice was like a stone in the river. Smooth, resilient. His hands trembled with every word he spoke, as if it took everything he had to maintain control. Pike bit his cheek to steady the feeling welling in his chest at the sight.

Vashar gave a sorrowful half-smile as though he understood Kael beyond his words. "It is a brave thing to leave your people. To join an enemy. Your ruler deserves no loyalty, this I know." He cleared his throat, closed the book before him, and stood. "Come. To be Xalthari, your eyes must open."

Pike glanced around as Vashar led them out and down the long hall. The man's words couldn't have been more cryptic. Looking at Kael, he saw a defeated man, head lowered and shoulders slumped. They were doing the right thing. Weren't they?

Around a corner, several rooms branched off the central passage. Pike looked at each one as he passed it. He wanted to know as much about this place as possible. There were more libraries, rooms with technology, and storage areas. He stopped. Looked back. There were no guards. That was what had been bothering him this entire time. Where were the warriors? The weapons? His skin tightened, and a spark crawled up his spine. Pike turned and ran to catch up with Kael.

There was an increasing sound of humming. Vashar led them into a circular room filled with Xalthari wearing, to Pike's surprise, black robes. They knelt, facing the center of the room in a large ring. At the center was a smooth slab of dark stone, and upon it was a body wrapped in the same black cloth. Vashar signaled toward an area for them to sit and walked to the center.

Kael knelt next to one of the robed figures, watching Vashar.

Pike looked at Auctor. "What is this?"

"A dead person."

Pike frowned. "Very helpful."

Auctor smirked back. "You're welcome."

Auctor knelt next to Kael. Pike's glare was burning holes in Auctor's back when Vashar started to speak. He knelt, trying not to look disrespectful of whatever was going on.

First, Vashar spoke in his language, then in common. "This is an unusual occasion. We have guests. They wish to observe."

Pike expected them all to turn and stare, but none did. They took a breath in unison and hummed.

"Since times before, we have returned wisdom to Xalthryn, it is wisest among wise. It grows, giving wisdom we might return." Vashar moved around the slab with smooth simplicity and covered the dead man's face, saying a few more Xalthari words: "Dhakim, return. Down into Xalthryn's heart, take wisdom."

He tipped the platform up at one end, and the body slid off with a hiss, disappearing into a hole at the room's center. All in attendance rose and filed out, heads bowed, while Vashar remained.

Pike stood and walked to the center, looking into the hole and its inky blackness. "What's down there?"

"Xalthryn's core," Vashar replied.

Auctor frowned at it. "Impossible."

"Ancient these holes. Deep. My ancestors built homes around them." Vashar waved his arms at the surrounding room.

Pike raised an eyebrow. "You didn't make them?"

"No."

Kael came up beside him. "We don't believe there's any use to the body after death. There's no ceremony or ritual, mere absence."

Vashar's eyes carried pity as he smiled. "Death comes with no escape. We believe wisdom returns to Xalthryn. It provides life in return. Through life, wisdom. As Xalthryn's seasons cycle, so do we."

"You don't fear death?" Pike asked.

"Wisdom is gained through life. A long life accumulates much. A larger gift to Xalthryn."

Kael nodded. "Even a short life grants a gift. Every gift is worthwhile."

Pike frowned. What he'd observed had been interesting, but it would take time before he could wrap his head around the idea of a planet storing wisdom.

Shaking his head, Auctor glared at Vashar. "Sounds like superstition to me."

Vashar smirked. It was the first time Pike had seen him look devilish. "Accusations from a child of Starlight?"

"I never believed in God or his Star. Ways to control the weak-minded."

"Perhaps Auctor does possess wisdom."

Auctor frowned. "Did we come all this way to learn about their afterlife, or are we going to fight?"

Snapping his head around, Kael glared at Auctor. "Don't mistake my intent, brother. We will fight. We will live and die next to the Xalthari. I would like to know who I stand with."

Pike watched, eyes wide as Auctor's righteous frown disappeared. The brothers stared at each other for what felt like an eternity.

Stepping between them, Vashar gave his disarming smile. "Come, rooms have been prepared. Rest is needed."

Nodding, Auctor turned away from Kael, who was still glowering at him.

Kael tensed as Pike touched his shoulder. "Let's get some rest."

Shoulders slumping, Kael's head bobbed, and Vashar led the trio into the maze of corridors.

Pike kept looking into each new room they passed and noticed a strange symbol stamped on a half-open door. He peeked inside. It was an armory; he would have to remember this. He looked around the hall, gathering any identifying markers he could before he fell behind.

Laughter echoed ahead. It sounded like children. At the doorway of the room from which the sound came, he saw it was full of everyday people. Children played and ran about between people's legs and under tables. Men and women talked and watched their children with wide smiles.

It hit him like a sledgehammer in the dark. Pike stared at the laughing children and smiling faces. He closed his eyes for a moment, and when he opened them, he was no longer looking at a room full of people but a firelit night sky. The house burned with a blaze like no other. This was home. His breathing became irregular, and his heart pounded.

*No, no. Not here.* Pike looked at the ground where she'd be. His sister, her body mutilated, cried out for him. But he couldn't move. No amount of effort could make his legs work. It was as it had been all those years ago. Staring, immobile, unable to help as the house fell and the inferno swallowed her whole. Breathing was impossible. His chest was crushed under the weight. He fell to the floor—not grass, but hard stone.

Someone stood in front of him. He squinted through his blurred vision, trying to see. It was a girl, not more than nine years old. His sister?

"Help," he tried to say, but all that came out was a wheeze.

Kael's and Auctor's voices sounded in the distance. Why were they here? This was before he had known them. Blinking hard, he looked up at the girl. Not his sister. Right, the Xalthari. He was on Xalthryn. His muscles ached, and the crushing weight lifted from his chest. He could breathe.

Kael lifted him and set him against a wall. "What happened?" He looked frightened.

Pike took a deep breath. "Nothing."

"Can you stand?" Kael's jaw was clenched and his eyes filled with concern.

Nodding, Pike pulled himself up. "Ain't nothing. I'll be fine."

Auctor frowned at him and continued with Kael after Vashar. Lingering, Pike looked back at the room, fists clenched tight. He almost wished he didn't know why; it would be easier. Burning fire of self-loathing engulfed him, rising from his gut and ending at his gritted teeth. He had sat by and let it happen. He hadn't even tried to stop it.

Looking at his hands left a sour taste in his mouth. How could he go on? The blood of how many families was on those hands, and all by God's will. The corps had done nothing except turn him into the same kind of monster who had butchered his family then asked him to slaughter these people. He looked away from those smiling faces, from those families.

Gritting his teeth so hard he could feel the vibration running through his face, Pike turned and walked after Kael. The corps thought they were bright and tidy, but they didn't know the monster they had created would realize what he was. It had been Kael's war before, but now it was his.

# Chapter 29:
## Offense

*"Putting the words Xalthari and offense in the same sentence is a joke—the heretics."*
—Auctor

The plan was solid enough except for one major flaw: it wasn't his. Auctor would've assigned himself a more active role. At least Pike wasn't here to steal all the fun. He'd volunteered to help move Xalthari refugees. Not an assignment Auctor would have chosen.

He frowned as the Xalthari scout ran down the hill. Out of breath, the young man shared his information with the group. Understanding Vekhara hadn't been a priority. He let Kael take the lead. And he kept watch.

Walking up to him, Kael nodded. "Good news."

Auctor smirked. "So, the outpost is where I said it would be? It should be an easy victory."

Kael's lips were drawn into a thin line, his frown deepening.

"Wait, do you hear that?" The sound was faint but unmistakable. "Landers," Auctor muttered.

They climbed to the hilltop and saw six landers had set down near the outpost and were unloading troops. Auctor grinned from ear to ear. sixty soldiers dismounted. With the outposts at ten, it meant seventy bodies. The Xalthari were debating something, and their chattering was getting quite annoying.

"What are they talking about?" Auctor asked.

Kael shook his head. "One of them thinks they should leave, and the others are trying to convince him to attack."

"At least most of them have some sense. We can win this."

Looking down, Kael winced. "I wish I had your optimism."

Auctor was sprayed with blood. He was getting ready to yell when the crack sounded. He threw himself to the ground right next to a dead Xalthari who was missing half his head. "Sniper!" he shouted. He was heard by many but understood by Kael alone.

He slid down the hill a meter or two to put dirt between himself and the enemy. It seemed the heretics got the idea, and one threw herself down next to him while more lined up nearby.

Auctor touched his face then looked at his hand coated in red and gray specks. Part of the dead man's head and brain by the look of it. They all hugged the ground in silence for a moment.

Kael's voice came loud and clear. "Are you alive?"

"Yeah, I don't think the sniper can see us behind the hill."

"This enough excitement for you?"

Auctor pulled a small mirror from his kit and crawled up the hill. Holding the mirror in his fingertips, he lay on his back, stretching his arm out. Troops had been organized into a formation and were advancing and looking up to see—

The mirror's glass disintegrated, disappearing from his grasp. As he yanked his hand down, the sound of the shot echoed past him. Eyes focusing, he gawked at his hand. "Still there," he muttered.

"They're coming!"

"Star's fury, they're attacking?" Kael asked.

He lay there a moment, looking at the sky, frowning. "We need a new plan."

"I hope you have one," Kael replied.

"I do," he said, smirking. "Move them all to the bottom of the hill inside the tree line." When they had assembled at the tree line, Auctor pointed. "Have them spread out and take positions with a good line of sight to the crest of the hill."

Kael started trying to explain Auctor's plan, and some of the Xalthari got the idea and were quick to find acceptable positions. Auctor took note of where Kael had set up then took a rapid survey of the terrain, and there it was, the best spot—and no one else had even thought of it.

Taking his position and readying himself, Auctor considered the time before the corps would emerge over the hilltop. A couple of minutes, no more. Those minutes came and went without a breeze whispering through the trees. He frowned, drumming his fingers on the grip of his rifle.

Kael moved up behind him. "Where are they?"

"You want to go look?"

"Why would they delay? The corps always follows through."

Auctor scanned the area; the dense underbrush in the forest made seeing either side of the hill impossible. He dismissed the thought. They weren't smart. Besides, he'd hear it if they moved eighty soldiers through the tangle.

"They could be stacking over the ridge to push in force," he told Kael.

Kael was quiet for a long moment. "Do you think Zero could be out there?"

"They made their choice, why does it matter?"

His brother sat in the dirt, staring down. "We might not be on the same side anymore, but it doesn't mean I don't care."

"Caring is for the weak, brother. You have to be strong if we are going to win."

Huffing a laugh, Kael stood. "I'm starting to realize we're different."

"No, not different. You need to get your priorities straight."

There was rustling to his left.

"Can't these Xalthari stay quiet?" Auctor asked.

There was a shot. As he turned to look, Auctor collapsed on one knee. The corps had flanked them. His leg was hot inside. Looking down, he saw crimson blood oozing from a hole in his leg. Then the hole burned like someone had put hot coals inside it. People were shouting all around, and a rash of weapons fire erupted from every direction.

He blinked as Kael wrapped a bandage around his thigh.

"Can you walk?" Kael asked.

He shook his head, grimacing. "Hurts too much to move."

Kael picked him up, carrying him on his shoulders. Frowning through the pain, Auctor couldn't believe what an embarrassment this was. His plan, his failure, and now he had to be carried out like a child. He was supposed to be the best, and this didn't make him look good.

Retreating with several Xalthari, Auctor watched behind them as corps troops advanced from the brush. His leg burned; it was like someone had added shards of glass to the wound. Baring his teeth, he grunted, muscling his weapon. He wasn't about to let them get away with this offense. Aiming as best he could, Auctor started shooting, his leg sending waves of agony through him. Corps soldiers were falling stars under his barrage. After managing to reload, he slapped the charging handle forward and fired, and more soldiers tumbled to the ground. His heart raced for the first time in an eternity, and he laughed.

"Are you alright?" Kael asked.

"Alright? I haven't had this much fun in a long time."

Kael's grip on him tightened.

The remaining few heretics ran with them as the soldiers gave up the chase. He smiled back at the carnage, the rush leaving all too soon, giving way to the pain in his leg. Letting his weapon drop, he watched it swing from its strap still around him.

After he had watched the ground pass by underneath him for quite some time, Kael slowed to a stop. "I have to check your leg."

Kael sat him against a tree and pulled out his med kit. As his brother removed the bandage, Auctor gritted his teeth, and as Kael ripped his pants open, he clenched his fists, grunting.

After rinsing the area, Kael examined his wound. "It's not bad."

"Not bad? It feels like I got shot with a rail cannon."

"It's shallow, and it went all the way through. Doesn't look like it hit anything major."

"Thanks, I'll let the heretic's doctor know you gave me a good prognosis."

Kael glared at him. "Hold still, I'll apply a new bandage. It's still bleeding."

"Alright, doctor, how long until I can walk?"

With a fresh bandage applied, his leg eased into an intense, dull throbbing, better than feeling like it was in a volcano.

Kael hoisted him onto his shoulders. "Gotta get you a real doctor. Not about to lose anyone else."

Auctor tried to rest but was irritated about being bested. How had they outsmarted him? Glaring down at the cyan grass passing by, he decided it wouldn't happen again.

# Chapter 30:
## Loyalties

*"The answer is not simple. First, you must ask yourself, what do my loyalties mean?"*
—Shepard of the Covenant

After placing the flickering holo-image on a shelf looking out over the circle of Xalthryn, Junova closed her eyes and pulled the second image from her pocket. She clenched her jaw, bracing for the light hum as the image flashed to life. Opening her eyes, her breath caught in her throat. Yet another good soul she had been unable to save.

Welling pressure in her chest brought tears to her eyes as she rested the image of Liora beside the others. She wanted to curl up on the floor and let it all out, but there was too much work to do. As she sat at her desk, the grav chair bobbed under her weight.

Junova was able to set up a dedicated comm link with encryption so she could speak with Kael. After activating the link, she waited.

"Captain?" His voice came loud and clear.

"Kael, it's good to hear from you."

"Likewise. Are you sure this thing is safe?"

"It's Hernz proof. No one but us can speak, listen, or trace this channel."

"That's a relief."

"Kael, I'm sending battle plans through the link. Hernz wants to crush the Xalthari before more reinforcements arrive."

"Seeing them now. It doesn't make sense to attack in a week when Justice arrives in four."

She sighed. "He doesn't see reason anymore, if he ever did. He thinks it will be a personal failure if he can't contain the situation without help. I think he fears what God's son will do to him."

"Thank you for getting this to us. I know it was a risk."

"How are things on the ground?"

"Auctor got hit in the leg two days ago, it's not bad, but he will be getting on his feet for this next one. Pike and I are doing our best. Have you heard from Justice?"

"Yes, I spoke with Captain Katsui and was surprised to hear he may favor our cause. We are supposed to be in contact today. I should know more next time we speak."

"Cause for relief, Captain, if we can't secure the space around Xalthryn...."

"I know. If Justice brought its fusion warheads to bear, nothing on Xalthryn would survive." Her comms panel blinked. "I've got an incoming hail. Stay safe."

The link went dead, and Junova switched it to the incoming traffic.

"Captain Junova."

"Yes, Katsui here."

"Captain, do you have an update?"

"I have spoken with a great deal of my crew. A few remained loyal to our God's son, but those have been dealt with."

After pausing a moment, she cleared her throat. "What about the soldiers you carry?"

"Nothing to speak of, they won't be a problem."

"I wish I were as confident as you."

"Oh, Captain, sometimes you must do what is necessary even if you don't like it."

She could hear his smile in those words. Trying not to think about what he'd done to those soldiers, she gritted her teeth. "Indeed."

"I'm happy to report Justice will be under the control of anti-Solovian nationals by tomorrow."

"What?"

"I had to persuade some of my officers, and it's easier to commit when you have a name to rally behind."

"I'll remember that."

He laughed. "The rest is in your hands, Captain. I think I'll miss all the fun."

"Don't worry, there will be enough for both of us when the child god learns what we've done."

She closed the channel and sat in silence for a moment. Maybe she was too cautious. Katsui had done in a few days what she had been working on for months . A week. That was how much time she had left. Hernz wanted her ship to assist in his feverish assault, and, if she was to prevent that, she needed the crew on her side. She wasn't about to flush them out the airlock. No doubt that was what Katsui had done.

The door chime pinged. "It never ends," she muttered, frowning. "Enter."

Reed walked in, stood tall, and saluted. "Captain."

"Reed, what do you have to report?"

"The precautions you ordered are in place. A great number of the crew are questioning their loyalties after...recent events. We can count on almost the entire crew to back your move against Commander Hernz."

"Thank you, Reed. Is there anything else?"

He looked at the floor, swallowed. "Ma'am, what should I do about her quarters?"

"Leave them for now. I'll handle it."

"Yes, Captain."

The door hissed shut behind him.

Leaning back in her chair, she rubbed the bridge of her nose, took a deep breath then stood. "It won't take care of itself," she muttered. Glancing back; the beauty of Xalthryn contrasted with the images of those she had failed. Resolve formed in her eyes, and she got into her hypertube and zipped off into the ship.

The hypertube spat her out a short walk from Liora's quarters. The crew she passed saluted and smiled, though their smiles weren't convincing. Then she was standing in front of Liora's door. How many times had she stood here waiting for the door to open? Liora would smile and say, *Captain, I'm happy you came.* Taking a ragged breath, she pressed the button, and the doors hissed open.

Junova stood there for a long moment, staring into the room, almost as if she expected Liora to meet her if she waited long enough. Taking a hesitant step inside, she saw the familiar sketches of constellations and the emitter she had bought for Liora. Throwing it away seemed an outrage to her memory, yet it couldn't stay here forever. She walked into the sleeping area. Kael hadn't even collected his entire uniform before leaving. She wiped a tear from her cheek and considered leaving it until Kael could be here. She still had to collect a few things as captain, but the rest could wait for Kael.

Finding the extra security pass and nav logs was simple enough. What she didn't like having to intrude on was Liora's personal log. There was nothing to decide. As captain, she had to read it in case it contained sensitive information.

Taking the pad out into the main room, she sat and activated the emitter. It projected a stunning garden world across the walls and onto the ceiling. The sound of rain filled the room with a soothing rhythm. Junova began to scan through the log, looking for pertinent information.

She hated this part, seeing someone's life laid bare, all wrapped up in neat lines of text. Page after page, she tensed more, her tongue hurting from biting it as she tried to maintain her composure. Hate was too polite a word. She loathed this, abhorred subjecting herself to reliving every day of Liora's life, and yet, there was no getting around it.

Skimming through, she focused on keywords. An entry caught her eye, dated four days before Liora had died. It referenced when Liora had brought Kael here after Pike had been injured in battle.

Junova's eyes stopped on a word. She closed them tight. "That's not what I read," she said aloud. Opening her eyes, she glared at the text. The pad slipped from her fingers and clattered to the floor. She shook her head. "No, I can't be the one..." she muttered. "I can't tell him. It would ruin him."

She snatched up the pad and shut it off. "I'll keep it safe. When this is all over, I'll ensure he gets it."

# Chapter 31:
## Together

*"Together, Xalthari will fight. Together, Xalthari identity will live on."*
—Xalthari Warden of Echoes

A giant chamber filled to bursting with Xalthari—the most he'd seen in one place—spread before him. Pike was beginning to understand their ways were different. They were not careless but intentional. They didn't fear death, not like he did. They laughed at him for sleeping with his rifle, for posting corps guards in halls and entrances. It wasn't that they didn't care, it was that they had certainty. The Xalthari held a quiet, dreadful confidence. Even if they died, their life had served a purpose for Xalthryn, and as long as their identity endured, they were never gone.

A large carved scene spread across the length of the rear wall depicting parts of Xalthari life. It was still in the process of being colored so much of it was still stone brown. On one end Xalthari grew crops of vegetables native to Xalthryn, mushrooms, squashes, roots. In the middle, hunters sought the fuzzy silver rats that scampered through the jungle. And on the other end, underground communes with small factories, historians, and families working together for the greater good of the people.

*It would look better once it wasn't brown.* Pike thought. Though he wondered if the Xalthari would expand it to include this alliance of corps rejects.

There was a growing number of corps uniforms among the Xalthari and the room of at least a thousand strong was a mix of drab corps cyan and green Xalthari robes. A checkered mix of dark skinned Xalthari with the whites, tans, and other various colored corps soldiers. Pike checked that Kael was close by in case he stuck his foot in his mouth. Offending the Xalthari had become his full-time job. At least, that was how he felt. Vashar had assured him they understood his ways were different, but that didn't change the looks he got when he opened his mouth.

Smiling, he nodded at Vashar. "Are you sure you want me to do this?"

"Translation to Vekhara is easier than common. Confusion on a battlefield is inevitable, best it be expelled from planning."

"Right." He swallowed.

Yelling in Vekhara, Vashar's voice echoed through the chamber. Silence fell, and he nodded at Pike.

Stepping forward, Pike cleared his throat. "The time has come. Hernz is planning an attack to crush us once and for all before his reinforcements arrive. His need for a swift and complete victory will be his downfall."

He nodded at Kael while Vashar translated.

"We are going to strike before he attacks us," Pike continued after the translation. "Captain Junova is already hard at work securing Radiance to deprive Hernz of support. We aim to catch him off guard and wipe the Starlit from Xalthryn."

Auctor walked out of a nearby door and took a seat. Pike frowned down at him. At least he was walking; it was a quick recovery.

"The primary assault will advance from the west," Pike went on. "Since the sunrise will put us at a significant disadvantage, we will use deployable barriers. Our objective is to draw their attention to this attack. It'll account for most of our combined forces to ensure the diversion works."

Everyone was listening in silence. Even the corps soldiers made no sound during Vashar's translation.

"The remaining company will be separated into two groups. Each will approach the compound from the northeast and southeast, attacking while the corps is occupied with our western assault. Once in the compound, you will move to secure all buildings and personnel. With any luck, Xalthryn will be ours by tomorrow night."

Pike sat down next to Kael as Vashar translated. Closing his eyes, he sighed. "Thank the Star that's over."

Kael chuckled. "I don't think the Star would approve."

"No, I imagine it wouldn't." Leaning back, he smiled. "This whole brown thing they've got going on is starting to grow on me."

"What?"

"The brown."

Kael was frowning at him. "What about the brown?"

"It's simple and low maintenance. It's logical."

"I never thought you'd say you like it."

"I ain't said I like it. I said it's growing on me."

Smiling, Kael shrugged. Then smile vanishing, "Do you think we'll see Zero?"

"We might, who knows where they'll be once the shooting starts," Pike replied.

"That's what I'm worried about. If they aren't at Hernz's side they will be fighting. Maybe fighting us," Kael said.

"If only they'd come with us."

"Yeah. It's Gatlin I worry about the most. The others... Well they might still join us."

Pike chewed on the inside of his cheek. "I hear you. The old drunk won't take kindly to us coming back. If he's on base, no doubt we'll have to fight him."

Nodding, Kael pulled something out of a pocket—his DEX card. "What do you think it says?"

Pike raised an eyebrow. "AWOL? Traitor? I haven't looked at mine."

Kael held it up to him. The screen was dark, displaying no information. "I guess once you're out, they shut it down."

Pike shrugged. "I ain't seen a reason why we'd still need it. Should get rid of them."

Kael slipped it back into his pocket and let his fingers linger for a moment.

As the crowd pressed out of the room, Pike looked to where Auctor had been. Gone. He must've left ahead of the rush.

"Are you ready for this?" Kael asked.

"Yeah," Pike said. "Vashar told me you and Auctor are assigned to the southeast team."

"We are."

"Some things never change."

Kael huffed a laugh. "True. I'm worried, though. He adapted faster to military life than I did, and watching him, I get the feeling he likes it too much."

"I've noticed. I wanted to believe he's trying to be a good brother."

"It's more than that. At least we'll be together for the assault."

Sucking in a breath of air, Pike knew what he wanted to say, but getting the words out was another thing altogether. He sighed. It was best not to leave things unsaid if you hadn't a reason to. "I ain't planning on having another funeral. Don't get yourself killed out there."

He stood to leave when Kael grabbed his arm. "You, too."

Nodding, Pike bit his cheek and walked away.

Pike met his fellow squad leader, a Xalthari named Anais. He was thinner and taller than most Xalthari, though his dress and features were unmistakable. Hawks talons were tattooed on his fingers, like those of the red raptors that preyed upon jungle rats. Together, Pike and Anais would be in charge of a cohesive platoon of mixed troops. Anais could speak a small amount of common, so at least they could communicate. The problem was with the corps soldiers. Xalthari held little to no animosity against them, but the corps viewed grudges in a different light. Getting them to work together would be challenging, but he would do it, and the first opportunity presented itself.

"Xalthari soldiers have been equipped with liberated corps arms and armor," Pike told the corps in his squad. "I'm making it your obligation to teach each one in our squad how to use their weapon."

Muttering came up from somewhere in the group.

"Do any of you have a problem with that?" Pike asked.

A man wearing a sergeant's uniform stepped forward. "I'm all for helping these here heretics keep their planet. We all have some problem with Hernz and his self-proclaimed God. How do I know they won't shoot us in the back? Many of us here have killed our fair share."

"It looks like you have a choice, Sergeant. Risk getting shot in the back or risk the soldier next to you being no help when you're getting overrun. I know which I'd choose."

The sergeant frowned and looked at the men around him. "Looks like we're school teachers now. Get to it, nova pace!" He walked up to Pike. "Look, sir, I have nothing against these people, but many men did. I hope you didn't take offense."

"No, Sergeant, and thank you. I was debating on how I'd handle the subject. You saved me there. I forgot how good it is to have the sergeant on your side."

The sergeant smiled and saluted Pike. "Glad to help, sir."

Anais caught Pike's eye and waved him over. "My understanding of Star technology is limited. My people have primitive designs." He looked down at the corps rifle.

"They ain't that primitive," Pike replied. "But I take your point." Pike picked up the rifle. "This here is your safety indicator. You will always have it set to safe until you're ready to engage. Pull your charging handle back and lock it in place. Press the release here to remove a magazine and insert a full one, ensuring it seats well. Depress the charging handle catch to release it, charging the weapon."

Anais nodded, and Pike continued. "Almost all the other parts are analogs to your weapons except for ammunition. The corps uses a caseless design to make the ammo lighter and easier to carry, as you see no ejection port. This weapon won't fire ammunition designed for yours."

"I appreciate it. A safety toggle is a wise inclusion. If we continue producing rifles, I will ensure they have these."

Huffing a laugh, Pike nodded. "At least you learned one good thing from us."

"Your people fight well. If this battle is to succeed, we need to fight together."

"I know. I've spoken with them. Many here fight for different reasons than you and I."

Returning to his room, Pike set down his gear and fell into bed. As he lay there staring at the ceiling, he was content. Frowning, he couldn't remember how long it had been since he had last felt this way. Perhaps years. It was ironic, on the eve of a major battle, after everything they'd endured, that he was almost happy. Could it be he was finally making a real difference?

He has been running from people and connections all his life. What a waste. The Xalthari had a tight community, and they were strong and happy. The road to letting others in wasn't over, but he'd made significant progress.

# Chapter 32:
## Condemning

*"Condemning yourself to a life of shadow is no life; walking in the glory of light is the only life."*
—Starlit Covenant

"What are your orders, Captain?"

Silence fell on the bridge; every set of eyes was on her. Her heart raced, and her temples throbbed. Junova rubbed them, an ache settling in her head. It was time. Hernz had ordered a rail cannon strike west of HQ.

Taking a deep breath, she spun her chair to face Reed. "Are we ready?"

He nodded.

"Then proceed."

Reed activated his console, and darkness fell upon the bridge. When emergency lighting came on, the two remaining loyalists on the bridge had been restrained.

One, her third in command, sneered. "It's too late, Captain. I've warned the others."

"Reed, have them taken to holding. And find out—"

An explosion rocked the ship, sending Junova flying. Hitting the deck headfirst, and the bridge spun. She got to her feet and stumbled back to her chair. "Are we being fired on?"

"Negative, Captain, the explosion was internal. It affected several systems, including drive and targeting control."

Sabotage. How hadn't she seen this coming? All her planning and careful progress, for nothing.

"Get damage control teams and security down there."

"On their way, Captain. I can check on the damage after getting these two to hold."

"Good idea, Reed."

Taking a few men from security with him, Reed escorted his prisoners off the bridge.

"What's our security status?" Junova asked her tactical officer.

"Captain, security is showing multiple weapon discharges throughout the ship. It looks like a war on the lower decks. All available crew not assigned to repairs have been activated to contain the situation," The officer replied.

"Keep me advised of any changes." Junova sat back in her chair, and the room spun. Her senses were returning. She took a minute to breathe and grasp the situation. "Security, I want everyone on the bridge armed. I'm going to help secure the lower decks."

"Captain, is that wise?" The officer asked.

Frowning, she stood. "It's what needs to be done."

"Understood."

Walking was a challenge. She must've hit her head harder than she'd thought. After taking a light projectile pistol from a locker, she entered the hypertube. Even though light was in its name the weapon weighed heavy in her palm. Black as the fleet uniform it matched, this weapon held enough power to kill a man. It's projectile, designed to fragment on impact, wouldn't penetrate the hull of any ship—or body armor for that matter. But fleet personnel weren't issued body armor.

What a star wreck this entire day had been. All her work to make the transition of power smooth had been for naught; it had still ended in violence. Perhaps Katsui hadn't been extreme after all. He didn't have a hole in the side of his ship—only a trail of a thousand frozen corpses. Junova shivered at the thought.

The tube flung her out to where the fighting was the heaviest. Shots rang out, sound deafening as it echoed through the ship. Yelling, cursing, and desperate screaming echoed between bouts of shooting.

Those were the ones making her tense. The sounds of war took on a whole new meaning when they came from her crew, her ship.

Gripping her pistol, she moved into the corridor toward the war. Two groups were fighting each other across a mess hall. Who was on her side? She ducked behind a table.

"Stand down!"

Quiet.

"Captain?"

She rose enough to see over the edge of the table. Both groups had stopped fighting, but now their weapons were pointed toward her.

"It's Captain Junova, stand down."

"She's a traitor!"

Shots rang out as she hit the floor. Peace wasn't an option. At least she knew where the loyalists were. Firing at the crew, her crew, Junova's teeth ground against each other like sandpaper with every shot until none were standing. She stood, unable to look at the death she had wrought. Most of the crew were with her. Reed had said as much. But not all. And now they were bleeding over the floor of her ship. The war for Radiance had started.

Security and other members of the crew assembled and formed several squads. The plan was to sweep every deck, securing any loyalists they found. Junova hoped they'd surrender, but she knew better. If they were loyal to God now, they would die for him.

Leaving the squads, she found Reed near the damaged section. "How bad is it?"

"Targeting control is almost back online, but we have a problem." Pulling up a holo display of the Radiance orbit, he explained, "The explosion was enough to push us into a decaying orbit. With the drives offline, we can't correct the drift."

Punching buttons on the display, she checked the calculations and frowned. "How long until our drive is fixed?"

He looked down. "Unless we gain engineering control soon, we won't have time."

Her eyes widened. "When did we lose engineering?"

"Twenty minutes ago."

"How many are holed up there?"

"Ten, fifteen."

Resolve formed in her eyes, and she gripped her weapon. "Reed, I believe we're the only crew available."

Looking at his escort, Reed nodded. "Yes, Captain."

"Time to fight for our ship, gentlemen."

Junova shot out of the hypertube, stumbling forward, and catching herself on a storage rack, gained her footing. Reed and the others tumbled into the room after her.

Someone groaned. "Tube must've been damaged."

"At least it spat us out in the right place."

Getting to his feet, Reed checked the corridor. "Clear."

Nodding, Junova waved security forward.

The room stank of ozone and grease. A flickering display showed temperatures and blinked out. They were two hundred meters away from the engineering room, but Junova felt closer to ash and brimstone.

Moving through the passageways and checking every room and corner was time-consuming, but being flanked because they hurried would be disastrous. The entire deck appeared to be deserted. This wasn't a high-traffic area, yet to see no one was unusual. Junova frowned to herself; these weren't usual times.

Checking the last corner before the engineering room, Reed waved a hand in a stop motion.

Hugging the wall next to him, Junova spoke in a soft voice. "How many?"

Two fingers went up.

"Can we take them?"

His head shook.

By the void, why couldn't anything be easy for once? Pulling him back, she peeked around the corner. They were standing guard by the door, and there was no way to do this undetected.

Looking at Reed, she furrowed her brow. "I'll take the far one, you shoot the other."

He nodded.

Kneeling, she rested at the corner to stabilize her aim.

Reed's knee dug into her shoulder as he readied himself. "Your call, Captain."

She took a deep breath, held it for a second, exhaled, paused at the end to steady herself, and squeezed the trigger. The two fell to the floor like they hadn't been alive a few seconds ago.

Reed and his men moved out, advancing across the charcoal floor grate. Junova hesitated. Pulling the trigger herself had made her stomach turn. She tried to convince herself it'd had to be done so others could live. Baring her teeth, she made herself move. This wasn't about her. Not anymore. It was about saving thousands of lives, and if she had to kill ten, twenty, fifty, she would.

Her fingers ached from grasping the pistol, and she adjusted her grip. This was it. They had no idea how many they would encounter or where they were. None had opened the door to check on their guards, but those shots had been loud. They knew someone was out here, giving them the upper hand.

"Reed, I have an idea." It wasn't good, but what else could she do? Waving at security, she continued, "You two on the right side. Reed, over here with me. I'm going to open the door. No one moves until I give the signal."

They nodded.

"When I signal, you two take the lead and cross left. There's a console you can use for cover. Reed and I will follow and cross right."

Another nod.

Her whole body tensed as the door hissed open. There was silence. She took an unsteady breath; the lack of sound was more unnerving than a hostile welcome. Pursing her lips, Junova frowned. "Move."

Darting through the door, security let loose a hail of weapons fire. It was impossible to tell if any shots were returning fire, so she slipped through, Reed following. Counting at least four as she dove for cover, Junova fired.

A storm of projectiles and thunderous cracks filled the engineering room. Breathing hard, her heart pounded in her chest. One of the security personnel took a shot to her face and fell to the ground, gurgling and sucking as air expelled from her lungs. Her flailing arms grasped for anything, then lay still.

Unable to look away, Junova stared at the corpse. She let the feeling rise in her like a fire being stoked. Bursting out in a tremendous roar, she aimed over the console and shot. Sparks flew, and waves of hot air vented from a ruptured pipe. Someone screamed as the jet of scalding gas blasted across several crewmen. She pulled the trigger until her pistol stopped firing.

Reed took her arm. She almost didn't notice through her rage and tears. "Captain, it's over."

Trembling, she took a slow, ragged breath and looked at him. The concern in his eyes was all it took to unleash the dam. Dropping her pistol, she fell limp into his arms. Her body convulsed with every breath between her sobs.

Reed held her tight. "You, get out of here, find a repair crew, and get to work on those engines."

"Yes, sir."

Holding her head with one hand, he closed his eyes. "It's over."

She sucked in an unsteady breath. "It's never over. There's more to do." She tried to move then slumped back into Reed's grasp.

"The repair crews can handle the drive system. Take a few minutes to collect yourself."

After wiping away her tears, she finally succeeded in pulling herself away from him. "No. I need to be there for my crew." It took all her effort, but she stood. "Reed, thank you. I would like you to oversee repairs."

"Of course, Captain."

She made her way to a tube, smiled at Reed, then zipped away.

Her quarters were empty. No doubt, the auto turret had been an effective deterrent. She pressed the comms panel and waited.

"Bridge."

"This is Junova, what's our status?"

"Most decks are cleared. However, there's still fighting near the rail cannons. One has fallen to loyalist control."

She closed her eyes. Of course, they had. "Does security have it under control?"

"No, ma'am. They are losing ground."

"Notify Reed I'm headed there and send any security crews available."

"Yes, Captain."

Cutting off the comms, she swallowed a lump. Xalthryn was still there out the window while those haunting faces sat on the frames below. Turning, she made for the tube, then stopped. Eyes widening, she glanced down. The floor was vibrating.

"No."

She turned back to Xalthryn's view in time to see the cannon shot enter the atmosphere. Sprinting across the room, she slammed into the tube and ran toward the cannons.

When she arrived near the rail cannons, she found a weapon and a room of security personnel sitting around. "Who's in charge here?"

A lieutenant popped up from behind a crate. "That would be me."

"Why is everyone on vacation when our rail cannon is firing on the planet?"

"Captain, I've thrown everything we have at them. The position is well defended."

"How many have you lost?"

"Twelve, sir."

Frowning, she looked around the room. "Are there schematics available for this part of the ship?"

"Uh, yeah. You can access them from here, Captain."

Pulling up the plans on the wall terminal, she looked them over. "Here, look at this, Lieutenant. You could've ended this without any casualties on our side."

Looking at the schematics, his eyes bugged out. "But, Captain, it would kill them."

Pointing at the bodies lining the corridor, she growled. "They don't have a problem killing us."

He looked down, shoulders slumping.

"Get your men together and close the bulkhead."

He nodded and pointed at several people, and they got to work.

Pulling up controls for life support, she found this section. From there, adjusting the ventilation systems and closing a few ducts was simple work.

"Bulkhead closed, Captain."

She hovered a finger over the button and hesitated. All eyes were fixed on her. With a single press, she would be condemning people to death. Hand trembling, Junova held her breath. The room shook, and a wave rumbled through the floor. She pushed the button and watched the oxygen drain from the rail battery.

Junova turned to the lieutenant, her lips a thin line. "Secure the battery."

No one moved or said a word as she walked back to the tube and was whisked away.

Arriving on the bridge, she was pleased to see everything as she had left it.

"I want to know where those cannons impacted," she said.

"Impact site is a kilometer west of HQ," tactical officer Haggen replied

"How'd they get this close?"

"Targeting came back online before the first shot. You should be asking me how they missed," Haggen said.

She sat in her chair, frowning. "Explain."

"I had control of the synthetic graviton radar when they tried to target. It wasn't hard to throw it off by a degree or two."

A smile tugged at her lips. "Good work, all of you. Status of the cannons?"

"Ready to fire, Captain."

She relaxed a little and activated comms. "Reed, report?"

"Captain, repairs are underway, and security reports the ship is ours."

"Good work, Reed."

They'd chosen her. Not all, but enough. The rest had either been silenced or subdued.

Standing, she walked over to view Xalthryn. "How about we give Hernz a taste of our cannons?"

"With pleasure, ma'am."

Cannons fired in sequence at Xalthryn, vibrating and echoing their roar through the walls. She didn't flinch this time.

# Chapter 33:
## Easy

*"Is it easy if it leads to pain, death?"*
—Xalthari Warden of Echoes

Sitting on a smooth, flat boulder, Kael watched the bright yellow and green birds flit between the trees, their chirping song a gentle balm to his aching soul. The blue glow of sunlight reflected off the leaves, highlighting their blue-green hue and silvery tops. How long had it been since he'd looked at nature?

Auctor sat next to him and started checking his weapon.

Kael chuckled. "I used to check my rifle five or six times before every mission."

"How could I forget? You always looked scared then."

"Still scared. I hide it better."

"Good, wouldn't want to make our friends nervous."

Kael frowned. "Can I have a conversation with my brother without being prodded?"

"No."

Sighing, Kael faced Auctor. "Don't you ever feel nervous or afraid?"

"Not often."

Kael stared off into the trees. "I envy you for it. I can't remember the last time I wasn't scared, nervous...." He looked down, gritted his teeth. "I was happy. For once, I wanted something besides following our father." Taking a ragged breath in, he looked back at the sky. "Now it's gone. She's gone."

Auctor continued his gear check. "I don't know what to say, Kael. We're both here because of you. I tried to stop you. Now, I have to make the best out of what we have." He stood and walked away as Kael stared at his back.

A rumble rolled in from the west. It sounded like thunder, and then the ground shook.

Kael put in his earpiece. "Pike, did you hear that?"

"Yeah, ain't nothing we have this powerful."

Kael frowned. "Could it be the rail cannons?"

"Has to be, but they aren't supposed to fire until we've engaged."

Kael checked his receiver. "I'm out of range. Can't contact Vashar."

"Same here."

Looking around at his squad, Kael rubbed his temples. "Should we move?"

"No, stick to the plan. Five more minutes, we can wait."

"Copy. And, Pike, stay safe."

"Don't worry about me."

Kael spent every second on alert, if alert meant pacing back and forth grasping his rifle like he'd die without it. His boots scuffed the ground where the grass had grown thin, and his hands became slick with sweat. Gnats buzzed all too loudly in the quiet dawn, passing by in swarms carried on the cool breeze.

It was time, the signal came, and they moved out.

Having reached the tree line, Pike spread out his squad. Looking through binoculars, he could see sentries on the wall and more running westward.

Smiling, he turned to Anais. "The diversion is working."

The Xalthari was gawking at the sky. As Pike turned, a fireball ripped through the sky and plummeted to the ground west of the HQ. If Junova lost the ship, they were dust.

His earpiece buzzed.

"Did you see that?" Kael asked.

"Yeah, something ain't right up there."

"I say you were right. Stick to the plan. Even if Junova's having problems, we might have a chance if we get inside."

"How long do we give her?" Pike asked.

"It'll take us ten minutes to cover the distance to the wall. I say go now."

Pike sighed, looked at Anais. "He wants to go now."

Anais smiled and nodded his approval.

Pike spoke into his earpiece. "Kael. Nova pace."

The Xalthari moved quickly and silently through the tall grass unlike the corps troops, who sounded like a herd of wild pigs, huffing and grunting, breathless and still not used to the gravity. Pike had forgotten how heavy he was in his first few months here. It was like an age ago now.

They were about three-quarters of the distance to the walls. Skidding to a halt, he called on his intercom, "Kael, look up."

Five, no, six raging fireballs flew out of the sky and crashed into the compound with a might he'd never seen. The sound was deafening, and the ground shook for several seconds.

When he looked up, large portions of the walls were gone like they'd never been built. Dust filled the air, and a silence fell as a hail of debris pelted them. Pike flung himself to the ground, covering his head as more significant bits of metal fell around them.

Debris stopped raining from the sky, and he stood. Besides a few nicks and cuts, everyone was ready and capable.

He tried his earpiece, but he got no response. Taking it out of his ear, he looked at it—dead. They had been too close to the rail cannon when it'd hit. No communication wasn't what he'd hoped for.

He urged his squad forward, and they reached the walls.

"Now the hard part."

"No, brother, now the fun starts." Auctor grinned at him.

Kael swallowed a stone in his throat. "I still don't understand how this is fun."

Stepping over debris and into the compound, Auctor looked back. "Because it's a rush."

Their mission was straightforward. Kael's squad would take the landing pad and UTC while Pike would take the training grounds and barracks. They would meet at HQ.

The Urban Tactics Course presented a unique challenge, though not because urban combat was dangerous. The Xalthari had no experience or training in this form of warfare. Kael did his best to train them before they left, but what could you do in a few days? Still, it was better than nothing.

Taking cover near the landing pad, two full squads were in standard defense positions.

Sitting with his back to the wall, Kael looked at Auctor. "Two squads."

"Not more?"

Kael frowned. "No."

"We have twice their number. This is easy."

"Alright, take your squad and rotate clockwise. I'll take mine the other way so we can catch them in a crossfire." As Auctor turned, Kael grabbed his arm. "Not too far, we don't want to shoot each other."

"I'm not an idiot." Auctor pulled away, waving his squad forward.

Kael led his squad in the opposite direction, moving cover to cover slowly and steadily. Peeking around his cover, Kael saw he had a clear line of sight to several soldiers. He readied his rifle and took aim.

Someone fell on a thin metal structure, creating a crash that alerted every soldier in the area. The defending soldiers opened fire on his squad, pinning them down.

"Easy," Kael muttered.

Projectiles zipped overhead and thudded into the wall around him. Some of his squad were managing to return fire. Kael poked his rifle over the edge of his cover and fired. It was inaccurate, but at least he was doing something in this mess. And where was Auctor?

It didn't take long to find out as the incoming fire stopped. Peeking out over his cover, he saw Auctor, standing tall in the midst of the fallen.

Kael frowned. "About time."

"I thought I was the stupid one."

Kael stood. "Fair."

"Collect ammunition and any extra gear you can. They won't need it anymore."

"Right."

Considering the injuries, they had been fortunate. One was wounded, and he could still fight. Not bad for their first real engagement today.

"Rally your squad," Kael said. "UTC is next."

Auctor nodded.

Having found no opposition at the training grounds, Pike and Anais made their way to the bunkhouses. He didn't expect anyone to be there after the cannon strike, but to his dismay, the place was crawling with Starlit. His squad split from Anais's; they would each take a side of the company street and clear the houses one by one.

One of the barracks had been obliterated. Scattered everywhere were wood splinters and chunks shaped like body parts.

"Somebody always pays the price," he muttered.

The majority of Pike's squad was composed of corps soldiers. While Anais's squad crept up to their position at the first house, Pike put his Xalthari members in the rear where they couldn't be seen. He marched his squad down the middle of the street, catching the occasional glance from the nearby soldiers.

His chest grew heavy as he came up to the first house. These soldiers looked like recruits who had been given real rifles. By the void, they were kids. They might not even know how to shoot a weapon yet. Pike skidded to a stop, his eyes growing wide as he spotted faces he knew: two of the corporals from training, Otho and Ford.

Stepping aside from a building, Ford locked his gaze on Pike. "Do my eyes deceive me? Look who's come crawling out of the mud." He flashed a cold grin. "Our little traitor's home to play."

Otho stood to the side, eyeing Pike, holding his weapon ready.

Trying not to glance at Anais, Pike put on his best poker face and smiled. "Guilty as charged. Do these kids even know how to fire their weapons?"

Scoffing, Otho tilted his head to one side. "Oh, they do. We made sure."

Pike's heart sank. So much for a peaceful resolution. Resisting the urge to glance around at the rifles in his direction, he focused on the two men.

Ford paced like he used to during training. "Looks like we have a standoff for ourselves. The question is, who twitches first?"

Every muscle in Pike's body was tense, ready to twitch at a moment's notice. He'd have to make the first move if he wanted to survive.

Slowing his breathing, Pike steadied himself. He didn't have to look back to know his squad had managed to spread out since they'd stopped. Fewer guns were aimed at him and more at their enemy. With a small gesture, he told Anais to wait. If this went bad, he'd still have the advantage of surprise.

All was quiet; even the air went still. Ford eased his weapon into a ready position. Gritting his teeth, Pike decided on his next move. Now, it was down to when. A couple of recruits shifted their feet, stepping back. Another adjusted her grip, glancing at Ford. Otho's finger moved a hair, but it was enough.

Pike dropped. His first shots ripped through Ford's chest, sending him sprawling. Otho got a few shots off before Pike could shift targets. Sweeping his rifle across the floor, Pike hit Otho in the legs and brought him down screaming. He was shot again and went quiet. Shots echoed off into the distance, and silence fell.

He stayed vigilant, waiting for anyone to exit one of the barracks. No one did. Either they weren't there, or they were holding defensive positions. Getting to his feet, he assigned soldiers to watch and took account of injuries. Nine dead and no wounded.

Anais's squad started clearing the barracks. One soldier kicked in the first door, and it flew off its hinges with a crack. Two shots were fired, and the all-clear was given.

Once his squad had stacked at the first door, Pike gave the signal. Someone had put a bunk up against this door, but the force of Pike's kick sent it crashing open. Men flooded into the room and called out. Empty.

He had just readied himself at the next barrack when weapons fire burst from the building, penetrating the walls. Several soldiers went down, including a Xalthari. Ducking, Pike returned fire into the building, sweeping its length. People on the ground groaned, breathing in thick gurgles.

Waving his men up, Pike kicked in the door, almost falling through it himself. He gained his balance and stumbled into the room where four soldiers lay, all dead. The bunkhouse cleared, he went to check on the wounded.

"Four dead, and six wounded. They won't be able to continue."

Could this get any worse? He stopped. Better not wish it into existence. With casualties mounting, he had seven men and women left. Anais had some deaths, leaving them with a total of fifteen. They'd be in a sorry state for a rendezvous, and they had two more houses to clear.

The next house was simple. In. Out. One shot fired. Walking up the steps to the last house, Pike hesitated. It had been his house during training. Memories washed over him of simpler times, though he hadn't thought so then.

As he got his squad into position, a thump came from inside the bunkhouse. He frowned. So much for being empty. He thought to shoot through the walls and end it.

A voice rang out. "We won't fight."

Pike thought for a moment. It could be a trap. Why, though? "How do I know you'll keep your word?"

A laugh. It was familiar, but Pike wasn't sure whom it belonged to. His eyes drifted down, and he watched as the door latch moved. His eyes bulged as the door yawned wide and a man he knew stepped out, grinning.

The UTC sprawled out in front of them, now a half-blasted war zone. Buildings collapsed and burned. Streets turned into rubble.

"Looks like you got your wish, brother."

Kael was frowning out at the devastation. "What's that?"

"Most of the buildings are gone. The heretics should have no problems fighting now."

"Don't call them that. We're allies now."

Auctor smirked. "Maybe."

"I have an idea."

"Oh, another brilliant strategy."

"Since the Xalthari are effective at non-urban combat, we should rebalance the squads. Put them together and assign the areas devastated by the rail cannon. Meanwhile, you and I will take the corps soldiers and clear the remaining buildings."

Raising an eyebrow, Auctor smiled. "You might be smart after all."

"I'll take that as a yes. Split them up and move."

"Yes, sir." Auctor gave a mocking salute.

The Xalthari were quite pleased to find out they didn't have to go into buildings and left before Kael's squad had organized itself.

The remaining buildings were located in groups near the course center, where Kael and Auctor focused their attention.

"If we split into teams of three, we can cover this faster," Auctor said.

Biting his lip, Kael scanned the buildings. "It'll be safer to stay together."

"We don't have time for that."

"By the void, it's the rule of three for a reason."

Smiling, Auctor turned and started splitting up the team into groups of three. Almost.

"Someone's going to be short a person," Kael observed.

"Isn't it obvious, brother? We don't need a third. Not while I'm here."

"I don't like it. Yet, I can't ask anyone else to lose a man for my benefit. Auctor, give them assignments. I need to sit for a moment."

Nodding, Auctor turned and started pointing out buildings.

Sitting on a chunk of wreckage, Kael looked at the wasteland. Pieces of a nearby building crashed to the ground as it burned. Holding a hand up, he let his eyes focus through his fingers, his hand a blur. How different would this moment have been if Liora was still here? He looked up at the sky, its cyan colors mixing with the black smoke. The acrid smell of burning debris assaulted his senses. Dropping his hand, he stood. There was work to do.

As usual, Auctor had to be first in. The first building had been a small house, and it was empty. Now, they stood in front of a multistory commercial building.

"There's going to be a lot of open sight lines in here," Kael said.

"Worried?"

Kael nodded. "Yeah."

Smirking, Auctor turned toward the door. "This will be easy."

Kael swallowed. He centered himself in front of the door. The hair on the back of his neck bristled. Pike had always had his back. He wasn't sure Auctor ever had. He kicked. The door burst open, and Auctor advanced. Something moved—a flash of metal. The rifle butt slammed into Auctor's face, dropping him like a brick. He lay sprawled on the ground, unconscious.

# Chapter 34:
## Snakes

*"A silent predator, a snake hunts prey, coils itself around it. Constricts. To a snake, it is a fair fight."*
—Xalthari Warden of Echoes

Jumping back, Kael aimed and shot through the wall. The projectiles hit with force against the metal building, and a few made it through. A soldier fell from behind the wall, crashing into the floor in a puff of dust. Dead. There was movement across the room. Kael fired again, hitting his target.

He glanced at Auctor and nudged him with his foot. "Wake up. Come on, I need you."

Nothing. Auctor wasn't getting up anytime soon.

Breathing slowly and deliberately, he adjusted his grip, keeping his weapon aimed into the dim building. He couldn't leave Auctor, yet it was too dangerous to move him. Or to stay. His eyes darted, watching. Nothing could escape his notice if he was going to survive. Hugging the outside wall, Kael peeked through the door. Quiet. Still. Maybe he'd got them all.

Glancing down at Auctor, he hesitated before readying himself at the doorway. His heart thundering, he looked through the doorway, visualizing the room in small movements, slices. After clearing as much as he could from the outside, he made entry, sweeping the walls and inner doorways. His boots crunched on fallen debris from ceiling material as he crept along. Sweat ran down his face and into his eyes.

There were two doorways, two rooms, left to clear. He looked back at Auctor, seeing his chest rise and fall. Still alive. Blinking the sweat from his eyes, he gripped his rifle tight and cleared the next room. It was small, empty.

Slow and steady, he made his way toward the last door. At a sound, he froze. Silence, but for the distant sound of burning buildings and weapons fire, met his ears. Entering the last room, he saw a lone stairway on the far wall and the body of the corps soldier he had shot lying motionless on the floor in a growing pool of crimson. He ventured a breath of relief and moved back to the entry.

Kael moved Auctor to a side room so he'd be out of sight—and safe, he hoped.

Cautious, he reentered the last room and approached the stairs. He hated clearing stairs in training. Too much could go wrong; it was so much space to cover alone. Taking a steadying breath, he readied his weapon and stepped up. With every slow step, he looked up, behind, to his sides, and forward, and checked the view below into the room. Hands trembling, he paused, readjusting his grip. He listened for any sound. For all he knew, the building might have been empty now, or the rest of those soldiers' squad was waiting for him. Kael had the sudden urge to swallow. Eyes darting, he took another step up.

Reaching eye level with the second floor, he scanned the room above. It was darker than below. Kael's finger twitched toward his rifle-mounted light; there was movement near the floor. Turning, he only just made out the boot as it kicked him. The room reeled, and he lost his balance and tumbled down the stairs. The air rushing out his lungs made a wheezing sound as he hit a step. Smashing into the ground, he tried to gasp, but the wind was still knocked out of him. His whole body ached, and his head pounded. Rolling himself over, his vision blurry, he saw a silhouette stalking down the stairs.

Frantic, he searched for his rifle. It was pinned under him. He tried to free it but couldn't. When he gasped again, air rushed into his aching lungs.

The voice came clearly. "It's been some time, lad. How's Zero's famous traitor?"

"Who...?" Kael wheezed.

"Did I knock your brains out?" He laughed. "I always said, don't expect a fair fight."

Kael tried to push himself up onto his elbows. The blurry silhouette stood over him; he could make out the corps uniform.

The man bent over, grabbed him, and hoisted him up. "Let me give you a hand. A man shouldn't die on his back."

His vision started to clear. It was Gatlin. The old soldier's face was all screwed up, snarling at him. Kael's eyes went wide.

"Recognize me now?" He pinned Kael against the wall.

Trying to resist, Kael grasped at Gatlin's arms and face, but his strength was gone.

Gatlin flashed a challenging grin. "The first time I saw you in battle, you was scared witless. You still had the globes to carry a man out under fire." He scoffed. "And I thought, this lad might make a decent soldier one day. How wrong I was." Spitting on the ground, he dropped Kael.

Managing to stay upright, Kael grabbed for his rifle. Gatlin was faster, landing a blow to his stomach. He held Kael against the wall, preventing him from falling.

"Good. You're learning. Too little, too late."

He punched Kael and continued to hit him in the face, chest, and stomach. Over and over. Every hit brought Kael closer to the edge of consciousness. His vision dimmed and sounds grew distant, as Gatlin's hands wrapped themselves around his neck. They coiled tighter and tighter. Theirs was a grip of iron. He couldn't breathe. White flashed in his vision, and he closed his eyes, but the flashes still came. The iron snakes loosened their grip enough for him to catch a breath. His eyes opened wide, and the iron coils tightened again.

"Can't have you die too quick, now can I?"

Memories flashed, and Pike's words from all those months ago came to him. *Damndest thing.... Can't leave fast enough.... It's the only place you want to be.*

To be home.

To see Liora, to touch her.

This was it, he was going to die.

His vision darkened, and Gatlin's face blurred.

Gatlin's head. Red mist. A voice.

"I told you not to die out here."

Gatlin's fingers uncoiled from his neck and slipped off. Air filled his lungs. The world rushed back in. Gatlin's body slumped to the floor and lay in a growing pool of red.

Back against the wall, Kael also slid to the floor. Turning his head, he saw two figures. Blinking, he tried to make them out. One looked at him with concerned eyes. The other still aimed down his rifle. He knew them. Who were they?

He was pulled up to his feet. "Kael!" the voice called. It was distant. Kael blinked again. The face was closer. Pike. It was Pike. He wasn't going to die.

The other voice came, closer now. "Almost dinne make it on time. Ye're blessed, lad."

Kael's eyes widened. Krennak? No. He must have been delirious.

Pike took him by one arm, and the man took the other.

Kael blinked. Gawked. It was Krennak.

"What are you doing here?" he tried to say, but all that came out was wheezing.

"Easy now, lad. Ye had tae life choked outta ye. We 'ave ye an' yer brother."

Kael drifted in and out of consciousness. He heard people yelling. He was aware of people running. He was still being carried. There were rifle shots.

"Almost there. HQ is close."

"Aye."

Smoke. Acrid. Thick.

"They've captured Hernz!" someone shouted.

Pike and Krennak put him down. His back was against something hard. He was sitting. Soldiers were running.

Everything went black.

Kael jerked to consciousness, gasping for air.

"You're safe, easy now." Pike's voice was a balm to his ears.

He fell back against the wall. Working his throat, he tried to speak. "What happened?" squeaked out.

"We won." Waving a hand at the destruction, Pike gave a weak smile. "Alandra, Ordan, and Qenni placed themselves near Hernz in the assault, and when the west walls fell, they took him prisoner. HQ captured without a shot."

Kael looked at him sideways. "Too bad we weren't so fortunate."

Chuckling, Pike slapped him on the thigh. Kael grimaced, his leg sore.

"What happened to Hernz?" he asked.

"I thought we should let Junova decide his fate."

Nodding, Kael smiled. "Yeah."

Pike groaned as he pushed himself up. "Shuttles are coming."

Leaning his head back, Kael stared into the smoke-filled sky. They'd won, and somehow, he was still breathing.

# Chapter 35:
## Sacrifices

*"You are judged by your sacrifices to the Star."*
—Shepard of the Covenant

Kael braced himself as the Htube spat him out near the bridge. He landed on his feet, and the sudden shock sent waves of pain up through his muscles. Gritting his teeth, Kael stood firm until the pain subsided.

The crew went about their business as if he wasn't there; the gentle tapping of fingers and affirmative chimes from accepted inputs filled the silence, punctuated by the occasional clunk of footsteps.

Taking a few labored steps, he walked into the strategy room where Junova and Vashar were already having a conversation. He nodded and received nods in return. Taking a seat, he gazed out into space. The inky dark looked calm with its array of twinkling stars. How many of those had Liora been to? Closing his eyes tightly, he could see her face and hear her voice. He would never know about the stars, as he would never hold her again. He took in a ragged breath just as the door opened.

Pike, Auctor, Alandra, Ordan, Qenni—his old squad entered, patting him on the shoulders with smiles and sitting around the table. He tensed, his body aching at the thought of Gatlin walking through the door. But he didn't. Gatlin was dead. Krennak entered, expressionless.

He glanced around the room and sat. A few minutes passed, and after greetings, the room fell into an awkward silence.

"Before Captain Katsui arrives, I must tell you about Hernz," Junova started. She caught everyone's gaze. "Hernz will no longer be a problem. He's dead."

The door hissed open, and a man stepped into the room. He was short, with narrow eyes too close together. He had long black hair and a round face. His skin was an olive color Kael had never seen before, and his uniform was the same as Junova's, black with a white star dominating his left shoulder, and five golden stars on his collar.

Clearing her throat, Junova stood. "Captain Katsui, it's good to see you in person."

He smiled. "Likewise, Captain Junova. How many years has it been?"

"Too many. I wish this were a happy reunion, but Katsui has some important information to share."

Smile vanishing, he leaned forward, palms on the table. "Indeed. It seems our little revolution has become a thorn in Solovian's side. The child god has ordered the four remaining battleships to cleanse Xalthryn and destroy us." He slumped back into a chair.

Raising an eyebrow, Pike eyed Katsui. "Are they like Radiance?"

"Vengeance and Lightbringer are the same. Harbinger and Absolution are equipped with fewer but more powerful rail cannons."

Silence took over the room for several seconds. Then Auctor pounded his fist on the table. "When do we leave?"

"Hey now, lad, do ye care to explain what ye mean?"

Scowling, Auctor scanned the room. "It's simple. If their target is Xalthryn and us, we should bring the fight to them. This time we choose the battlefield. Open space would give us room to fight back."

Rubbing his chin, Katsui looked thoughtful. "The idea has merit. The question remains, how do two of us win against four?"

Kael bit his lip. "Junova's ship has rail cannons and a large missile stock. Katsui, what are Justice's armaments?"

Katsui and Junova looked at each other for a moment before Katsui replied, "Justice was built for planetary bombardment. In space, it's almost toothless."

"What do you use for bombardment?" Kael asked.

Another shared glance. "I have an accompaniment of one thousand twelve megaton fusion warheads. Launched from our launchers, they deorbit and impact predetermined places on a planet. Without gravity to assist deployment, they are worthless."

"One thousand?" Alandra muttered.

Pike whistled. "Corps is always serious."

Looking at Junova, Kael raised an eyebrow. "How many missiles does Radiance have?"

"More than two thousand." As the words left her mouth, Junova's eyes widened. "Katsui, does your ship have any missile launchers?"

"No." He looked perplexed.

"I think it could still work." She brought up a schematic of Radiance on the wall display. A cutaway of the ship appeared, and she touched a screen highlighting Radiance's launchers. "If we remove a dozen launchers, can you install them in Justice?"

Katsui's eyes lit up as he smiled. "I could do it in a day."

"Good. Now the hard part. If we remove the explosive warhead and guidance from some missiles, we can fit a fusion warhead in them. The drawback is they wouldn't be able to track their target."

Katsui paced to the viewport, his small stature exaggerated against the void. "Like a dumbfire fusion torpedo. If we retrofit enough missiles and use remote detonation, tracking won't matter."

Nodding, Junova looked at everyone in the room. "Any questions?"

Vashar stood. "My people will come. We will help in your battle."

Wincing, Kael shifted his weight. His whole body hurt, and these chairs were not comfortable. "You don't have to come, Vashar. Xalthryn is free."

"No. Until this child ruler is stopped, Xalthari will never be safe."

"Thank you." Junova stared out into space. "I'll have Reed send shuttles when you're ready."

Vashar nodded. "Then I will prepare my people."

"Get to work. We leave orbit in two days."

Kael sat and stared off into the void as most of the others left. It was starting to look like the war would never end. One victory led to another battle, and so on. He was tired. Junova sat next to him. Krennak stood, hesitated a moment, and looked at Kael, mouth open. Then he closed it and left, the door whispering behind him.

Junova keyed the display, and a personnel file popped up. "Your father's record."

Kael gawked at the information as it scrolled by in front of him. "I never thought I'd know what happened to him."

The file started: *Ezra Vallen. Sergeant. Age at death: thirty-eight.*

"Three years after," he muttered. "I was sixteen when he died. Thank you for telling me." He gave a weak smile.

Junova's jaw worked. "I thought you should know." Pushing herself up, she winced. "I...I haven't packed her room. I thought you should. If you want to, that is."

He nodded, taking a shaky breath.

She left, and he leaned forward on the table, gazing at his father's life rolling by on repeat. His fists clenched, and his nails bit into his palms. Heat rose in his cheeks; he was glad Hernz was dead. Kael hoped Junova had made his last moments torture.

The door whispered open.

"Kael." It was Vashar. "I give my thanks. Your sacrifices to my people have been great."

Swallowing hard, Kael nodded. "You opened my eyes. Without you, I don't know if I ever would've left the corps."

"I asked a question, no more."

Kael tried to huff a laugh. "What am I supposed to be when it's over?"

Vashar sat. "Once your ruler is gone, there must be another. A person fair and just." He pointed right at Kael.

"No, I could never."

Smiling, Vashar shook his head. "I remember a verse. Star shines on those who feel undeserving of warmth. It does not worry over such matters. Take warmth you're given, without it, frost is all that waits."

"That's the Starlit Covenant," Kael muttered.

Vashar grinned.

He'd heard the verse before as a child, but he hadn't understood it then and wasn't sure he understood it now. He nodded anyway. Warmth was enough for now.

# Chapter 36:
## Tool

*"The six are a tool to spread the Stars' light across the galaxy."*
—Shepard of the Covenant

Auctor surveyed the dark void between the outer armor and inner hull. Its few connections were solid armored struts tying them together like sutures in a wound. It had been sealed and filled with air so they could start work on the launchers. What he couldn't understand was how the crew of Justice could work in such a disorganized mess. Tools were strewn haphazardly about the floor. Plasma torch lines were wrapped up in the wiring. It was a wonder the ship even flew. He ducked through the hatch. He could help with the missiles instead.

With a smile, Auctor gawked at the warhead storage: a thousand perfect, organized, clean fusion bombs. The squad was here, too. He wasn't the only one who hated a messy workspace.

Pike was struggling with a missile casing too heavy for one person, so Auctor stepped in to help.

"Thanks, those things are heavy."

Auctor shrugged. "What do you need help with?"

"We are removing the existing warheads from the missile bodies, and the next station is removing guidance and mounting the new bombs."

Skyler R Ostrom

"I'll help remove warheads first."

"First?"

Auctor smirked. "Can't I do both?"

Nodding, Pike pointed. "You can start on those. And be careful."

Turning, Auctor looked at his tools. He was always careful; how dare Pike assume he wouldn't be? Taking up his tools, he got to work ratcheting open the modular latches.

"It's good to see ye, lad," Krennak said, walking over. "I could use help down 'ere."

Pike turned to him. "Ain't it the truth. Could always use an extra hand."

"Where do I start?" Krennak asked.

"Auctor's got those. You can help with these. Together we can push these through quick."

Glancing back, Auctor frowned at the two men. Working on the same missile was a waste of time. He tried to ignore them as they rambled on about many unimportant subjects. By the void, it grated his nerves.

No one ever talked about his contributions. Why were the smart undervalued?

Dismounting warheads was easy. He was done here. Auctor stood and walked toward the other station.

"Where ye goin', lad?" Krennak asked.

He didn't look back. "I'm going to work over here." He kept walking.

Alandra, Ordan, and the annoying one, Qenni, were working on installing the fusion warheads.

"I want to help."

They all turned, gawking at him.

Qenni chuckled. "You want to help?"

He frowned at her. "Yes."

Raising an eyebrow, Alandra looked at Ordan. "Get him started."

After hesitating a second, Ordan waved him over. "It's simple. We aren't planning on using the guidance, so cut the wires, unbolt it, and toss it into this pile." He pointed at a heap of units, rolled the missile onto a rack, then lowered a warhead using the crane. "Once you have it in place, the attachment points use the same latches as the original warheads. Tighten them down, and move the completed missile to stock."

Auctor started by removing the guidance system. Once he'd completed the entire process several times, he was confident in his ability. He set down the tools and left.

"Going to the mess?" It was Ordan.

Auctor waved a hand without a word.

Before getting in the tube, he considered staying to help. It would surprise him if they finished on their own. His plan was taking shape; he would be back, though not to help.

It would be a tool, a last resort if the situation called for it, one no one would even consider securing. Auctor watched the tube opening yawn wider as he approached it. With a whisper, it spat him out into an inky blackness. Perfect. Lights off meant he was in the clear. Grabbing the handle, he flipped the switch. Lights buzzed on in sequence throughout the storage bay.

Auctor made his way to the first station, where there was a missile on the workbench. At least he didn't have to lift one. He picked up the tools, released the explosive warhead, and set it aside. While rolling the missile body onto the rack, he caught the tip of his finger under the edge as it settled.

Yanking his hand away, he lost a tiny strip of skin. Blood oozed from his wound, dripping down his hand. With a flash of anger, he almost kicked at anything, but he stopped himself, remembering where he was. He wiped his bloodied hand on his pants. Activating the lift, he moved to the next station.

The missile came across smoothly and easily. He cut the guidance wires, unbolted it, and tossed it aside; it was trash. He brought a fusion warhead down slowly to a gentle rest using the crane. Using the ratchet latches, he tightened it down. He smiled; this was too easy. Using the crane again, he transferred the missile onto a conveyor and shipped it off toward the hangar.

It zipped along the tubes, taking a minute to reach the hangar. While he waited for it to arrive, Auctor prepared one of the cargo drones. It was from Radiance, so setting its system to return home was simple.

The cargo floor opened, and his missile rose from below. Auctor grinned. Here it was, and it was his. Loading it on the drone was an easy crane transfer, and he activated the drone's return once it was done.

He stood grinning, watching it leave, a flash of something predatory in his eye.

"What are you doing here?"

Grin vanishing, he spun around. Katsui.

"I was seeing one of the last cargo drones off." Not quite a lie.

Katsui's eyes narrowed, and he looked out at the drone. "Good." His lips twitched upward in a smile that unnerved Auctor. "Wouldn't want any trouble, would we?"

"No. I'm finished now, I'll join my squad."

"Very well."

Auctor moved as fast as he dared while trying not to look suspicious. Katsui huffed a laugh and glared at the drone as Auctor threw himself into the tube and was whisked away. It'd been close, but he'd got away with it. And now, when the moment came, he would be holding the winning hand.

# Chapter 37:
## Flame

*"Identity is an eternal flame; it shapes life, it shapes death."*
—Xalthari Warden of Echoes

He rode the air, eyes closed, fists balled, and arms planted against his side. Pike hated the Htubes and wouldn't have used them if there had been a better way to travel through the massive battleship. Feeling a slight shift in the current, he cracked an eye open and saw the exit fast approaching. He braced himself as it shot him out, boots clapping against the deck.

Sighing, he looked out into space. The stars glimmered in silence. The viewing deck spanned the height of two decks and ran along almost a quarter of the ship's length. Steps led down to a viewing platform with chairs, benches, and tables for the crew. Starting down the steps, he marveled at the bronzework lining each one. It was elegant and out of place in a warship—art on a ship built to kill.

Seeing a silhouette against the transparent alloy, Pike stopped in his tracks. He'd come here for the quiet, counting on the fact that most of the crew would be busy preparing for the upcoming battle. Shoulders slumping, he turned and began up the stairs.

"Don't leave," a hushed voice said.

Pike stopped, swallowed, and turned back to the dark outline below. "I didn't mean to interrupt."

The voice came louder, and he could tell it was a woman. "You aren't interrupting. Please, come and sit."

After starting to take a step forward, Pike hesitated. He wanted time alone, but what was the harm? He continued down the stairs toward the shadowed figure and sat at a respectful distance.

Taking a deep breath, he peered through the window. Starlight curved in slow, silent arcs through the inky black, refracting like it danced across still water. He smiled, knowing Radiance was moving faster than light, yet the stars were like lanterns, gentle guides lighting the way.

Glancing at his silent companion, he pursed his lips. Should he leave? She had asked him to stay. Pike closed his eyes, listening to the constant low hum of the ship. It had unsettled him at first, but now it was a strange comfort; it was like he knew he was safe as long as he could hear the life within the ship.

He glanced at the woman again then decided to leave and started to stand.

"Please stay." The voice was clear now. It was Junova.

He froze, half seated, then sat down and stared at her.

Her voice sounded solemn, filled with regret. "I used to love watching the stars. Before Corvallion." She sat unmoving, a statue in the dark. "I remember the cannons raining his judgment down upon the planet. Every sound and vibration through the ship as they fired. Watching the silent video feeds of cities reduced to flame and rubble."

Pike closed his eyes and clenched his jaw, seeing his own family home in ruins.

Her breath was slow and ragged. "They weren't soldiers. They were men, women, and children, my family. They tried to surrender. I let them believe it might save them. I gave the order anyway." She went silent, her breathing blending with the ever-present hum of Radiance.

He stared at the void of floating stars for a long while. "When I was a boy, my family was murdered. I was too afraid to run, too frightened to help. I stood frozen and watched as my sister called out for me, her body mutilated." He clenched his fists and closed his eyes. "Our house was on fire, and it fell on her. Swallowing her in flames. I can still remember her screams as if it were yesterday. When I could move, I ran, and I've been running ever since." Taking a deep breath, he bit the inside of his cheek.

She stood, her boots sounding against the deck. "I have to prepare."

He nodded as she walked up the stairs. There was a whisper of air from the Htube as she entered it.

Opening his eyes again, he saw the stars were there waiting, moving. Time stopped for no one. Not even them. He wished he knew whether he was still running...or too afraid to stop.

# Chapter 38:
## Justice

*"The light of God's Justice may dissolve a world of shadow."*
—Starlit Covenant

"Captain, ten minutes to contact. All four ships, as expected," Astronav Izzani reported.

"Good. Bring us to a stop. Get Katsui on comms." It wasn't good, though. Her stomach knotted at the thought of the battle ahead. Even with their secret weapon, the outlook was grim. She glanced over at Reed, who was overseeing crew manning the array of tactical stations. Sometimes, in quiet moments she wondered if he questioned her and their goal. Frowning to herself, Junova knew it was a foolish thought, he'd been the most faithful and steadfast second she'd ever had. And a good friend.

"Captain Junova. I see our prey falls into the trap."

"Katsui. You always were optimistic."

"I see no reason to change. I have a little under twelve thousand megatons of fusion missiles."

The words took a moment to sink in. Under? Wouldn't he have twelve on the dot? Perhaps he had some other plan, so she brushed it off. "You're first up, my friend," she said. "Don't forget about those cannons."

He laughed. "Never. These missiles will outrange anything they can throw at us."

"I'd say go with the Star, but I don't think it would approve."

"Good one, Captain. In that case, shadow and void guide you." He chuckled and cut comms.

It was up to him now.

Shifting in her seat, Junova surveyed the bridge. "Tell Zero to get up here. They will want to see this." She paused. "Bring the feeds online."

Across the bridge, live image feeds from Justice flickered to life. One clear picture of the incoming ships showed frigates and destroyers in close formation with the battleships.

"By the void," someone muttered.

Junova fought the urge to swallow a lump. "I want all crew at their stations. When Katsui has done his work, I want to be ready."

Reed glanced over. "Yes, Captain."

Zero arrived on the bridge, and Junova spun her chair to face the squad. "You will want to see this."

Upon seeing the screens, all faces sobered. She turned around. It was a hard fact to face. If the ship was disabled, there was nowhere to run or hide. All were welcomed to death by the vacuum of inky black.

Kael pointed at a screen. "It's begun."

Missiles poured from Justice like angry red ants. Rocket glare distorted the image as each missile shot forward. Frigates and destroyers spread out, and battleships changed course. Point defense weapons came online, firing streams of orange projectiles.

From this distance, even chaos looked slow. PD disabled many missiles, but far more missed their mark. Knuckles white, Junova grasped her chair. In silence, they watched the spectacle unfold.

A flash.

The image distorted.

A white-blue ball grew like a new star was being born. Then it vanished.

Once the image cleared, wreckage remained. The battleship was adrift. It had been half vaporized, leaving a cutout of its interior like a grim display in a museum. There was no sign of its escort.

A cheer erupted around her, and Junova allowed herself a smile. They knew these weren't standard missiles. The remaining battleships wouldn't make it easy. She didn't like how close Katsui was, either; he would be in cannon range soon.

"Reed, how many missiles has Justice fired?"

"Estimates are around two hundred, Captain."

Frowning, Junova glared at the screens. She didn't want to place all her hopes in Katsui yet, but his crazy scheme might work.

An orange, hot projectile flew past Justice, missing by a few meters. Any closer, and Katsui wouldn't be able to outmaneuver those cannons.

Two frigates collided in a spectacular display of fire. One reactor venting plasma melted a hole in the other frigate, creating an explosion that fragmented both ships. Parts of the ships drifted outward, creating a debris field that disabled several incoming missiles. One missile slipped through the debris and detonated the aft deck of the second battleship. When the flash died out, half the ship had disintegrated, leaving the fore section dead in space.

This time, the cheer was cut short by a projectile skimming across Justice's outer hull. It cut two image feeds and left a yawning wound from bow to stern. The entire bridge held its breath as Justice launchers went silent. Junova gawked at the images, her shoulders slumping.

"See if you can get Katsui on comms."

Silence.

Comms flickered to life and static roared in the background.

"Junova," Katsui coughed. "Half the ship depressurized, and we have fires where there's still air. The launchers are out. I still have three hundred warheads over here. I can't think of another way to deliver them."

She swallowed. "You can't."

"It's been a pleasure knowing you, win this for Justice." He cut the link.

"Katsui," Junova shot to her feet. "Can we help him?"

"No time, Captain. He's engaged his drive at full power."

She watched as Justice turned, not retreating but rocketing forward, a war god committing to one last charge. The third ship tried maneuvering out of Justice's path but was too slow. A rail cannon fired from the fourth battleship, its projectile piercing Justice from ventral to dorsal, leaving a gaping hole. It started losing power as it contacted the third ship. They seemed to meld together for a long moment, bits breaking off and spiraling away. The images distorted and flickered out with a flash.

Junova fell into her chair and stared at the black screens.

"Captain, I can confirm detonation. The last ship was close enough for the EMP to wreak havoc on its systems, but it's still operational," Haggen said.

"Which one is it?"

"Absolution."

Closing her eyes, Junova gritted her teeth. Absolution was one of the two names she had least wanted to hear.

Someone was next to her. "Bad?"

Opening her eyes, Junova nodded at Kael.

"What can we do?"

"Its cannons are bigger than ours, and the projectiles are faster. We need time to alter direction after they fire, which means distance. Distance—"

"Our cannons are less accurate," Kael finished.

She nodded. "If anyone has an idea, I want to hear it."

"Absolution has changed course to intercept. Fifteen minutes until they are in reliable weapons range."

"Navigation, can you buy us more time?"

"Maybe a few minutes, Captain. The drives are still not one hundred percent."

Rubbing the bridge of her nose, Junova took a slow breath. "Launch missiles. Try to take out the escort ships."

"Right away, Captain."

Qenni was gawking at a battlefield display. "Captain? Does Absolution have missiles?"

"Yes, why?"

"They're not firing them."

They weren't. How had she missed that?

"Maybe the EMP disabled their launchers," Pike said.

Reed glared at the display with Qenni. "We can hope."

It wouldn't be enough. Absolution's cannons fired slower than Radiance moved, but she could never close the distance enough to guarantee a hit. One hit from those cannons, and Radiance and everyone aboard would be dead.

Auctor made his way over to the battle display and watched for a moment. He looked hesitant.

She frowned at his back. "Auctor, what do you think?" At least three members of Zero were frowning or raising eyebrows at her, but she didn't care.

Auctor straightened and looked at her with an unnerving intensity. "Do we win?"

She studied him for a moment. "No."

Auctor smirked. The back of her neck prickled at the sight. "I can save us," he said.

She wanted to gawk at him, mouth open, but creeping suspicion kept her in check. "Explain."

He walked out onto the bridgeway like he was on a stage then turned and smiled. "I have a fusion missile."

Now she was gawking at him, mouth ajar. As was the entire bridge. She wanted to ask how, but there wasn't time. "Where?"

He shrugged. "The landing bay, in a cargo drone."

She frowned. There wasn't enough time to load it into a launcher. "Do you have a plan?"

Grinning from ear to ear, Auctor walked to the drone console. "I can fly it."

Stalking over and wearing a frown of his own, Kael glared at Auctor. "They will shoot it down. It'll never work."

"Hold on." Krennak was rubbing his chin. "Yer gettin' ahead o' yerselves. One time, I was assigned to protect a government official durin' negotiations. We used landers an' flew tae one wi' our official in tae group's center. A tight formation, dinne leave a gap. Lost a few good men but completed our mission."

Junova snapped around, looking at Reed. "How many drones can we launch in the next five minutes?"

"Uh, about half our complement. Twenty."

Now, Ordan was glued to the battle overview. "I don't think it will be enough. The missiles aren't even scratching the escort."

Kael was still frowning at Auctor. "What if we time the drones so they travel with the missiles?"

Junova allowed a slight smile. "It might work. Everyone, get to work."

Drones launched and in formation, Auctor prepared to follow the next wave of missiles.

"Nav, how long until they can hit us?" Junova asked.

"Two minutes."

Spinning her chair, she swallowed. "That's how long you have to pull this off. We'll keep launching missiles after the drones leave."

Auctor nodded, focused on the console.

"Nav, they know our evasive maneuvers. You'll have to use manual control."

"Understood, Captain."

Junova watched as the drone feeds filled the screens where Justice had been. A wave of nausea washed over her. This was their one hope. All their lives rested on a missile thief. And Katsui knew this. She remembered his count of under twelve thousand megatons. Did he know Auctor had one? She shook off the unease but would have to watch him more closely.

"They know we're up to something. Remaining frigates are positioned to protect Absolution."

The image feeds flashed with yellow streams of PD projectiles. Some missiles and a drone were hit. The wreckage was carried forward by momentum, screening against some incoming fire. Passing near a frigate, several missiles retargeted and veered off. They struck the frigate, disabling it.

A flash showed on the screens near Absolution. Junova's eyes widened. "Nav—"

"I see it, Captain. It's going to be close."

The drive sputtered and shook as navigation pushed it harder. Spotting a red dot in the distance, Junova stood. It came in near the starboard side. The deck vibrated, and the whole ship shook. An ear-piercing metallic grinding rattled through the bridge.

"Where are we hit?"

Reed examined his console. "I'm getting reports. It hit the ventral aft section. Two decks are vacuum. Engineering and drives still intact."

Sighing, she fell back into her chair. It wasn't good, but it could've been much worse. "Status, Auctor."

"I'm close."

She frowned. "Does anyone have details?"

Breaking his gaze from the overview, Pike glanced at her. "Ten drones left. No missiles."

Tapping her fingers, she watched the screens. "How long?"

"Thirty seconds."

An eternity. Worse yet, Absolution would get another shot.

It didn't take long for the shot to come. This time, she watched it come in from above and strike a port cannon battery. The delay between contact and vibration was seconds and several more seconds for the sound. Covering her ears, she grimaced. Out of the corner of her eye, she saw the image feeds flash bright white and black a moment later.

Mouth agape and eyes wild, she turned to Reed. "Confirm contact."

He watched his display. "Nothing. It's gone, we did it."

The bridge didn't cheer. There was no triumph. There was only silence and the weight of everything they'd survived.

# Chapter 39:
## Coward

*"A coward chooses to be blind to themselves. Then, is a person calling themselves a coward seeing their true self, or is their view obscured?"*
—Xalthari Warden of Echoes

He hung silent, in inescapable morbid awe. His view wasn't glorious but one of death, one of bodies lilting through an endless void, one of steel careening unbounded into oblivion. His breath kept him company, its dull hiss offending in the tight confines of his suit. Not unlike a canyon carved into a planet's face, the wound yawned before him. Kael placed another metal bandage across the gaping flesh.

Pike closed his visor as the welder sparked to life in a faint glow of blue. Flameless, the evidence of its functioning was a tight white point of heat flowering against the hull. There was a spark, and vapor expelled from the wound like steaming breath on a cold day. He leaned in, supporting the welder with one gloved hand as the beam sutured steel in silent intensity.

Finishing the weld, he gazed out at the stars. Radiance spat verdant plasma from its drive as they propelled toward destiny. After placing the final slab of metal, Kael waved him over. Pike bound the metals together, sharp golds mixing with dull grays to form a scar across the ship. Such was the prize for surviving war.

After entering the airlock, Pike sealed the outer hatch. Air rushed into the space around him, hissing like a hurricane. When the pressure stabilized, the inner door groaned open, and Pike stepped through. He removed his helmet and placed it on a shelf, and the crew helped him remove the unforgiving suit. Sitting on a bench, he toweled the sweat from his face.

Sitting next to him, Kael dried his head and arms. "I don't think I'll ever get used to how hot suits are."

"I'll add it to the list of jobs we don't want."

Both men chuckled.

Glancing at Kael, Pike gave a weak smile. "What's waiting for us?"

Taking a deep breath, Kael stared at the floor for a long moment. "It started with the Xalthari. Vashar fights for his people's identity. Freedom to exist as they are and not some identical servant of the Star." He balled his fists. "What awaits us is an end to oppression. An end to senseless murder."

Frowning, Pike put on his shirt. "Is it worth the cost?"

Putting on his shirt, Kael stared at him expressionlessly. "What would be the cost if we didn't?"

"I don't know. What will we do when we've won? We've been pushing hard for so long. What's next?"

"There will be a new ruler who is fair and just. Someone who can reshape the Starlit into a society welcoming all."

Raising an eyebrow, Pike looked at Kael sideways. "You?"

Kael huffed a laugh. "No. Though Vashar might think otherwise, he told me of ruling when the time comes. I don't want it."

"We should decide who it will be."

"I thought it would be obvious."

"Not Auctor, I hope."

Kael shook his head. "Junova should become ruler. It seems the right choice. She has experience with command and negotiation. She cares about people on a level most in a command position don't."

"I agree. We should talk to the others about it."

Kael nodded. "We're almost there. Everything we've fought for has led us to this moment. Tomorrow we'll land on a new world and fight so countless millions don't have to see what we've seen, feel what we've felt."

Taking in a slow breath, Pike nodded. "It's going to be dangerous, and...I don't want to lose anyone else."

"I know." Kael's throat bobbed. "We're Zero. They can't kill us." Kael clapped him on the shoulder.

Pike appreciated the thought even though it was a lie. No one was invulnerable, a fact they both knew too well. Nodding at Kael, he turned away. "I better get ready then."

Pike stalked from the room into a hypertube and was whisked off into the ship. His quarters were about one hundred meters from the nearest tube, and Pike used the opportunity to run. As he sprinted down the corridor, the crew leapt out of his path, their boots clanking across the deck plating. His blood coursed, thumping in his temples, and his breath came fast. A bulkhead light flashed as he passed it, casting his shadow against the bronze wall in hard lines.

Coming to a stop, he opened his door and flung himself onto his bed.

Eyes closed, he lingered in the moment, feeling his chest rise and fall and his heart thundering in his chest. The cool air from the ventilation system was a small reprieve from the heat welling inside him. Clenching his fists, his nails bit into his palms. He didn't like the quiet. He had too much time to think, to fear the future, and to be haunted by the past. This had made him run, so he could distance himself from the quiet, from people. Joining the corps had been him running away from his past while trying to avoid a future of pain.

Where could he run now? That was what scared him. He might leave Kael and the others if he had a way out. Not because he didn't care but because he couldn't see them hurt like his sister. What if he were helpless? What if he had to watch them die in agony, too? He closed his eyes even harder. A tear ran down his cheek.

He was a coward.

# Chapter 40:
## Words

*"In his words, he'd stored his ghosts, memories, wisdom, and peace."*
—Unknown

The corridor stretched quiet and solemn, its bronze walls dull under the soft white light. Kael's company was an alcove containing a looming statue of God, face shadowed, the Star ever-present above its head. The lack of prayers murmuring in the corridors left an odd, irregular hum emanating from within Radiance.

His hand was placed flat on the door before him, and he stared forward, silent and tense. Crew walked by, quite evident in their attempts at concealing their curiosity, trying not to catch his eye as they glanced back with solemn looks, their muffled footsteps fading.

His fingers slid across the cool surface as he pulled his hand away, feeling every imperfection and detail. He touched his pocket. Reaching inside, he grasped the war-torn paper and held it in his trembling fingers. It had been wet, a corner torn, and yet the constellation Liora had drawn was still visible.

"Obralon," he muttered. "So I can always find you."

Jaw clenched, he took a ragged breath and slid the paper back into his pocket. The air was clean, sterile, odorless. The door hissed open, and he stepped into the dark room. Light filtered in from the corridor for a moment then vanished as the door shut, leaving him in total darkness.

He stood alone in the inky black for a long moment. The only sound was his breath whispering against the walls of the small space. The scent of her perfume still lingered in the air—flowery, light, and sweet. His fingers trembled as he reached for the light, hesitating before activating it. The room was as he'd last seen it. However, it was heavier and smaller without her presence, as if her being here had given it life. Given it meaning.

He stepped farther inside, stopping at the holo emitter. Flipping it on, he watched the walls transform into a beautiful garden world. Trees rustled in a breeze, and birds flew about. He pressed a button, and the projection changed to Liora's favorite: waterfalls. He closed his eyes and stood listening to the babble of water in the stream, the distant crash of water below the falls, and the sounds of birds flitting in the trees.

Kael fell into the chair surrounded by constellations and gazed at the moon-adorned sky.

"Better than maps," he muttered.

But the room didn't answer.

As his eyes shifted to the violet waterfalls, their serene beauty that had once filled him with wonder now gave him only sorrow. An emptiness filled his chest, and he overflowed with an agony so sharp it made him clutch at his heart. Tears streamed from his eyes, and he curled up in the chair, sobbing.

Memories flashed through him. *Found the floor. Hello to you, soldier.*

"I'm not a soldier yet," he muttered between sobs. "We'll never see Syrelis, not together."

The waterfall answered with its steady rush of water. Sucking in a ragged breath of air, his body tensed between sobs. If he'd woken when she'd left, if she'd told him she was going...it should have been different. Junova had unassigned her; she wasn't supposed to have been there. It had to have been Hernz, Junova had said it herself. Thank the void he was dead and rotting.

Face all screwed up somewhere between anger and despair, Kael knew it was useless to consider alternatives. They would serve only to cause more pain. It would not be daring to hope but hoping for the impossible.

Hands still shaking, he clenched his fists, trying to steady them. He knew the words, the ones he never got a chance to tell her. "I love you, Liora," he muttered. "I...I loved you." Closing his eyes tight, he could see her face, her eyes set against the Emerald Star.

A flower of beauty he'd taken for granted back home, the Emerald Star. A simple thing turned into a symbol of her beauty, the Emerald Star. Pulling his knees into his chest, his tears renewed. A flower he would never look at the same way, the Emerald Star. A rose by any other name, the Emerald Star. His body shook, and he wailed in agony.

Once his tears had dried up, he sat staring into the falls. His feet in the stream below were enveloped by a rush of distorted photons flowing around and over them toward the rushing falls. The water chuckling and his feet, dry and warm, gave him a feeling of disconnect with the environment.

A sense of numb exhaustion enveloped him. Pushing himself up, he flicked off the emitter. There was one room left. After approaching the door to her bedroom, he paused, remembering the last time he'd stood here.

She had led him straight to the spot before the door and told him to wait. After several minutes, she had opened the door, smiling, taken his hand, and led him inside.

Raising his hand, he stared at it as he recalled the soft warmth of her fingers against his, the simple strength behind her pull as she had guided him, a subtle squeeze urging him forward. Taking an uneven breath, the door whispered open, and he stepped inside.

His uniform jacket was still on the floor. He'd forgotten it. His eyes scanned the room, unchanged. Absurd in its state of emptiness, the bed ruled the room like a testament to a life lost and a heart crushed.

Closing his eyes, he turned away. Kael couldn't bear to look upon it for another second. The memory ate at him like rust in his heart.

He left the bedroom, and the door whispered as it closed, becoming a ghost haunting his memory. He shuddered.

Everything left of her was here. And yet, there may have been something to the Xalthari belief. Perhaps some of her was with Xalthryn now; some of her wisdom might live on. The thought brought him a modicum of peace though the hole inside him remained.

He gritted his teeth. He'd return to Xalthryn and give her a proper goodbye.

"After it's over," he muttered.

Letting out a sigh, he resolved himself. He had to see this through for Liora, his father, the Xalthari. For all who had suffered at the hands of their god, a false god.

# Chapter 41:
## Blood and Bones

*"Blood. Bones. These remain after death, after wisdom leaves."*
—Xalthari Warden of Echoes

As he exited the tube into the docking bay, the ever-present pungency of grease permeated the air. No matter how often Pike came down here, he never got used to the odor. Looking around at the controlled but urgent activity, he shrugged his shoulders. At least it wasn't brown.

Vashar was organizing his men, meshing integrated units of Xalthari and corps soldiers under one banner. Boarding shuttles was an army to rival anything that might be waiting for them planetside. Continuing to the far end where Zero was boarding their shuttle, Pike slowed a moment, listening to the clatter and voices droning throughout the bay. There was no quiet before this storm.

As he went to put his gear on the shuttle, Pike was distracted by raised voices. Peering around the far side of the shuttle, he saw Kael and Alandra engaged in what appeared to be a heated debate. Frowning, Pike dropped his gear in his seat and went to see what the problem was.

Stabbing her finger in the air, Alandra frowned. "I'm not a sergeant anymore. You should be in charge."

Sighing, Kael waved a hand in dismissal. "That isn't important. You have the experience and training."

"I'm not Zero's leader anymore, you are. They respect you and listen to you, Kael. I'll support the squad, but I won't lead anymore." She turned and walked past Pike and into the shuttle before Kael could get in another word.

Kael stared into space before acknowledging him.

Pike shrugged. "She's right."

Throat bobbing, Kael nodded. "I know." He sat on a crate. "It's not like I want a way out. I don't feel ready for this."

"None of us do, but we trust you to lead us. You've made the hard choices and haven't led us astray." He grasped Kael's shoulder. "Let's change the galaxy together."

Nodding, Kael stood. "Together then."

Zero was now aboard the shuttle and seated. The shuttle ramp folded in, and the door squealed closed. Pike winced at the sound. Couldn't they spare some grease for that?

They all watched the display as Radiance settled into orbit. There were no signs of other ships or resistance of any kind. Had Solovian been so desperate he had sent everything he had?

The shuttle's floor vibrated as the rail cannons fired upon the planet's surface. Then they launched, exiting Radiance, and turned about, facing the planet. Ordan switched the display to a live feed, and Pike gawked at the visual.

It was the most beautiful planet he'd ever seen. It looked like a blue and white jewel hanging among sparkling stars in the void. Wisps of white clouds swirled and streaked across the sky like a painter had taken a brush and spread them out. Great blue seas enveloped most of its surface, with several continents forming its landmass, a stark contrast to the ten percent surface water of Xalthryn. Its yellow sun gave off a warm, inviting glow as if to say, "Welcome home."

They all looked nervous as the shuttle landed, but not him. He anticipated the rush as the shuttle door opened, and they filed outside. Auctor stepped out onto green grass as he gazed up at the palace looming before him. Sounds of battle in the distance got his blood pumping. His eyes filled with the whites and golds of the massive structure. He didn't care about architecture, but this symbolized power, a lot of power.

Vashar's presence was evident, as armored soldiers were strewn across the grassy courtyard. Pools of red coated the green grass.

Qenni kicked at a corpse. "Their armor is like Hernz's."

Alandra scanned across the bodies. "Solovian's personal guards. There will be more in the palace."

Moving ahead of them, Kael glanced back. "They can still be killed. How effective is it?"

Pursing her lips, Alandra frowned. "Direct hits should penetrate. Shots coming in at an angle could glance off."

Kael nodded. "Alright then, make your shots count."

The doors to the palace fortress must have been over ten meters high and sat wide open. Auctor frowned at them for a moment. If one wanted to be viewed as a god, perhaps making people believe you needed such a tall door lent weight to the deception. Auctor could see no other reason for such an impractical display.

Inside the doors, a long and over-decorated hallway presented itself. Perfect white floors met bronze walls, which continued to a sky-blue ceiling. Identical golden statues lined the length of the hallway. Each statue had a rose-gold crown with a glimmering yellow gemstone set into it. He almost scoffed at God and his Star.

Movement at the far end caught his attention. Soldiers scurried about setting up barriers and what looked to be an automatic turret.

He waved a hand at Kael. "Soldiers ahead."

"I see them. Pike, Ordan, and Qenni take the left side. Use statues for cover. Alandra, Krennak, Auctor, with me on the right side."

The defenders knew they were there yet waited far too long to fire. Letting Auctor get too close was a mistake, proof he was better.

253

Once the shooting started, it became clear the defenders were overconfident. That was when Auctor got to work. Popping out from his cover, he aimed and fired, hitting two before returning to his cover. They looked confident; they thought themselves untouchable.

Projectiles hammered the walls and statues around him, splashing gold and plaster through the air and onto his uniform. His ears rang, and his nose seared with the invigorating smell of burning propellant.

A grin spread across his face. These weak gods and their weak soldiers didn't stand a chance against him. His heart pounded, and as the rush kicked in, he shot again, bringing more soldiers crumpling to the floor.

And then it was over.

The defenders lay dead or dying. The rush ebbed, leaving emptiness. He glanced at his weapon and pulled the magazine for a count.

Behind him, Kael would be preaching peace and unity. Pure nonsense. Let him. Auctor dealt in realities.

He slid the magazine home with a click and checked the chamber. Still more to do. Still more to kill. A smile tugged at the corner of his mouth: thin, satisfied, empty.

Ordan's voice came from behind. "Couldn't they put a lift in this place?"

Trying to catch his breath, Kael stopped for a moment. "What, stairs are too much for you?"

A chuckle erupted somewhere down the line.

Krennak stalked by. "Be glad yer not fightin' uphill."

Frowning at his back, Ordan continued up the stairs.

Kael shook his head, pushing himself forward. At the top was a small empty room. It looked much like the rest of the palace but with paintings in place of statues. Ordan and Qenni slumped to the floor, looking exhausted. Alandra joined them, finding her place to sit. Auctor watched the exit from afar as Pike and Krennak checked the next room.

Walking up to a painting, it looked old. It's brush strokes were thick and heavy with paint. A night sky swirled, and the stars appeared as bright beacons, like lighthouses guiding ships to safety among the jagged shores. Moonlit hills rolled in the distance, stopping at a valley where a slumbering town lay on the edge of a wood. Even then, there was an idea of stars guiding souls.

"Kael."

Kael spun to see Pike waving him over.

Pike nodded toward the door. "There have to be twenty of them in there."

Gritting his teeth, Kael peeked into the grand room ahead. The defenders were well placed around the room to cover a door opposite. In the middle of the room was an odd spiraling monument jutting from the floor like a stone tree. The column of sorts looked to be made of the same white stone as the floor. Along the wall, there were several alcoves with small altars. They looked large enough to provide cover for two people.

He turned back to Zero. "Ordan, Qenni, you go left. Krennak, Auctor, go right. Alandra and Pike will go up the center with me."

Everyone nodded, lips in tight lines, except Auctor, who frowned.

Ignoring this, Kael stood at one side of the door. Looking at Pike and Alandra, he swallowed. "We go after they clear the door."

Ordan opened the door, and he and Qenni slipped through, followed by Krennak and Auctor. Auctor fired on the defenders before they made it to cover and hit two. Kael frowned. Now the defenders were shooting back, making it more difficult for him, Alandra, and Pike to push up the center.

Forced to wait, Kael held position as rifle fire rained plaster and splinters around them. He waited for a moment when several soldiers ducked, receiving fire from Zero, then he sprinted out with Alandra and Pike. The three slammed into the column, hugging it for safety.

Kael pulled a starburst grenade from his belt and lobbed it toward the defenders. It exploded in a spectacular flash of light and with a sound sharp enough to make your ears ring. He peeked around the column and shot. When his rifle was empty, he pulled back and reloaded his weapon.

Ordan and Qenni tried to use the flash as cover to move up, and Qenni took a projectile to her right side. Ordan pulled her into cover and applied medical aid. Kael shot around the column again with Alandra kneeling next to him. This time, there was a yell, and several soldiers fell.

Auctor was separated from Krennak and pushed forward from cover to cover until Kael lost sight of him. Krennak followed suit as Kael ducked out to shoot. When he fell back into cover, a silence settled in the space.

"It's clear, ye can come out."

Standing, Kael saw Krennak and Auctor checking bodies. Armored soldiers lay strewn across the floor, their crimson blood a stark contrast to the white marble. Turning his attention back to Qenni, Kael ran to her side.

"How is she?"

Qenni frowned up at him. "Don't ask him. I'll be fine. Might need some stitching."

Pursing his lips, Ordan applied pressure to her wound. "She'll live alright. But I'd better stay with her."

Kael nodded, gave Qenni a quick smile as he stood. He turned away to glare at Auctor. "What was that?"

Auctor stared at Kael expressionlessly. "I killed them, didn't I?"

"That's not the point. You left your squad-mate behind."

"He should've kept up." His eyes were filled with a challenge. "You're not going soft, are you?" Taking his place at the next door, Auctor smirked. "Am I going to have to do this by myself?"

"Everyone, stack up on the door," Kael said through gritted teeth.

After Qenni got hit and his fight with Auctor, Kael became less emotional and more reserved. He fought like a man with a singular purpose. Pike kept himself behind Auctor at all times and watched his every move. Auctor had always been off, but he'd never been this unpredictable. It was almost like he didn't need the rest of them anymore.

Pike took his place at the door behind Auctor. The plans showed one room between them and the throne chambers. They pushed through the large double doors. The room wasn't filled with soldiers or weapons. Tall, thick glass cases lined one wall, their contents lit with dim lights. They were filled with people. Each case had a small metal plate at the bottom of it engraved with a name, a range of years, and a number. The bodies looked decayed to an extent but had been preserved somehow. Even the clothes hadn't disintegrated over time.

The other wall was lined with partitioned bookshelves, each with a name matching one of the glass tombs. Books filled all but two cases, on which the metal plates were blank. Those tombs were also empty, as if waiting for their tenants.

Alandra examined the most recently deceased body. "They're all God."

Kael looked at her, eyebrows raised. "What do you mean?"

"Look at the dates. Each one starts when the last ends. It's every man who ever called himself God of the Starlit."

Kael glared into the case. "Remember when we joined the corps, God's decree? He said he wasn't immortal."

"Ain't forgot, took it to mean he couldn't live forever. There's no more than a hundred years between these," Pike said.

Tapping on the glass, Auctor chuckled. "I didn't expect anything less. A god with blood and bones."

Kael stopped in front of the two empty vessels. "That means his son is, too."

Looking at the two empty tombs, Pike adjusted his rifle strap. "Ain't a coincidence those have been put in here. With both empty though...Solovian's father must still live."

Kael frowned at the glass then over at the barren shelves. "It doesn't matter if he's alive, we must finish this."

"Agreed." Pike nodded. "This rot goes deeper than Solovian." He waved a hand at the row of bodies. "A millennium of oppression and injustice."

Kael's eyes filled with determination. "Let's breach this door and end this once and for all."

Grinning, Auctor took his place at the door. "A pity they built all this for unworthy men."

Glancing at Auctor, Pike lined up behind him.

Taking a position opposite Pike, Kael touched his zippered pocket and gave him a nod. There was nothing left to say.

# Chapter 42:
## Gods

*"The Gods themselves were a tool. A means to an end that has long since been forgotten. The time for Gods is at an end."*
—God of Gods

They breached the final door.

A long hall stretched forward, its white tiles separated by gold inlay. Tall windows arched over each side, spilling sunlight across the floor and filling the room with a warm glow. At the far end was the throne. Wide steps led to a marble platform wrapped in gold. Above, the ceiling rose into a high dome. Eight guards in full armor head to toe lined either side of the hall. Their gray armor thick and jointed covered every part of their body, and they wore closed faced helmets.They stood still as the door opened not even turning their heads to look.

Solovian sat upon the throne, arms draped on the rests. Skin an alabaster white, and hair of gold, he appeared to be about Kael's age. Thin and despite his seated position tall, he wore a white robe with a gold-trimmed collar resting on his frame like it was stitched with the haughtiness of a thousand gods.

Behind him, a transparent chamber held a frail skeleton of a man. Hairless, skin of gray ash, he must've been over a hundred years old. Tubes fed into his chest pulsing as if pumping liquid, and the hum of machines filled the silence. It looked to Kael like the machine must be keeping the old god alive, while his son Solovian, sat on the throne. A pretender. A murderer.

Zero entered, weapons raised. Kael, Alandra, and Krennak took one side. Auctor and Pike took the other. This is the root of oppression, Kael thought.

Solovian didn't flinch. "So, the rebels arrive." He tapped his fingers on a rifle Kael hadn't noticed. "This is how God ends, is it? Not with fire, but with heretics and rebels. My own weapons." He laughed, and the sound echoed in the open chamber. "Couldn't think of anything more original?" Solovian shook his head. "Well I must say I am quite impressed you made it this far ." Looking back at the old man in the machine he continued. "When was the last time a revolution made it this far, father?" The old man didn't answer. Looking at Kael, Solovian pursed his lips as if in thought. "Hmm, I'd say about a hundred and fifty years ago. But then they didn't even manage to land on this world let alone reach the throne. Unless you count raining down in tiny pieces as landing." He chuckled.

Stepping out into the center of the room, Auctor smirked. "You love to hear yourself talk, don't you?"

Rage flashed in Solovian's eyes as they snapped from Kael to Auctor, but the man kept his composure. "I am God, when I speak people listen."

Auctor stood there expressionless and blinked. You aren't God. If you were God we wouldn't be standing here."

"Ha, but I wanted you here, and you are here," Solovian replied.

"You're lost in your own delusion," Kael said, taking position next to Auctor.

"Delusion? No. Clarity. My entire life has been decided. I am he who continues what my father and all the gods before him started. I am the Star, and my light will bring another hundred years of peace to our galaxy."

"Aye, like tae peace on Xalthryn or a hundred other worlds we destroyed in tae name o' God," Krennak spoke, his voice filled with disgust.

"Yes, like those," Solovian said. Then rubbing his chin he continued. "The death of those Starless heretics makes our peace possible. It simply wouldn't do, letting them spread their false way of life among the Starlit."

Auctor adjusted his grip on his weapon and Kael glanced over, placing his hand on Auctor's arm. Relaxing his grip on the rifle, Auctor's jaw worked as Solovian spoke.

"What I am, I am for all of you. Without me, you'd all be nothing. Without my father you might not have been born." Solovian scoffed. "I am God, as I am the Star, yet I am not free. I'm a slave to my rule. Bound by duty to preserve the Starlit. A prisoner here to ensure all under my rule have peace. If a few thousand heretics have to die for that, then so be it."

Taking a step forward, Kael gripped his rifle. "The Xalthari didn't even have space travel, how could they be a threat to us?"

"Why wait until they are?" Solovian waved a hand in dismissal. "It's no use speaking with you. You'll never see what it means to rule. What it means to hold the lives of an entire race in your palm and be expected to shepherd them." He sneered. "Go on. Finish what you've started. Take your place upon this throne. You're no better than I am."

Kael raised his rifle.

The chamber stilled, and no one moved.

Kael held his weapon tightly, sights on the man who killed for power, who had stripped away the lives and identities of so many people. His finger rested on the trigger. Then lifted.

He lowered the weapon. "I can't kill the monster without becoming one. It's not what she would've wanted. You're not a god. You never were. You're a man grasping at power."

Solovian blinked. His eyes narrowed. "I knew you wouldn't kill me. And even if you did, you who are my slaves, my weapons, would serve to be the gods of tomorrow." He laughed.

Kael turned to Pike, nodded, and walked toward the door.

There was a movement, a rifle shot. Kael spun around to see the rifle falling from Solovian's limp hands. Red stained his white robes as it spread from his chest. He fell from the throne and sprawled across the stone floor.

All eyes were on Auctor. A gentle wisp of smoke rose from the barrel of his rifle.

Kael stared, frozen. His choice had been shattered in an instant. "Why?" he whispered.

Lowering his weapon, Auctor scanned the guards along the walls. "I had to, he was going to shoot."

The guards remained motionless, quiet in their positions. There was no joy in it, the corpse of a broken tyrant. Kael stood for a long moment. He wasn't sure he believed his brother. Not entirely.

Kael and Pike neared the chamber where the old god lay. A guard stepped away from the wall—Kael tensed, raising his weapon. Stopping, the guard lowered his rifle and set it on the ground. Each of the eight followed suit and approached the life support sarcophagus and knelt facing God with their heads lowered. Hesitating a moment, Kael continued to the old man's side—guards remaining motionless.

He lay there, his eyes open, staring up at nothing. Or so Kael thought. His eyes locked onto Kael's, and his breath came faster. He opened his mouth; it looked as though he was trying to speak. Kael lifted the transparent cover. Air hissed out and slid away.

It was hard to imagine how he was alive. His skin was paper-thin, wrapped around his bones. His eyes were sunken back into their sockets, and dark rings surrounded them.

Bending over, Kael leaned in to hear the old man's words.

They came softly, slowly, barely even a whisper. "My son is dead?" Kael nodded.

The old man shut his eyes. "The time for gods is at an end." A weak smile spread across his lips. "Let the heretics be free. Let Xalthryn be free." And opening his eyes once more stared at Kael. "Now, let me die."

Kael raised his head and stared at the old man. His finger hovered over the power switch. A dying man's last wish. Closing his eyes, Kael hesitated. Now that he was here and the old man a vision of death in front of him, Kael didn't want to kill him. Looking upon the frail being, a tear glistened in his eye. He pushed the button and watched as the machines hummed to a stop and the man's chest lay silent, still. It was done. God was dead. Kael didn't know how to feel. But he thought he'd feel relief, triumph, something. There was only the finality of his mission complete and a numbness he couldn't wrap his fingers around.

Pike was standing next to him. "What now?"

"Now we talk to Junova."

# Chapter 43:
## Hope

*"The Star may have been a false hope, but our future is not."*
—Captain Junova

Staring into the dim green glow of the screens, Junova's eyes glazed over as lists of dead or captured scrolled past them. These were the names of all those who had given their lives for freedom or Solovian—opposed in life, together in death. Rubbing her eyes, she leaned back. This would be her first change, notifying families of their deceased loved ones. No matter the effect, people had a right to know, and the Starlit had been wrong for breeding false hope.

Taking a deep breath, she gazed out at the blue jewel below. Her eyes shifted to the photos: her family, friends, and Liora. Those lives she had taken on Corvallion had sparked the change sending her down the path of rebellion.

"We won, but the cost of change was too great," she muttered as she clenched her fists. "The price of blind loyalty." Turning back to the display, she flicked through the captured loyalists, sighed, then activated comms. "Reed?"

"Here, Captain."

"Start organizing prisoners by planet of origin and arrange transport. I'm sending them home."

He paused for a moment. "Of course, Captain."

"And, Reed, no need to call me captain anymore. Radiance will find a new captain."

"Yes, Cap...Junova."

She cut the link.

Pulling up a list of ships, she identified one of sufficient size. It was scheduled to leave dry dock for its shakedown cruise within the week. Its name was Hope.

Clicking comms, she connected with Vashar.

"Junova, pleasant as always."

"I have arranged a ship for you. So, you and your people can go home whenever you wish."

"Much gratitude."

"How long will you stay?"

"Some of my people wish to return, others would stay awhile. We will decide when it is time."

"I understand. Thank you, Vashar. Without your people, we could never have won."

"No. Junova, Kael, many others, deserve thanks. We have been saved."

Closing her eyes, she smiled. Vashar's humility and kindness never ceased to amaze her. The Starlit could learn much from the Xalthari. "Thank you. Safe travels, my friend."

"Likewise."

The channel went dead.

These were her last official acts as captain of Radiance. Now she would rule the entire Starlit and its worlds. It was time to go. Standing, she took the holo photos from the window and deactivated them. Everything else would be sent down later. Placing the small projectors in her pocket, she scanned her room one last time before powering off the workstation.

With the door hissing closed behind her, Junova entered the Htube. It whisked her off toward the bridge; she had to make one final stop before leaving. The Htube spat her out in a whisper of air, and her boots clanked on the deck as she landed.

When she entered the bridge, all the crew were at their stations, focused on various tasks. Reed was the one who noticed her presence. He stood tall, smiled with kind eyes, and said nothing. She scanned the bridge from the screens where she'd watched the death of Justice to Liora's Astronav station, which was still empty. The statue of the dead god watched over the bridge like some eternal reminder of her sins.

Junova's eyes fell back to Reed. His lips were in a thin line. He saluted, his eyes glistening in the light.

Junova saluted him, nodded, then turned and walked away. She didn't look back.

# Chapter 44:
## Knife

*"The blade itself is not a weapon but a tool. A knife can carve out futures and erase the past, silence mouths and make them speak, and although small, its weight cannot be denied."*
—Unknown

God's palace rose in front of her like a great giant sitting on the edge of a precipice, watching over it's kingdom. The white-and-gold structure hinted at command and power, but in reality, it represented genocide, oppression, and corruption.

Upon her request, Kael had found an adequate location in one of the palace's wings for her command, with rooms nearby and a view of the surrounding lands.

Entering her new rooms, she scowled at the massive space, a monument to a sick kind of opulence, no different from the rest of this place. After setting her belongings on the large bed, she peered out at the balcony, at the land beyond.

It was a picturesque view. Deciduous trees with amber and purple leaves stretched across the horizon, separating blue sky from green grass. A small lake could be seen hiding among the trees. Sweet smells of flowers carried on a cool breeze brushed her cheek. To think this place was the seat of something so vile.

She took the holo photos from her pocket and set them on a shelf near the fantastical view. If anyone deserved peace and beauty, it was them. Flickering to life, Liora stared at her. The girl's eyes were filled with dreams and adventure.

A distorted image with smiling faces appeared next to Liora. Junova gazed at them for a long moment.

She took a deep breath and walked down the hallway to her new command. It wasn't so much a bridge as an office, but some equipment was familiar. The room colors were identical to the rest of the palace. That would have to change.

Kael was sitting in a chair, gazing out a window. He gave a small smile, which she returned.

Waving her hands about the room, Junova glanced at her surroundings. "This is it, then?"

He nodded. "The throne room is much more your style." He shrugged. "But this will have to do."

Chuckling, she shook her head. "I'd be a queen on God's throne. A goddess by all accounts." Laughter echoed in the chamber, dying out to somber silence. Junova sat in a chair much like the one from her room on Radiance. "Where is everyone?"

"Pike and Krennak are helping Vashar shuttle his men and equipment to the orbital shipyard. Qenni is still recovering, and Ordan hasn't left her side. She's been transported to a hospital." He sighed. "Alandra has been helping me clean up the mess. Someone had to pick up the bodies and keep Solovian from falling into the hands of any loyalists."

She cocked her head, raising an eyebrow. "We can't hide his body forever."

"I know. We thought launching Solovian, his father, and the rest of the pretenders into the sun might be fitting. Total obliteration."

She leaned back, her gaze soft on the ceiling. "Live by the Star, die by the Star, and shine forever within its embrace."

Wetting his lips, Kael looked down. "Ever since he shot Solovian, Auctor has been more distant. He's been brooding, and he won't talk about it."

She stood and walked to the window. "I hope you're not suggesting I talk to him."

"No, not at all. It's.... He worries me. I haven't felt I can trust him for some time now."

Junova stared out at the gardens, the sky, the trees. "During our battle with the Starlit ships, Katsui knew Auctor had one of his warheads. I've been playing it over and over. I keep coming to the same conclusion. I want to know why Katsui didn't outright tell us."

Kael frowned at the ceiling. "Maybe they planned it together, or Auctor stole it? But it leaves the same question. And if Auctor stole it, what was he planning on using it on?"

"That's my worry, Kael. Katsui gave me a hint he knew a warhead was missing. The captain wanted me to know but without tipping off Auctor."

Throwing his hands up, Kael shook his head. "Then we may never know, now the missile is gone. I can talk to him, but he's as tight-lipped as a spy."

"All I can do is tell you to keep an eye on him."

Kael let out a sharp breath. "Easier said than done."

Junova faced Kael with a stern look in her eyes. "I want your advice. What should I do about all the planets still serving the Star? Rapid change could send them into chaos, but if I move too slowly, I may never bring about real change."

He stared at the floor for a long moment. "I remember a quote from the Covenant. It says, 'Light reveals and blinds in equal measure, the wise see the difference.'"

Her eyes narrowed. "Are you suggesting they are so blinded by faith I could effect change in the name of the Star and they wouldn't notice?"

His head bobbed. "It would be slow, yet the Starlit Covenant could be eliminated. Replaced by a new way of life, one where all can live together in peace, sharing different cultures and identities."

"It sounds impossible."

He stood and rested a hand on her shoulder. "Not impossible, a dream."

Her smile was soft. "Dreams can become reality."

He turned to leave.

She grabbed his arm. "Where will you go?"

"I was thinking of going home. It's been too long since I've seen my mother. Since I've seen home. Someone has to tell her about my father."

She held onto his arm a moment longer, as if this was the last time she'd see him. "I understand." She released him. "What about Zero? What will they do?"

He shrugged. "I don't know. There is no corps anymore. I'm sure they'd stay if you asked them."

"I may. Kael, I'll arrange a ship to take you home whenever you're ready."

Kael smiled. "Thank you, Junova. For everything."

"One more thing." She gazed at him, her lips a thin line. "Believe people can change. I'm one of many standing as proof of the possible. Don't become what you fought."

Kael frowned, looking confused, then nodded.

And with that, he was gone.

Spinning her chair around, Junova gazed out the window. Work could wait a few more minutes. The quiet felt different now. Before, quiet had been a moment of calm between battles during which anticipation built, but now it felt wrong, like it was ready to be cut at any moment.

Pushing open the windows, she let in the warm breeze and closed her eyes.

"Beautiful, isn't it?"

She hadn't heard the door open.

That voice.

Auctor.

Turning her chair around, she gave him a tight smile. "Yes, quite beautiful."

He was sitting in the chair Kael had been in, not a meter from her.

"How did you get in here?" Junova asked.

Smirking, he waved a hand. "I have my ways." His smirk turned into a disarming smile. "An odd time to unwind. But you never really stop, do you?"

Junova glanced out the window. The warm breeze moved through her hair. "I've found ways to have peace."

"Peace. Still chasing that dream?"

"I have to."

Auctor tilted his head. "Why?"

"Because if I didn't, someone like you would."

He laughed, though not loudly, and the warmth didn't reach his eyes. "Unfair. You don't know me that well."

"I know enough."

"Do you?" He leaned forward, elbows on his knees. "If I were Kael or Pike, I'd be flattered. But I think you don't like what you can't predict."

She met his gaze. "I don't like what I can't trust."

Auctor's smile faded as he stared at her. "Do you think you should be our ruler?"

Her eyes narrowed, and her body tensed. "I did not ask for this, I was chosen."

"Ah, yes, chosen by the shortsighted fools of Zero. They have no eye for the future. What the Starlit could become."

Swallowing a lump in her throat, she glanced around the room, searching. "And what is that?"

He laughed again, the sound cold and empty. "Even you don't know. That's disappointing. And I used to think you were clever."

She stood, scowling at him. "Enlighten me."

The little smirk returned, and she wanted to smack it off his face. "Solovian. The gods. All blind. All afraid. The Starlit is power. Power to shape the universe into anything you want. Not something to be wasted squabbling with heretics on backwater planets."

She leaned forward, tapping her fingers on the desktop. "Let me guess, you think you should've been God?" Her voice was full of disdain.

Leaning back in his chair, he shrugged. "Yes."

Pushing off the desk, she gritted her teeth. "Power is not a tool for self-gain. That's why Solovian fell. He misused his power to harm people."

"No, he fell because he didn't understand the power he wielded." Auctor scowled at her. "Solovian was no more than a fool playing at being God. I am no fool. And I will rule." His fingers drummed on the chair's arm then stopped. He bared his teeth at her, and before she could react, he was over the desk and had one hand around her throat. He squeezed tightly, and she fought. "Now you see how powerful I am."

Her chest ached as she gasped for air, but none came. She swung her fists, kicked, scratched, and grabbed at his face, anything. But Auctor was unfazed. He pulled a knife from his belt, grinned wide, and rammed it into the side of her chest. Her body lurched, and searing pain shot through her.

Terror and disbelief struck her as the silver steel, red with blood, drew out from her body. A warm trickle of blood ran down her side, soaking into her shirt. The strength drained from her arms and legs. Her heartbeat slowed and became uneven. The world dimmed. Sounds faded.

Auctor plunged the knife into her chest, but there was no pain. No weight. It wasn't her body. Not anymore.

Light returned, and she was seeing herself. Seeing Auctor. Death, her death, played out like a play in front of her eyes. Cold, it was very cold. There was so much left to do, how could it end like this? A shiver swept the room, and Junova resigned herself. At least she had the chance to redeem her past. And even though those she murdered could never be brought back, perhaps now she could see them again. Her sins erased.

The knife rose, and she felt nothing as it pierced her body again.
The world fled from her, first sound, then light, then breath.
Then there was only darkness.

# Chapter 45:
## Monster

*"A hunter still hunts a monster if it lives in an abyss. They only need to remember they shouldn't stare."*
—Xalthari Warden of Echoes

"Kael." Pike's voice sounded shaken, unsure.

Kael turned from the console.

"It's Junova." Pike didn't need to say another word. His face said it all.

Kael's breath caught in his throat. Rage flashed through him. "Who?" His voice was clear, demanding.

"The medics tried, but she was stabbed through the heart. Bled out before they got there."

Kael grabbed Pike by the collar. "Who?"

"I examined the security cameras. It was...Auctor."

Kael's teeth gritted, and he shoved Pike aside. His boots echoed down the hall, up the stark white stairs, and past the guards. Every step struck the ground like it owed him.

Inside the grand hall, he found Zero waiting. Alandra leaned against a column. Krennak sat in a chair, arms crossed. They knew.

Kael didn't need to ask where Auctor might go. He knew. He went up the stairs to the ruler's museum and into the throne room. He stopped at the door, Pike on his heels. "Wait here."

Pike opened his mouth as if to speak but didn't say anything. Kael entered alone.

Auctor sat upon the throne like a king watching a peasant come to plead for an audience. Kael marched right up to him and grabbed him by the shirt, pulling him off his pedestal.

"How could you kill her?" His voice was as rough as broken glass and not much more than a growl pulled from somewhere primal.

Auctor smiled. "She was weak, brother. She couldn't appreciate the power you'd granted her. I can." His voice was smooth, gentle, like a blade sliding back into its sheath. Not loud, not harsh. Calm, cool, and confident. He wasn't boasting. He believed what he said was the truth and wanted Kael to believe it, too. But his truth was poison wrapped in honey.

Kael's face screwed up with rage, and his fists shook. "I can't accept that. She was trying to make people's lives better."

"So am I."

"No!" Kael threw Auctor down the marble steps, hands trembling, covered in blood. Junova's blood. He fell to his knees and roared out in agony.

Auctor, getting to his feet, laughed. A cold grin spread across his face. "You see, brother, not even you can kill me."

Pushing off the steps, Kael jumped through the air and into Auctor. Both men hit the ground, groaning.

They rolled.

Punches flew.

A knife skittered across the floor.

Getting to his feet, Auctor licked blood from a busted lip. "So, we fight? After all I've done for you? The people I've killed for you?"

"For me? No. You kill for yourself." Kael got to his feet, panting, pained. His head was a whirl of thoughts and emotions, rushing and overwhelming him.

"Then prove me wrong." Auctor came at him like a raging bull. After dodging the first blow, Kael tried to counter but caught an elbow to the face, sending him sprawling. As he lay on his back, Auctor came into view. "You see, brother? I'm better than you. The sooner you accept that, the sooner we can get to work."

Kael rolled over, pushed himself up, and swung at Auctor's knee, sending him crashing to the floor.

Grunting from the pain, Auctor got to his feet, limping and grinning. "You had too many distractions, brother. I started with Liora."

Kael blinked, and his face went slack. "What?"

Auctor's eyes lit with something vicious, predatory. "Of course, you don't know." He laughed a cold, menacing laugh. "And you thought it was Hernz. A simple matter. Changing the duty roster." He smirked. "Flying off on a suicide mission, little hope of returning."

The breath caught in Kael's chest. Everything went still. "You?" His voice was weak. The walls closed in, and Kael fell to his knees. "You wouldn't."

"Oh, but I did. Junova tried so hard to have her removed from the roster, too. All in vain."

Kael couldn't breathe. Not with Junova's blood on his hands. Not with his brother smiling. There was death in his smile. Kael's body wasn't his own, his mind an iron veil of rage. He wanted to stop the smile. No, he needed to.

He let out a roar, charging forward. Auctor tried to duck, but he wasn't quick enough. Kael caught him under the chin with his fist. Both lost their balance; Auctor stumbled and fell. Kael slid across the smooth marble and landed face-first, bashing his nose on the floor.

Memories flooded in, and it all made sense. Auctor's suspicious glances. His unusual greeting the morning she had died. He'd seemed so pleased that morning. Affectionate. Now, Kael saw it for what it was: gloating. Victory disguised as care. The words flashed in his brain like a sign. *We all have a choice, brother. Sometimes you need a little push.*

Groaning, Kael turned over to find Auctor already standing. "This isn't how I wanted it to end. I hoped you'd leave the dead where they belong. And you'd look to our future. Now I see you aren't strong enough."

Kael's breath hissed through his bared teeth. A lone tear ran down his cheek. "I never had a brother, did I?"

Throwing his hands up, Auctor paced about the room. "Now he sees, unblinded by the Star's light. If it weren't too late," his grin was predatory, "if you'd noticed sooner, you might've been able to save dear Liora." His voice dripped with venom.

Pushing himself to his feet, Kael stabbed his finger toward Auctor with violent purpose. "Don't you dare speak her name. Never again." He roared the words.

Auctor smirked like he'd already won. He opened his mouth and began to speak. "Li—" He got no further.

A crack tore through Kael the instant it happened. Everything moved as if it were in stop-motion. Like lightning, he closed the distance to his brother, the murderer. Kael had him by the collar with one hand. His forehead cracked into Auctor's nose, and they were on the floor. Kael hammered at Auctor's face, again and again, until his fist was bloodied and Auctor lay limp on the floor. He looked down at his hands. Blood. His brother's. Soaked into his skin, down his wrist, into the cuff of his uniform. Auctor had changed, but so had he. Kael had crossed something. And he didn't know if he could come back.

A voice told him to stop; it came not from a person, not from Auctor. It was a soft voice inside him, and it begged, pleaded with him to stop. And he remembered his own words. *I can't kill the monster without becoming one. It's not what she would've wanted.*

He backed away, eyes wide on the bloody pulp lying in front of him.

Kael glanced at a couple of guards, stiff as statues, at the far end of the hall. "Guards, take him into custody. Tend to his wounds and throw him in the brig."

Their armor clattered as they strode across the hall. Picking up Auctor and carried him out, leaving the doors wide open.

Pike walked in, scowling. "I knew there was something off about him, but I didn't think he'd do this." Seeing Kael, Pike's scowl faded. "You let him live?"

Kael lay slumped on the floor. "Yes." His voice cracked, weak.

"Why?"

"I can't kill the monster. He's still my brother."

He wasn't sure which hurt more—what Auctor had taken from him or what he had almost become to take it back.

Kael's fists clenched. He slammed a fist into the floor with a dull crack. "Damn him," he hissed through gritted teeth. "Damn him." His chest heaved, and his breath was ragged with fury and pain.

Pike flinched at the sound but said nothing.

Kael's voice broke. "He killed them both."

Pike crouched beside him, his hand hovering before it landed on Kael's shoulder. "I know."

Kael didn't collapse. He sat there, shaking, almost unable to contain the fire burning through him. He wouldn't cry. Not again. But as the gods were ash, he wanted to.

# Chapter 46:
## Deserves

*"Who deserves to live here? It's not for me to say, I feel sorry for them all."*
—Warden of Eesbex

"I have come to know Star people. Death is different. I offer my grief to Junova's life." Vashar's voice was hushed, smooth, a voice which might calm a crying child.

Kael sat in Junova's white and gold office. The space was filled yet empty. He nodded. No words were appropriate.

Giving a pleasant smile, Vashar stood.

Kael stretched out a hand, pleading with him to stay a moment longer. Vashar paused, and Kael met his gaze. "Will you take Junova with you and pass her wisdom on to Xalthryn?"

Bowing his head, Vashar held his arms out wide. "Junova will find rest among Xalthari."

Kael gazed out at the gardens, a weak smile on his lips. "She would've approved." Then, remembering Vashar standing before him, he regained his composure. "When do you leave?"

"Within a week, perhaps less. My people desire their home."

"I understand."

Vashar left, the old palace door creaking behind him. Kael stared at the door for a long while. He understood the Xalthari's longing for home. How often had he wished to see home since he'd left? More than he could remember.

He'd planned on going home after Junova had settled in. But now, how could he? Someone had to take responsibility. Vashar had championed him before Zero, and it was settled in their minds, the logical choice: Kael, ruler of the Starlit.

He scoffed. He was a broken and battered pretender.

There was a knock at the door. It groaned open. Pike walked in, followed by Krennak, Ordan, and Qenni. Pike wore a frown as deep as a canyon. "We need to talk about Auctor."

Kael bit his tongue, nodding.

"What do ye plan on doin' wi' him?" Krennak asked.

Taking a deep, ragged breath, Kael stood and walked to the window, glaring at the manicured beauty. "He will stay in prison."

Someone slammed a fist down on the desk, and Kael tensed.

"It's not enough." Qenni's voice was like a swarm of enraged hornets. She'd never sounded angry before. At worst, she complained when forced to eat nutrient blocks. "What he did...it's unforgivable. How can you let him live?"

"I will not become him! That's why. To kill for the sake of vengeance is no better than murder."

"Then let me do it." Pike's voice was cold, controlled.

Kael shook his head. "No. Even to condone his death would fracture everything we've fought for. We'd be no better than Solovian, than any monster."

Krennak stepped forward, arms crossed, his voice like a disappointed drill instructor. "He is a monster, Kael. Ye canne keep a monster locked away forever."

Ordan, silent until now, leaned against a far wall, his eyes darkened by shadow. "This isn't Justice. Junova deserves better." He paused. "Liora deserves better."

Kael's knuckles whitened on the windowsill. "Don't you dare tell me what Liora deserves." He turned toward them, teeth bared. Spit shot from his mouth as he spoke. "My decision is final. Auctor will be sent to Eesbex. He will live out the remainder of his days rotting on the ice."

They all stood, blinking for a moment.

Qenni's voice dropped to a whisper, but the venom remained. "The blood he spills next will be on your hands." She stormed out, slamming the door behind her.

The silence left by Qenni's exit lingered too long. Kael didn't move.

Ordan exhaled through his nose, disgust curling the corners of his mouth. "I thought I knew you. I was wrong."

Krennak walked out muttering something Kael couldn't understand.

Pike lingered by the door, his jaw muscles working. "You'll wish we'd killed him. We all will." He swallowed hard. A flicker of pain passed through his eyes, brief and buried, before he looked away.

Kael gave no reply and didn't move a muscle.

Ordan brushed past Pike and vanished into the corridor.

Pike's eyes softened, then he spoke, his voice firm and low. "It's been decided. If you won't reconsider, we will leave and find our way."

Chest heaving in long, slow breaths, Kael glowered out the window. "Don't you think I care? Junova was my friend, a mentor. I have to think about the bigger picture now. It's my responsibility to rebuild what we tore down. I didn't want this. I would give my own life to bring Junova back."

Pike's boot clapped on the marble floor as he took a step. "You know she forgave herself. I hope you don't waste it."

For a moment, Kael thought Pike might say something, anything, else. But he didn't.

Kael turned, but Pike was gone. He stood alone. The sound of the wind outside was like a distant scream.

He stood by the window until the sound of their footsteps faded. His breath shuddered. Liora, Junova. Both gone. Both murdered by his brother.

He sank to the floor, head in his hands. The silence wrapped around him like frost.

"Liora," he whispered. "I miss you. I don't know how to do this without you."

# Chapter 47:
## Mistake

*"Staring into the devil's abyss was a mistake. A mistake I won't repeat."*
—Pike

By sunrise, Pike's quarters were packed. His bedroll was folded with military precision, his satchel packed, his boots laced, and his jaw clenched tight like that of a man walking into battle—or away from one.

After tying his bedroll to the bottom of the satchel, he donned it and took one last look around at the sickening decadence.

Krennak leaned in the doorway, arms folded. "Ye ready to go?"

Pike nodded.

They arrived in the main hall at the same time as Qenni. Her face unreadable, eyes still burning from the fight with Kael.

Ordan came last, carrying his rifle and a silence to set men on edge. They all looked at Pike and, without a word, set out toward the palace doors.

They had almost gone when Alandra stepped into their path, frowning. Her voice was calm but final. "You don't all get to run away from him."

Pike stopped, his lips a thin line. "We're not running, but we can't stand by while he does nothing. He is letting Justice die."

"You're choosing to burn the bridge behind you," she said. "He may be wrong. He may be broken. But at least he's trying to make this galaxy a better place. Do you think turning your back on him will fix this?"

Pike didn't answer. None of them did; they didn't have to. Silence was her answer.

The others kept walking. Alandra didn't follow.

At the palace gates, Pike stopped. "There's something I need to do. I'll meet you at the starport."

He went back into the palace, down the marble stairs, and into the prison below.

Somewhere, the marble gave way to damp, mossy stone. It smelled of stagnant air and mold. The steps wiggled beneath his boots, each one more unstable than the last. With every step, the air grew colder, like the breath of Eesbex had traveled across the stars. Far below, water dripped like it was counting his every step. A door at the base of the stairs looked centuries old. It groaned on rusty hinges as he pushed through it and into the prison.

There were five cells, all empty except for one. The aged and damp bars had rusted; the once black metal was stained with red decay.

Pike stood before the cell, arms behind his back, eyes fixed upon the battered devil inside.

Auctor looked up and gave a weak smile. His nose was bent to one side, his lips crusted with scabs of dried blood, his face swollen and lumpy with black and purple bruises, and there were dark rings around his eyes. "Come to do what my brother could not?"

Pike didn't flinch. "No. I came to look upon a murderer who should be put to death."

Auctor leaned forward, lips curling. "Then look." He chuckled. "How does it feel to look into a mirror?"

Pike scowled. "You're no mirror of mine."

"Really? You haven't killed?"

"It's not the same," Pike snapped. "I don't kill for my selfish gratification, for power."

Smirking, Auctor leaned back against the mossy wall. "Keep telling yourself that. Maybe one day you'll believe it."

Pike's jaw locked tight as he remembered Auctor had gunned down a terrified tech, a man who couldn't have fired a shot if he'd tried. He opened his mouth then closed it. There was nothing else to say.

As he turned to leave, Auctor jumped up, snatching the bars, his eyes wild. "You think you've made a choice, Pike? You haven't. You're a shadow owned by him. You'll come back. You want what I have. The truth."

Pike froze, his hand on the door.

Auctor's voice dropped to a venomous hiss. "Kael's mercy is your prison. Mine was a gift. One you'll beg for when the walls come crashing down." The bars rattled under Auctor's grasp. "You're not leaving because of his mercy. You're leaving because you're afraid. You belong to him because of it. Keep running, Pike. Maybe one day you'll outrun your past."

Pike didn't look back. He stepped through the door and let it slam shut behind him, rattling on its hinges. The haunting laughter followed him up the stairs, scraping on the walls like a knife dragged across stone.

Back in the sunlight, where green fields flowed and blue skies marched on forever, Pike arrived at the starport.

Krennak sat on a crate, nodding to him. "What did ye 'ave to do?"

Pike worked his jaw and looked at their shuttle. "A mistake."

He walked past Krennak, stopping at the shuttle's ramp. The others were on board, waiting. Pike turned around and looked at this world one last time. The purple and amber leaves were falling from the trees now, leaving a carpet fit for royalty on the ground beneath. The old gods' palace remained fixed like a macabre reminder of what power, corruption, and obsession could do to a galaxy.

His chest pained. Kael had not come to see them off, and he couldn't blame him, not after their fight.

Krennak approached him, touched his shoulder, and squeezed. He spoke in a low voice. "Time to go." Krennak walked past him and into the shuttle.

Jaw clenched, Pike hesitated, hoping Kael might appear. But he did not. Pike turned and stalked into the shuttle, and the doors whined closed behind him.

Thrusters blew verdant plasma, and the shuttle lifted. Pike sat with Zero. Hum of the engines filled the silence, but he was alone. A thought stuck in his mind, a wedge in his musings. It was a niggling doubt he was running, not from his past, but from his future.

# Chapter 48:
## Light

*"When starlight fails, many find their eyes open, their path changed."*
—Xalthari Warden of Echoes

Green plasma flared from the shuttle's engines as it punched through the puffy white clouds, carving a glowing verdant canyon into the once serene sky. Kael's fingernails dug into the window's edge.

A gentle and cool breeze whispered past his ear. He fell back into his chair, letting it spin from his weight. A pad lay in the center of the desk before him. Picking it up, he read. It was a missive to every planet contained within the Covenant. Only a few lines had been written. He should start here, with a dispatch. Where to begin? What to say?

He tossed down the pad, frowning at it. He might know what to say if it came to him in time.

The door opened, and Vashar stepped in. "Kael, it is time. We leave."

Kael's jaw tightened, and he swallowed. "I understand. Safe travels to you all."

Eyes narrowing, Vashar nodded. "It is appreciated." He paused. "I sense Kael is troubled."

Eyes landing on the pad, Kael picked it up. "Junova was writing to the colonized worlds...before everything happened. I should continue her work, but I'm lost. I've never done anything like this."

Vashar took a deep breath, and his expression softened. "Your heart will help. Stay true to your path. Starlit Covenant will help."

Kael wasn't sure he understood, but he would try. "Thank you."

Vashar smiled, turned, and left the room.

A knock came at the door.

Alandra stepped in.

Brows furrowed, Kael stared at her. "I thought you left with the others."

"No." She took a seat. "I never told you about my brother."

Raising an eyebrow, Kael set down the pad. "Your brother?"

She winced. "He was my twin. We joined the corps at eighteen, like you." Looking down, she took a deep breath. "A few years in, we were on a mission together. He didn't come back." Meeting his eyes, she continued. "For years, I sought vengeance against the Starless. It was the one thing keeping me going. Until you showed up in my squad."

Sitting back in his chair, Kael remained quiet.

"At first, I thought the cycle couldn't be broken. But then it changed, you changed it, and I knew it was God's fault he died." Alandra took a ragged breath. "You showed me I could be free of anger. You showed me a better way." She gazed out the window, eyes distant. "I understand why you can't kill Auctor. And I want you to know you have my full support going forward. I believe in what we are trying to build."

Kael swallowed. He wasn't quite sure what he should say. So, he said all he could think of, his voice soft. "Thank you for trusting in me. For trusting in our future. I'm glad you decided to stay."

She gave a weak smile, shifting in her chair. "There's work to be done, and I've kept you long enough." Standing, she walked to the open door. "Thank you, Kael."

He gazed out the window, at the vista stretching before him, at the distant snow-capped mountains on the horizon. How had he never spotted them before? He smiled at the beauty. And he smiled because

Alandra had stayed. He understood what losing a brother was like. Maybe that was why she'd confided in him. Yet, it wasn't the same. One had been a betrayal, the other a true loss. Nevertheless, her support filled him with hope that the future could be better.

Closing his eyes, he focused on the movement of his chest and the cool autumn breeze caressing his hair. He wished the others had stayed. He wished Junova were here to guide him. But it was impossible. Or was it? He remembered her last words. *Believe people can change. I'm one of many standing as proof of the possible. Don't become what you fought.* Maybe that had been her way of telling him he could change, too. He no longer needed orders. The future didn't have to mirror the past.

Now he had to find his own way, forging a path forward for a galaxy of people. As he opened his eyes to the warm sunlight streaming through the window, a line from the Covenant echoed in his mind, words he hadn't thought of in years.

*Truth is a light too bright for some to see; wisdom lies in knowing when to turn away.*

"Knowing when to turn away," he murmured.

Turning back to his desk, he picked up the pad and stared at it for a long time. He knew starting fresh was right, but it left him with nothing to work with. This would be all him. So, he wrote:

*You didn't hear the cries.*
*You didn't see the cannons rain terror from the sky on Xalthryn.*
*You didn't see the bodies of men, women, and children.*
*You didn't know there was a war.*
*That's not your fault.*
*It was kept quiet by design. The Star blinded all who need not know the truth.*

*I don't send this message to accuse. I send it because the fighting is over. Because you should know.*

*We fought, not for glory or conquest, but to end a system built on oppression. A system demanding conformity and obedience, calling it peace. A system punishing difference, calling it justice.*

*The tyrant who built the old galaxy is gone, a pretender god who committed genocide for his own twisted goals.*

*Our work has begun.*

*You don't owe us thanks. You didn't ask us to fight. We don't ask for your obedience. But if you believe a better way of life is possible, where your name, culture, and voice don't have to be erased to belong, you are part of this, whether you knew it or not.*

*The Covenant says, "The star does not change, it is we who turn away from its glow."*

*Then let us turn away, not into shadow, but onto a new, absolute path. We will not fear the dark. We will make our light.*

*Many of us gave everything so the galaxy could open its eyes. Now it has the chance to see what we have become. May we all step beyond the lines they drew and chart our path.*

He set the pad on the old wooden desk. A cool breeze swept through the room, a gentle caress on a spring day. This was the beginning, and much work lay ahead, but it was a step in the right direction.

# Chapter 49:
## Shattered Stars

*"Our victory was bittersweet, our path strewn with shattered stars."*
—Kael

Reed stood straight, his arms behind his back, as Kael stepped out of the shuttle. The ship's interior was a stark contrast to the palace's white and gold. Charcoal and bronze dominated the space, and the air was oily thick with burnt plastic and hot circuitry; there was an undercurrent of graphite lingering in its midst, a smell he wouldn't soon forget.

Kael gave Reed a weak smile, which he returned. Reed's eyes were sunken and dark, with puffy bags forming underneath. "It's good to see you, sir."

Kael flinched. He didn't like it, Reed calling him *sir*. "How is Radiance and her crew?"

Reed's head tilted down. "The ship is fine, but the crew.... Morale is low. With Junova gone, many feel hopeless."

Stepping closer, Kael spoke softly, his voice low. "And you?"

Reed's jaw worked as he glanced about the bay. "I'm trying to keep myself together. For the crew. It's been difficult. She wasn't our captain, you know. She was family. She believed in a life we forgot could exist." His eyes said otherwise, as if he felt the nightmare hadn't ended and he wasn't sure it would.

Kael took in a ragged breath, holding back his own emotions. "Reed, you're going to be the captain now. You know this ship, her crew. There is no one better qualified to keep her going."

Reed nodded, though Kael wasn't sure if he believed it. He turned and walked over to the hypertube. "There's something I need to show you."

Walking over, Kael raised an eyebrow. "Where are we going?"

"Captain's quarters." Reed disappeared into the ship.

Kael looked at the tube for a long moment. When had he last been in those quarters? A memory came like a knife in the dark, and Kael's breath caught in his chest. That morning he had asked Junova where Liora was. It had been an eternity ago, yet the memory was crystal clear, as if it had happened yesterday.

He blinked, clenched his jaw, and stepped into the airstream. A few seconds later, he was standing next to Reed. Finality hit him as he looked at her quarters. The charcoal-black floor and bronze walls were barren; all that remained was her desk and chair.

Arms behind his back, Reed walked over to the window and looked at the world below. "It was my duty to pack her things." He pointed at a lone pad on her desk. "Except that. Junova said you should have it if anything happened to her."

Kael slowly stepped forward. "What is it?"

Reed turned, eyes down. "It belonged to Liora." He stalked out, stopping in the open door. "About the captain. Junova. Where is she?"

Kael's fingers trembled. "I asked Vashar to take her ashes to Xalthryn. It felt right that the Xalthari keep her memory."

Wiping a tear from his cheek, Reed nodded. "Kael, I'm sorry." The air whispered as he entered the tube.

Swallowing, Kael took a slow, hesitant step toward the desk, and he gazed down at the flat gray surface with the small pad in its center. He almost didn't want to look at it. He almost turned away. Almost. He had to know. He had to know what was so important that Junova had kept it for him.

The grav chair bobbed as he sat at the desk. He picked up the pad and ran his fingers across the cool metal. Finding the switch, he powered it on.

The pad flashed to life and showed a list of files by date. He selected one, and it opened, revealing a journal entry. Each breath came slowly, purposefully, as he scanned through the entries.

*I met a soldier today. Okay, a recruit. He was interesting and smart. I taught him how to fly a lander. I hope to see him again.*

His smile was soft, and he selected another entry.

*I saw Kael again today. I transported his squad out to God's temper. He was worried about failing, so I bet him a surprise if he won or a favor if he lost. I know he'll win.*

He looked out at the blue sphere suspended in the inky void. "Have you been here?" he murmured. Taking a deep breath, he looked at the next entry.

*I taught him how to fly the shuttle. He was a little rocky at first, but caught on quick. Of course, he won the bet, so it was time I paid up. I brought him up to Radiance and showed him the holo emitter. We watched the violet falls for hours. It was the best night of my life. So far.*

It was a good memory. He could still remember his amazement watching her room transform for the first time. Kael sat smiling for a long time. Then he remembered; he pulled the tattered paper from his pocket and unfolded it.

Her constellation was still there. Maybe he would see her world, her home, before returning to his. He slid the paper back into his pocket and opened the next entry.

*I found out he didn't come back today. Junova tried to help, but I feel lost. Hopeless. I never dared care for anyone before Kael. And now I might be alone.*

The words hit him like a gut punch. He knew the feeling all too well. He closed his eyes. A tear ran down his cheek. The familiar, hollow ache crept back into his chest. To read about her pain made it worse.

Opening his eyes, he braved another entry.

*He's alive! I almost can't believe it. I cried when Junova told me. I will fly with Zero tomorrow, and we will save him.*

A smile tugged at his lips. She had been with Zero, but they had gone to the wrong location. He sighed. Another date, another entry.

*I'm taking him to Radiance when he's released from the infirmary tomorrow. Junova approved him to stay a few days. I can't wait. There's so much to talk about.*

He closed his eyes. A shaft of light. Her eyes had been hazel. Gold and green glinting in the sun. Her lips. A kiss.

He exhaled through his nose, slowly, deliberately. He had never told her—told her that he loved her. Opening his eyes, Kael read the last entry.

*Today's the day. I'm going to tell him. I think he'll be scared. I am, too. But he should know.*

*I think.*

*I think he'll be a good father.*

The pad slipped from his fingertips and clattered to the desk. Kael blinked. Drew a ragged breath. Stared out the window for an eternity.

Images flashed of that day. The note.

*Last-minute order. I have to fly. I have a surprise for you. See you tonight.*

Was this the surprise?

She'd never had the chance to tell him.

He'd found out too late about their child.

About all of it.

"No," he whispered.

His thumb brushed the tattered paper. No emeralds. Nothing but shattered stars. He pressed his forehead against the window and let the silence swallow him.

*"I face my future and embrace my shattered star."*
—Kael

# Acknowledgments

This book exists because of the people who believed in it and in me, even when I didn't. Thank you!

Rebecca for listening to a thousand ramblings while encouraging me to continue writing.

Michael Dawid E5, for generously allowing me to interview him about his service in the United States Army during the height of the Middle Eastern conflicts. Imparting his wisdom of military structure.

Cierra Jade Craney a Licensed Marriage Family Therapist (LMFT) with her Masters in Counseling Psychology at the University of San Francisco, for helping me build the psychological profiles that made my characters real.

Dennis Fischer for a brief discussion, which launched me into a world of dialogue improvement.

Danille Dyal, who edited The Shattered Star with care and determination, uncovering every flaw and helping it shine.

Christian Storm, for designing the striking cover of The Shattered Star, which turned an idea into a visual masterpiece.

And to the readers—whether this is your first sci-fi novel or your hundredth—thank you for giving me your time and trust. I hope something here lit a star in the dark for you.

# Join Zero Squad

## Get Exclusive Updates from The Shattered Galaxy

When you subscribe, you'll get:

Exclusive sneak peeks at upcoming chapters and side stories

Early access to cover reveals, launch dates, and special editions

Behind-the-scenes insight into character arcs, world-building, and the writing process

You'll also receive a free digital short story set in the Shattered Star universe before the events of this novel, available only to subscribers.

Sign up here at:

https://skyler-r-ostrom.kit.com/shatteredgalaxy

Or scan the QR code below

www.ingramcontent.com/pod-product-compliance
Lightning Source LLC
Chambersburg PA
CBHW020944260626
47169CB00006B/1804